The Narrow Path

The First Storm

The Narrow Path

The First Storm

Sherlock Holmes and
His London
Through the Eyes
of Scotland Yard

by Marcia Wilson

Edited by David Marcum

MX Publishing

ISBN Paperback 978-1-80424-653-5
ISBN AUK ePub 978-1-80424-654-2
ISBN AUK PDF 978-1-80424-655-9

Published by
MX Publishing
335 Princess Park Manor, Royal Drive,
London, N11 3GX
www.mxpublishing.co.uk

David Marcum can be reached at:
thepapersofsherlockholmes@gmail.com

Cover Design by Awan
Illustration of The Yarders by Marcia Wilson

Sherlock Holmes and the Scotland Yarders

by Marcia Wilson

Further adventures forthcoming . . . .

Author Foreword
by Marcia Wilson

Looking back, it was a strange time. High school in the late 1980's meant Tolkien, King, Christie, and Poe were always checked out of the school library, but we had multiple copies of Sherlock Holmes on the shelf. If students were going to apply for English-oriented scholarships, by gosh, we were going to read the good stuff, and that meant short stories with murder and mayhem. In emulation of the masters, our choices were usually ACD or . . . Hemingway. It wasn't much of a contest. Hemingway didn't have a demon glowing Death Hound on the moors.

High school segued into college, but we had *Mystery!* re-runs on PBS, even if we had to visit people to watch it, and besides Jeremy Brett, we had Christopher Plummer's compassionate Holmes against Jack the Ripper, a role that shattered the domination of Rathbone and Bruce. Our classmates swore it was necessary for our sincerity as fans of Sir Arthur to see it.

If that sounds like pithy stuff for high schoolers, my generation had a flexible relationship with media – or even power grids. Even if they existed, they weren't exactly as reliable as the sun coming up every morning. The further into the West Virginia panhandle you got, the bigger the library room in the house. Even the poorest of houses, be they on blocks or wheels, had at least one shelf of sanity to rely on when the power was out, or the brownouts made hash of anything but AM radio. When a flood took out the local libraries, it was devastation.

There was media, but there wasn't enough – there's never enough – but as far as the books printed in the wake of Sir Arthur . . . it really was never enough. You were lucky to find something in a thrift store or library sale, and your odds were no worse than combing the bookstores in the mall. Oh, for the days when there was more than one bookstore in a mall. If something was found, readers had to buy it on faith that it wasn't a waste of their time.

Look, our standards weren't low, they were desperate. We made a lot of poor book-buying choices, which were hastily returned to the ecosystem of flea market sales for some other poor shmuck to buy up. One girl, bless her, would donate the books after carefully penciling in every sin the authors made against Canon, history, plot contrivance,

1

and attempts to pair Holmes up with a romantic partner. I like to think she cackled as she returned the much-improved dreck to the public. She always cited her sources . . . .

It shouldn't be a surprise when we wound up obsessing, ever so slightly, with what little we could find that wasn't terrible, and (*Hooray!*) didn't go against The Canon. I wonder if anyone has ever tried to list all the knockoffs and illicit print runs out there. Probably not – I'd like to think nobody could be that crazy.

Fan fiction was the outlet for a crying need that had hit breaking point. Paper fanzines of decent quality were even harder to find than a decent paperback on the shelf – you have never bought a pig in a poke until you've combed through a hand-printed zine catalog, squinted at the type, and decided to spend your allowance on what sounded the most promising – and too bad the cover art was rarely as good on the inside.

Fanzine editors lived in the twilight, trying to put out their passion projects between the obligations of home, family, and keeping a roof over their head, as well as hanging on to entire drawers of receipts to make sure a rival 'ziner didn't get spiteful and report them to the IRS. (That actually happened.) Zines were non-profit only, which is partly why the zines we could afford were always shipped Media Mail on whatever paper was on sale. If you were very lucky, you got your order in three weeks.

Maybe we shouldn't talk about the pastichery in animation . . . .

The Internet found its feet and bloomed with forums and places to hide and talk about the lack of stories, and that led to posting paper zines online, and people began writing fresh stuff, online, and showing it for reading and/or critiquing. Almost overnight there were clubs, groups, and social organizations that could get their fix on the stories between the boom-and-bust world of conventions and newsletters.

There were friendships made that I miss to this very day. The sheer power of a small number of people who were intelligent, thoughtful, and mindful of Canon encouraged so many of us. They helped with research, knew how to spell, and learned different languages in this world. They reviewed books, scrounged supplies, and let us know if someone was copying our plots just a little too much for comfort. Plagiarism and how to address it was a real eye-opener when it came to intellectual property that wasn't yours to begin with, but you could claim the OC's (Original Characters) were yours, and debatably, your unique perspective on the people, places, and things created under the pen of Sir Arthur.

I was a fan of these fans. They were amazing and – honestly – damn good writers. *Damn* good. They were role models. They read the whole Canon, and they kept track of everything, and they led us to places like *fanfiction.net*, where we could post with a minimum of fussing.

I could write about anyone I wanted, but it was partially out of respect for these writers that I began to veer away from making just one more story about Sherlock Holmes and Dr. Watson. I loved the stories, but part of their appeal was their world. And there was a lot to that world that was relevant today. Methods may alter crime, but motives rarely do.

At the time, there was a pretty well-represented group that was pro-Watson, and they wrote some of those "damn good stories" with Watson as the protagonist – or at least, a powerful, equal voice. The Granada series was a huge influence, as well as the Russian series, and throw in some of "the radio show" for good measure.

These fan writers may have loved the tight scripts and drama of the Rathbone and Bruce approach, but as they grew up, they said, collectively, "Man, that was bad for Watson!" There were other words, much less polite. Burke and Hardwicke were a positive force for the shift in the thinking that pointed out Watson was *not* an idiot and we couldn't do a decent job showing how smart Holmes was by surrounding him by idiots. This had already been tried, during Classic Dr Who, and nobody had been left happy about it. Nobody blamed the actors for doing their job too well.

Fine, I thought, *there are a lot of really good writers writing for Watson. I can do that.* But I also caught on that if Watson illuminated Holmes by writing of the man from his point-of-view, *maybe I could write about Watson through other people's eyes.* The question was: *Who?*

Enter a re-visit to the Granada Series, and "The Norwood Builder".

I make no secret of the fact that I am heavily synesthetic. Face blindedness comes with its own challenge, and I have to train myself to recognize people. With an irony that approaches opera-grade comedy, I literally could not tell Holmes from Lestrade in Granada's "The Norwood Builder". Also, Lestrade made me angry when I was a hero-worshipping teenager watching the show with other hero-worshipping teenagers. *How dare Lestrade challenge Holmes? Couldn't anyone see Holmes was the smartest man in the room?*

Older adult me revisited that part of my life and went *Oops!* because there were some of those Fanfiction Demigods that rather liked Lestrade and had plenty of backup reasons. I wish I could remember the name of the one who mused, *"Colin Jeavons is the only actor who could be bulldog-like and also ferrety."* I was doing a lot of research at my job, and that included the Victorian era and law enforcement. Somehow it all started clicking together, piece by piece.

A writer whom I regret losing (her entire message board went the way of LiveJournal – only, it vanished for good. Poof. No trace) challenged me on whether or not Lestrade was stupid. He knew more than he let on, she said, and I . . . kind of said, *"Oh? Prove it."*

Ouch. She did, lining out events in "The Boscombe Valley Mystery" and "The Second Stain" and a few other bits and pieces, and I ate crow. A lot of it. I was wrong. Still, I could at least write with this new perspective. Bad as it was to be wrong, it would be worse to stay with it.

Add to this a sleep disorder that can politely be called *insomnia*, and a marriage turning into a nightmare of violence, and no health insurance – but writing was the cheapest therapy out there . . . Lestrade slowly woke up and came to life. I'll blame Colin Jeavons for knowing what the writers wanted out of the scripts. It's on him.

"Trust your characters," my old English teacher would say, sternly, so I did. I wrote short stories that could connect with others to make a fuller piece. A necklace is made one bead at a time. I wrote at night. I had to. I needed to stay awake, listening to any sounds that might be my ex-husband's return to stalk us – tampering with my car, crawling under the house, draining the well his own children needed to drink from, and taunts to the police that tried their best, but could only work within the limits of the system. They failed, but it was the system that failed. They cared, and they shared my rage that when the ex was finally brought to justice, it was too late for one of his victims.

There is only so much a policeman can do against so much collective injustice out there. If Sherlock Holmes had existed on that force, they would have begged for his help against my ex-husband. They knew he could go where they couldn't, and they would know when not to ask the awkward questions about how information was collected. They would have sniffed and said, "Well, that's a pity," and

4

shrugged and did things according to the law – *their* law – but not expecting civilians to follow the same oaths they swore.

I empathized with Gregson's ability to buck the rules, and I empathized for Lestrade's inability to do so. The Yarders took on their own lives and, without knowing it, the job had changed. I was now sitting back and watching the stories unfold, writing them as fast as they told them. They had a lot to say. They still do, but the stories are whispering now. We are safer, there is no need to listen for danger. I am learning how to sleep.

More years ago than I'd like to recollect, I received an email so startling I forwarded it to my sister before a family dinner at the pizza parlour. It wasn't a fantastic day. Before long I would be needing their help to flee across the country in the middle of a winter snowstorm. The mood was glum. We were subdued.

My sister looked at me over the table and said with uncharacteristic bluntness, "You impressed that man."

That man was David Marcum.

Marcia Wilson
February 2025

Scotland Yard's Story
Editor Foreword
by David Marcum

Back in 2008, it was still a different Sherlockian world from today.

In those days, the quest for more excellent Holmes adventures beyond the pitifully few sixty Canonical adventures was still quite difficult. Each year, only a few slipped through the needle's-eye clutch of the moribund major publisher model. (In fact, if one is still publishing by that route, then this fact remains true.) But there were many Holmes adventures waiting to be revealed, and they just needed an outlet. Is it any wonder that the Internet was that path?

Holmes pastiches have been around since William Gillette's 1899 play, *Sherlock Holmes*, showing that Our Heroes' adventures did *not* have to pass across the first Literary Agent's desk. Some amazing and accurate adventures appeared on the radio in the 1930's, courtesy of visionary Edith Meiser. And the door kept getting wider, with more radio shows, films, and the occasional book giving us more traditional, authentic, and Canonical Holmes.

But it was not enough.

In 1998, *fanfiction.net* was created, allowing another outlet for sharing Holmes's adventures, wherein those who had discovered them could get them directly to starving readers immediately, without facing the impossible discouragement of the faceless soul-dead major publishing model. I was fortunate to discover the site a few years after that, and began to visit regularly to read and print and archive stories about the True Holmes. There are thousands of Holmes stories located there, but many are parodies, or anachronistic, or related to modernized and offensive simulacrums, or with incorrect ghost-busting leanings. Others were clearly written by individuals who have no clue about Sherlock Holmes, or have hijacked him for their own agendas. These stories may be ignored, even if they have to be waded through – for buried in the muck of this backyard goose lot, for those who take time to look, are some true and rare jewels.

And in April 2008, the beginning of a couple of stories were posted, "An Ordinary Meeting" on the tenth, and "Truth is the Critic" the next day, both as written by an author going under the curious sobriquet of *aragonite*.

"An Ordinary Meeting" gives details of Lestrade's first consultation with Sherlock Holmes, and "Truth is the Critic" is written from the perspective of the Scotland Yard inspectors as they read *A Study in Scarlet* – and providing their reactions when see how Watson has described them. These were well written and interesting, and this approach really hadn't been attempted before.

(To be accurate, there had been some stories about the Yarders, but they were inconsistent. For instance, M.J. Trow's long Lestrade series veers wildly from legitimate mysteries to unreadable parodies, with particularly bogus attacks on Sherlock Holmes, and Trow inexplicably gives Inspector G. Lestrade the first name of "Sholto".

In "Truth is the Critic", *aragonite* was already painting the Yarders – Inspectors Lestrade, Gregson, Bradstreet, and Hopkins in particular – in well-rounded and respectful ways that hadn't been seen before. They had their own life stories beyond The Canon, and weren't just the inspector *du jour* appearing in this-or-that Canonical tale. Who knew then that this new author, slipping quietly onto the scene, had such an overall vision for these individuals, with fully realized details about their personal lives, their backgrounds and histories . . . and a plan for a massive overarching adventure that would span decades in their lives?

Over the next few months, more stories quickly followed – "A Cookout in Cornwall", "Route to Madness", and "Just Inspector Will Do" (my all-time favorite of these works, relating the events on the Paddington platform when Mary Watson awaits her husband's return from the Continent in mid-May 1891. I re-read it every year on Reichenbach Day.) But on April 17th, 2008, *aragonite* raised the stakes, publishing the first chapter of a novel, *A Sword for Defense*, the first of a massive story arc relating what Watson and Lestrade and the other Yarders faced in the months after Holmes's supposed death at the Reichenbach Falls.

While keeping one story going would overwhelm many authors, *aragonite* – whomever he or she was – had even greater ambitions. New stories and chapters began to be posted at a feverish pace. A week after *Sword* started, another serialized novel began, *You Buy Bones*, telling how Watson, in early 1882 and fresh from his first year living with Holmes in Baker Street, comes across a monstrous crime that directly and personally affects the Scotland Yard inspectors. And a few months after that, *aragonite* started another novel that served as a prequel leading to *Sword* called *The MoonCursers*, telling of Lestrade's

7

own terrifying adventures in late April and early May 1891, occurring at the same time Holmes and Watson were playing cat-and-mouse with Moriarty, on their way to a fateful encounter in Meiringen.

Over the course of that summer, nearly every day brought some new chapter: Sometimes another episode in *A Sword for Defense* or *You Buy Bones* or *The MoonCursers*, and at other times a seemingly stand-alone story that that filled in some crucial and interesting aspect about the Scotland Yarders that only made the overall painting richer and deeper.

Imagine if Charles Dickens were writing and publishing three serialized novels at once, and adding in short stories too. And they were going straight from being written to being posted for public consumption as soon as they were complete. And clearly the overall storyline wasn't being generated along the way – there was a *plan*, for little threads mentioned here and there about Lestrade's boyhood or Bradstreet's family had massive importance much later.

Over many months during this time, *aragonite* was also constructing another massive work, *Test of the Professionals*, which related the events after *You Buy Bones* and served as a set-up for *A Sword for Defense*, telling us much more about Lestrade's past, his unfortunate and dangerous life-long connection with Professor Moriarty's agent, the truly evil Jethro Quimper, and the escalating and terrifying events surrounding his courtship with Clea Cheatham.

In August 2008, with all of this going on, *aragonite* started another brilliant novella, *A Secondary Stain*, the *other* events of "The Second Stain", in which Lestrade was not as clueless as he appears in Watson's manuscript, actually working behind the scenes to assist Holmes's investigation. It was the brilliance of this story that finally prompted me to write a fan letter.

Using the fan fiction website's messenger feature, I emailed an extensive message to *aragonite* in October 2008, and soon received a wonderful and informative reply.

First, I learned that *aragonite* was really Marcia Wilson. In subsequent communications, I learned that *aragonite* – which curiously I'd never looked up before then – is calcium carbonate used by marine organisms to build their shells and skeletons. Since aragonite can be found in cave formations, and since Marcy is a caver – the evidence of which can be found in some of her stories brilliantly dealing with caverns and London's Lost Rivers – I suspect that's why she chose the unusual pen-name.

Over many emails over many years, Marcy has explained to me that she wrote so prolifically in those early years because she had insomnia, and that was a very productive time to write. She also could *see* all of these scenes, and almost couldn't write fast enough to convey them. In her very first reply to me in October 2008, she explained, how she approached telling the Yarders' story, and why she named Inspector G. Lestrade *Geoffrey:*

> *I've never liked the playing down of characters. It's a lazy way to pump up the character in your mind. I have to be very careful not to wander into the Fangirlyverse. Usually I deal with it by giving a character a name I dislike, and for some reason, I dislike Geoffrey so naturally I stuck it on the poor guy.*

She also explained that:

> *I was so bleeding tired of writing against another person's notions on Holmes and Watson that I just went to another character that I rather liked. (When I was younger, I hated Lestrade. He should have been kowtowing to Holmes' genius like all of us!) Later on, I realized that it took a pretty remarkable man to refuse to see Holmes in a reverent light. [The] clues about Lestrade were subtle and interesting. There had to be a reason for someone who was supposed to be such a good cop to stay a police inspector after his initial promotion. I made him a Celtic Breton out of a half-thought. I was seeing Colin Jeavons in my head, and he's so Welsh he's probably half-Neanderthal! Being a Breton or a Channel Islander would have made [Lestrade] an English citizen, but he would not have been accepted as an equal in race or status by many people.*

Our communications continued, as did her writing. By early 2009, *A Sword for Defense* was complete, and the next book in the ongoing saga, *The Narrow Path* had commenced. Those were great days to be a Sherlockian and to be reading *fanfiction.net*, as there were other great authors there as well – *Westron Wynde* and *KCS* among them, all with powerful and correct understandings of the *True Holmes*. These authors were writing for the fans, and also for each other, and I was privileged to be in contact with many of them. In a few years, Marcy and *Westron*

Wynde – who turned out to be amazing pasticheur Sarah Bennett, whose works are slowly being made available from Belanger Books – began to take down their online works and publish them in real books. (It was at this time that I let Marcy and Sarah read my first Sherlock Holmes pastiches, written in 2008 and at that point seen by no one but my wife, and with their encouragement I started publicly publishing my stories too.)

Marcy initially published *You Buy Bones*, along with some related short stories, in 2010 (from Lulu Publishing. That version is now out of print.) Next came *Test of the Professionals: Leap Year* (2013, also from Lulu and out of print), also collecting the original online novel and working in some supplementary material.

In 2015, I came up with the idea of *The MX Book of New Sherlock Holmes Stories*, and of course Marcy was in the initial list of invitees. Since then, much of her writing has been turned to contributing stories to these anthologies, having submitted nearly two-dozen. Through these books, she became associated with MX Publishing, who issued a new edition of *You Buy Bones* in 2015, as well as splitting *Test of the Professionals: Leap Year* into three planned smaller volumes. The first two, *The Adventure of the Flying Blue Pidgeon* and *The Peaceful Night Poisonings*, were published by MX in 2016 and 2017, respectively. Unfortunately, due to a combination of events, the third part of *Test* – the much larger piece called *Leap Year* that relates the exciting conclusion to that narrative – was not published.

So for the wider public, those who were never able to read Marcy's massive *ouvré* on *fanfiction.net*, her available works consisted of these three novels, and her well-respected stories in the MX anthologies. (Unfortunately, Marcy, Sarah Bennett, and several others were forced to pull their Sherlockian content from *fanfiction.net* several years ago after some of their works were stolen – copied-and-pasted and then republished under other author names by way of Amazon's self-publishing program.)

In late 2024, I was in the process of working toward assembling and editing the final volumes, Parts 49, 50, 51, and 52 of the MX anthologies, a process which would continue into early 2025. While looking around in my computer files, I found something I'd forgotten: Years earlier, I had saved and formatted the files for five of Marcy's novels – those relating to Watson and Lestrade's adventures during The Great Hiatus. Since the late 1990's, I've printed and archived every traditional Canonical Holmes adventure that I've found online –

thousands of them – and I have over 175 binders of pure Holmes adventures – including all of Marcy's now-withdrawn stories. But luckily I had these novels as Word files. And I had an idea . . . .

I contacted Marcy, who hadn't had time in several years to think about publishing more of her works, and asked if I could shepherd these five novels to publication – *pro-bono*, just because I was passionate about other people reading these incredible stories. Marcy was willing, and so I started editing with great enthusiasm – even as I was supposed to be editing the final MX volumes, stories for which were rolling in every day.

It soon became apparent to me that to publish these five novels without readers knowing the events of the missing *Leap Year* would be a confusing mess. Too much happened in these books that continued from what happened in *Leap Year*. Clearly, that missing volume would need to be edited and published too. And while I was at it, why not re-edit the previously published three books – *You Buy Bones*, *The Adventure of the Flying Blue Pidgeon*, and *The Peaceful Night Poisonings* – into an overall cohesive narrative?

MX Publisher Extraordinaire Steve Emecz, THE Sherlockian publisher and the Sherlockian Gutenberg – the man who made Sherlockian publishing accessible to real people instead of guarding a narrow doorway, or deciding that Sherlockian publishing should only be available for a very narrow cadre of self-described elites – was enthusiastic, and ready to proceed immediately. But I needed to actually finish editing the nine books first. It was a joy, and a labor of love to do so.

I had read all of these books serially as published, hopping from story to story as new chapters appeared, back in 2008-2011. But to read the story now, in one place, in order and available in its entirety, made it even more amazing – and exciting for the thought of new readers able to discover this magnificent world: *Sherlock Holmes's London, as seen through the eyes of the Scotland Yarders.*

Even as I dug deeper into Marcy's Scotland Yard adventures, I was remembering the other stories – the previously mentioned *A Secondary Stain*. Her Yarder's Christmas novels, *Gunnysack Goose for Christmas* and *A Mouth of Ivy*. Short-story collections like *Devilry* and *It's All in a Name*. Other novels and novellas like *The Muse of History*, *Ghosts in the Making*, *Courage Rises*, *The Kings and Queens of London*, and the World War I narrative, *The Days of Our Years*. I had amazing fun editing the first nine books that are being published in

2025, and with any luck, I hope to be able to edit the rest of these, along with a collection of Marcy's MX anthology contributions, over the next year or so, in order to fill in Marcy's *Great Scotland Yard Tapestry*.

There are certain authors who "own" other Canonical characters by taking hold of them and defining them. The late Carole Nelson Douglas was Irene Adler's chronicler. Michael Kurland gives us the best portrait of Professor Moriarty. Will Thomas has absolutely defined Barker, Holmes's hated rival on the Surrey Side. The late Gerard Williams claimed Dr. Mortimer (even if only for two books), and Susan Knight is easily becoming the definitive voice of Mrs. Hudson.

But Marcia Wilson tells the True Story of the Scotland Yarders – and presents an amazing viewpoint of Holmes and Watson along the way.

I've said it many times before, and can't say it any better now:

Marcia Wilson has found Scotland Yard's Tin Dispatch Box.

David Marcum
January 2025

The Narrow Path

The First Storm

Chapter I – The First Storm

Inspector Gregson was rarely taken aback by the weather. Some men had old wounds – broken bones, metal bits from battle stick stuck in them – perhaps a sensitive head. He, however, had a wife who had a particularly exquisite sense of smell that had somehow remained intact despite a lifetime of London.

But Elise was out with her family on one of *those* jaunts, the sort that lasts all day and finishes with bulging sacks of stuff, and the gruff man had forged without this morning. So accustomed was he to her barometric reports that he had quite forgotten to pay attention to his own senses. Enough of his brain was devoted to just rising, dressing, eating the bread and tea she had thoughtfully left for him, and then getting out the door.

So it was with a slight sense of surprise and a much larger sense of self-annoyance that he rounded the corner on his way to New Scotland Yard and found himself staring into the rising front of soggy grey atmospheric bile.

"Oh, no," he groaned aloud. A troupe of urchins – Gregson recognized them as the reprehensible malcontents off Lestrade's street – paused on their pelt to shelter with a puzzled look. Elise would kill him if he came back to their apartment with a coat soaking wet and stinking of the factory-smoke coming off the estuary.

And speaking of Lestrade . . . Gregson hurriedly put his back to the grimy bricks, hoping for a scrap of protection, noting Constable Lions was headed for cover on the other side with an unseemly haste in his heavy coat and boots.

. . . if that wasn't Lestrade himself, exposed in the mews, running like a member of the peerage pursued by anxious bankers.

"Hurry, man!" Gregson felt victim to his own temptations, and cheered him on although it looked fairly well hopeless. The clouds were boiling like that stuff the theatre put in the witches' cauldron whenever they did *Macbeth*.

Lestrade gasped to a halt, literally stopping his momentum by putting his palms up against the bricks by Gregson's side.

The heavens opened.

"*Holy God!*" Gregson blurted. He stared in a mixture of disbelief and reluctant admiration at the seething brew above their heads. "Look out!" They pressed themselves as close under the eves as their bodies allowed. The first of the water running off the roof-tops was always the worst and it hadn't rained in over a month. It drizzled down in thick, black strings, painted with thirty-two days of soot and cinders, feathers, small bones, plane-leaves, chips off tile, slate, paint flakes, bird and animal droppings, cloth, twigs, dead lengths of ivy, loose bits of crumbling brick and mortar

Lestrade grabbed his Derby in both hands and tightened it about his skull like a bottle-cap as a half-eaten rat plopped out of the sky to land in a mass at their feet. Maggots crawled out of its thin rib-cage. A puddle – more soup than water, mixed equally with roof-top effluvium and fresh horse manure – collected around the dead rodent.

"You know," Lestrade spoke through the intricate fence-work of perfectly clenched teeth. "There are over fourteen-thousand lost umbrellas in the Missing Claims department. Fourteen-sodding-thousand. And *we* can't afford to purchase a single one."

"We should have a statute on them," Gregson agreed. "Of course, can you imagine the damage *Punch* would do to us?

The little man shuddered as if he was cat, not man, under the wet. Both had sudden fantasies of a painful cartoon drafted up of an improvident Bobby supplementing his pitiful income by hawking lost umbrellas on the street. The possibilities were simply infinite.

"I wonder how long this is going to last?" Gregson finally wondered.

"I don't know, but at least the water coming down is merely grey now." Lestrade sighed. He looked tired – of late, a common occurrence with him. It was a little disturbing.

"Too right. And no longer textured." Gregson shivered under his coat. "Awfully late in the year for rain." His breath smoked in the thickness of the air. "I'd much rather it be snow."

"One last cleaning of the *ton* before winter, I suppose." Lestrade commented. Unlike Gregson, Lestrade was a small furnace. His breath steamed as violently as the vapour coming off his shoulders. Gregson had never seen Lestrade more than slightly discomfited by the coolness of the clime, and he always felt it unfair. He himself had a severe allergy to the cold, especially when it was *wet* like this. [1]

"Your people hail from sunny France," he complained. "Why aren't you cold?"

Lestrade blinked at him, askance at this peculiar attack. "We hailed from Cornwall and Wales *before* we fled to the peninsula, you know," he pointed out. "Have you ever seen Snowdon in January?" He tucked his hands inside his arms. "This isn't like you, Gregson. Shouldn't you be making a clever comment about how we're getting nowhere in the Funeral Home scandals?"

Gregson shrugged. The movement almost took him from out of the protection of the eve. "I'm helping Hopkins too, y'know. I *know* what kind of problems you're having."

18

Lestrade blew out his breath. "It's awful," he said bluntly. "We've tried everything we can think of, but it still looks like we might have to apply for an exhumation or two."

Gregson had expected the news, but winced anyway. "*That* won't go over well," He proved his gift for understatement. "Not with the Ministry breathing down our necks for anything it thinks we're doing poorly."

"At least they haven't gotten wind of this mess . . . yet." Lestrade pointed out.

"Too true." Gregson shook his head.

More rain. A gust blew mist into their faces. Lestrade burrowed under his muffler, resigned to his fate.

"Well, Lestrade, I suppose I owe you an apology."

Lestrade met that comment with the suspicion it deserved. "How so?"

"I once told Mr. Holmes you didn't have the sense to come out of the rain."

Lestrade chuffed. "Kind of you," he said evenly.

Rain.

"Heard from Watson?"

"He can't really enter this case until we have something to show for it." Lestrade folded up the edges of his muffler to cover the bottom of his chin. "I appreciate the man's instincts, his willingness to keep up with the advances in science, and I *certainly* appreciate the fact that he's not a bad tracker . . . but we don't have anything for his medical analysis yet." He blinked as the wind changed direction. "I was on my way to meet with Hopkins. He was investigating some church records that might prove useful."

"There are too many dead people to keep track of." Gregson complained.

"I'm sure that's how these parasites managed to avoid detection all these years."

The rain was halting to the point where they could see the street on the other side. The Inspectors watched as poor Constable Lions poked his head out from his own shelter, looked both ways, and resolutely squared his shoulders. The big man appeared to sigh, reluctant but determined to do his duty, and he stepped into the open street. Standing water met his uncomfortable boots. He was probably already soaking wet. Walking inside his heavy wool uniform would keep him warm to an extent . . . as long as he *kept* walking.

Dry if not cozy, the Inspectors watched him go with a piling caseload of guilt. When it approached avalanche proportions, Lestrade squared his own shoulders and faced forward. Gregson could only follow. They might have the luxury of plain clothing, light shoes, and the freedom to huddle

19

out of the weather, but it was impossible to enjoy that comfort when their fellow policeman was out suffering for less than half their own wages.

And it wasn't as though *any* policeman made enough to brag about. Lions was paid roughly the same amount as a ditchdigger. One-hundred-fifty pounds. The absolute minimum required for marriage. The Inspectors made more by fifty, but it was eaten up in the same rate. Just putting his two sons in school cost Lestrade an easy two pounds a year. Cheap enough on the outside, but that didn't cover their clothing or books or school supplies. Gregson had heard that the first-born was a bright little button, craving paper and ink more than other children did toys and sweets. That cost money too. Chalk and slate did it more than not, like it did most children.

Gregson suspected Lestrade was stretching his funds to the last farthing to make certain his children never had – or suspected – the kind of schooling he had. Gregson couldn't blame him. Education had been bad enough when they were that age, but at least Gregson had the luxury of being sent to a Dame School with his older brothers. The small man had been much less fortunate. Like all too many children, he had known only the lot of the "ragged schools" – six half-days of education to the very poor and orphan children. Although Gregson had not been subject to that misery, he did not wish to contemplate it. It was one of the reasons why he and Elise were childless.

The other and more important reason, of course, was in Elise herself . . . .

Still, we somehow turned out all right . . . somehow . . . .

Reminding himself of that always worked . . . for a while. It was too easy to remember the hollow anguish in Bradstreet's eyes back in '82 when his three youngest children died of winter ails – and nearly their mother too. Lestrade had nearly lost his wife the same way with the arrival of their younger son.

Gregson wasn't certain how those men could continue on after that sort of loss. Elise was the one thing in his life he could rely on, and thoughts of anything that could endanger her made him half-mad with fear.

Lestrade slowed, politely waiting for the bigger – and naturally clumsier – Gregson to catch up. Rain speckled tiny dark freckles the dome and rim of his hat. Those large dark eyes regarded him with a little puzzlement mixed with a bit of impatience. Gregson could read the thoughts: *Can't he wait until we're at the Yard before he starts woolgathering?* It made him smile to himself. Their rivalry was not the same bitter thing it had been, ten years ago. In its absence both men felt a sort of unspoken relief. It had held them both back, even though the war had been under the tacit approval of their superiors, who carried the attitude that "grist makes bread".

Gregson had once believed that.

"Where are you headed today?" the larger man asked.

"After work? Unless something shows up, straight home." Lestrade's step faltered just slightly as a dying gust swept a fragrant wind into their faces. "I don't care to be caught at the office when the Chief brings in his new guest for inspection!"

Gregson snorted through his nose. "You have to wonder who it will be this time," he noted as they skirted a rapidly expanding puddle. The same boys that had ran past Gregson before the storm were running past them again. Lestrade paused and shouted something in a mash of syllables Gregson – as usual – couldn't fathom. One boy paused long enough to give a saucy answer in return, but the grin on his dirty face melted as Lestrade said something right back, quick as a fishwife. As one, the children teemed off with the group-control of a school of fish that already knew where it should head.

"Honestly," Lestrade switched to English – he probably thought Gregson had even understood him. "I don't understand some of these boys anymore."

"I have a hard time imagining you as a boy myself, Lestrade." Gregson noted.

Lestrade spared him a hard look. "I guarantee you, Gregson – The older you get, the harder that will be."

"I'll take your word for it – Bother!" They avoided a stinking rivulet just in time. "All right. If Hopkins and I were to see you today, after work, would you be available?"

The little man paused, tilting his head to one side curiously. "I wasn't planning on being anywhere, if that's what you mean," he said carefully. "Have you learnt anything yet about this funeral scandal?"

"I'm not sure. But it wouldn't hurt the three of us to start meeting on a regular basis and pool what we know. The three of us ought to be able to learn something, you know."

"One can only hope!" Lestrade spoke just a bit sourly for the perspective. He stuffed his hands in his pockets. Like most men who couldn't afford a tailor, his outer-clothing hung slightly too large for his frame. While it gave him a greater freedom of movement (a vital thing in a dangerous situation), it gave the wrong impression that he was smaller than he really was. "It's settled then. You and Hopkins come over whenever you're both ready. I'll be at home."

"And why wouldn't the three of us meet at my place? Or Hopkins?"

Lestrade gave him the look of scorn he deserved. "I'm not about to go *anywhere* near your house at the hours of supper without your wife present. And Hopkins . . . While I wasn't there at the time he invited over those cronies for Youghal's birthday, I certainly heard all about it. We'll be doing him a favour by keeping the hospitality duties away from his family."

"I admit, I feel sorry for that boy." Gregson smiled weakly. "Were our mothers ever that protective?"

Lestrade did not smile back. "I wouldn't know," he answered seriously.

Gregson swallowed down. Stupid, he thought. "This evening it is," he promised. "I will see you with Mr. Hopkins then."

Lestrade nodded. "We'll have supper for you."

"You needn't go through any imposition, Lestrade."

"I'm not. We need some sort of excuse. Just tell the others I lost a bet and had to provide a free meal or something." Lestrade looked like he didn't care what anyone thought of him for such a loss. He didn't look he cared either way. "And warn Hopkins about Paddington Street, would you?"

"Absolutely," Gregson chuckled. "We'll see you then."

Lestrade watched him go. Gregson walked like a stiff, aching rheumatoid and it was no wonder. It made him shake his head to think of what the bigger man went through on a regular basis.

He was a bit of a prig, and he *never* hesitated to rub his better brains into Lestrade's self-worth, but Lestrade always wondered if Gregson would survive one winter to the next. His normally white face would tinge with blue. His tallow head would chill with frost, and his hands shook constantly. But damned if he would go through double-effort to make certain no one had cause to say the winter hampered his ability to work. From one tenacious man to another, Lestrade respected that.

NOTE

1.   Reynaud's Disease.

Chapter II – Rabbit

Cooking smells met them at the doorway. Gregson paused to grin at Hopkins, who was nervously glancing up and down Paddington Street, one hand never far from his money, his fob or his watch. "Ever eat at The Lancashire Rose?" Gregson asked him point-blank.

"Not often," Hopkins admitted. "Perhaps two or three times. I don't often have the time to sit down and eat." Which was a polite enough lie to avoid confessing that his relatives hated the idea of their promising scion dining with lower-middle-class workers at a charity organization.

"Well, you're in for a treat. Not that it was bad before he married. That landlady's a marvel with a tureen . . . It's a wonder Lestrade doesn't weigh twenty-stone," Gregson paused to analyze the mingling odors. "Some people are just lucky, I suppose." He shrugged. "Then again, as much as *he* gets about, I daresay a pound of treacle on bread every day for a month of Sundays wouldn't bulk him up . . . ."

Hopkins was eyeing a cluster of children playing stick-hockey with soggy lumps of horse manure for pucks. It was possible he hadn't heard a thing his companion had said.

"You needn't worry about your wallet with those three," Gregson assured him as he knocked on the door with his knuckles. The handle of the doorknocker, which was a ghastly snarling monster crossed between a lion and a Chinese pug, gave him the chills every time he saw it.

Even Gregson was surprised to see Mrs. Lestrade had answered the door. The tiny woman paused to brush damp hair from her forehead. She was wearing a pullover cooking-apron with a dusting of flour here and there.

"There you are. We've been expecting you." Clea Lestrade smiled up at the two men. "You're just in time. I was setting out the side-dishes to cool a bit."

"I hope we're not putting you to an indisposition, Mrs. Lestrade." Gregson quickly put his hat on the rack, glad to do something with his hands.

"Not at all. Mrs. Collins is off to see her family, and my brother brought us enough brown and blue hares to feed a brigade this morning." She sighed, momentarily stymied. "I suppose I'll turn a few into tomorrow's cooking lesson . . . ."

"How goes the charity?" Gregson wondered with an ease that flabbergasted Hopkins. Business was chancy enough of a polite subject, but to a woman, and a married woman at that, he wouldn't expect it of the bigger man.

"Well enough that I can turn it over to my assistants in a few months." Clea beamed. "And then I can concentrate on my cooking school. Mr. Hopkins, let's get your coat off and up. It's damp out still."

Hopkins followed, fully awkward as they circumnavigated out of the narrow hallway and into a large kitchen. The young man realized then at the size of the place that the entire lodgers' building must have been a glowing private establishment at one time. Only a full math of servants, a large family, and a consistent influx of guests would explain the size of the fireplace, though it was now superfluous against the iron cook-stoves lined up, one on each side. Both were operating. The warmth emanating into the walls reminded their guests of the growing seasonal chill.

In the furthest corner, where it was no doubt cooler against the original stone walls that started the building (Hopkins guessed a few hundred years ago), Lestrade and his little sons were kneeling before a wash-tub, sleeves rolled up as they soaked fresh pelts into a peculiar-looking solution.

"Remember, you have to *squeeze*, not *wring*," Lestrade was warning an earnest-young tanner just in the nick of time.

"There's a blood-spot on yours, Nicholas," the smaller boy pointed out.

"My hands are too big for this!"

"Your hands are hardly larger than mine, *Mab*," their father pointed out. "But you can stop now . . . time to wash up." With that casual look a farmer gave the wandering beeves when they wandered back home, Lestrade rose to his feet, reaching for the wash-basin set close by.

In the meantime, Martin had lifted up a prodigiously sized grey and white hare skin, beaming in triumph. "Look," he told the newcomers. "*Konifl.*"

"*Blev*," his father corrected absently. "*Honifl* is what you *eat. Blev* is what you turn into mittens . . . Get your hands in here, Martin. You're having supper with your mother, and she wants *clean* hands on her cooking."

"Yes, sir."

Lestrade flicked his glance to a second sink not far from Gregson's hands. "Might want to use that one, gentlemen . . . I *guarantee* it doesn't have blood."

"I assure you, I've been up to my elbows in much worse this week." Gregson agreeably picked up the cake of soap. It looked home-made and he gave it a cautious sniff. It was a creamy white and smelled of . . .

rosemary? He noted belatedly (some detective) that delicate fossil leaves of that very plant were stamped along the soap.

"You have an odd look on your face," Lestrade commented as he saw to the cleanliness of his sons' hands.

"Is the home-made soap or store-bought?"

"Home-made. Who can afford that store-bought stuff anymore?"

"I'd agree with you, but how'd you get it to look like store-bought? Store-bought is white."

Lestrade sternly produced a towel, scrubbed Martin's fingers, and examined them closely. "I didn't. But I saw the women putting pipeclay into the mix. *That* made it white." He tended to his own hands with obvious relief. "Draws poisons out of the nastiest wounds, let me tell you."

Going by Hopkins' face, Lestrade was an exotic individual indeed. Well, so be it. Gregson didn't grudge Hopkins his being raised in a better economic era than their own – nor would Lestrade. But once in a while they were reminded of the differences. Like now. Hopkins was luckier than he'd ever know. He'd probably never had to "make do or do without" in his childhood.

Clea Lestrade re-entered to collect the trays for her supper with the boys. "I'll leave you alone, now." Clea paused to smile at her husband on the way out. The maid followed with the remnants. Gregson was privately amused to see Hopkins' discomfiture at the quick smile Lestrade returned to his wife. It would seem the younger man had not reconciled their host's fierce reputation from the street. He probably thought that awful gorgon door-knocker was an extension of Lestrade's personality.

"I thought you disliked rabbit, Lestrade." Gregson lifted an eyebrow as they settled to the plank table.

"Not at all. I just don't trust another person's word that it *is* rabbit." The smaller man lifted his own eyebrow. "One of my wife's brothers was invited to a hunt the other day, and I'm beginning to wonder if he didn't clean out three whole droves of hare in the meadow."

Hopkins started on a baked apple wrapped in bacon. Soon warmth pervaded inside and out and he felt himself relaxing. This time of the year, it was inevitable to find apples or vegetable marrows or parsnips into the cooking. Just as well he liked *all* foods. "Has anyone heard from Dr. Watson of late?" He asked. "I'd heard he was going to attend that little meeting at Barts over dating corpses, but I never saw him."

Gregson shrugged. "Watson's easy enough to miss in a crowd," he offered as he passed the salt bowl. "I suppose that's how people wind up saying the most *outré* things in his presence . . . They don't really *see* him."

"It's possible he didn't attend." Lestrade opined. "I spoke to him less than ten days ago, and his wife was fighting an upper-chest cough. [1] It turns out we were both in line at the chemists' for our own remedies, and he was worried about the last batch of syrup he'd bought for her."

Gregson frowned uncertainly. "Don't most women get a cough during their confinement?"

Lestrade shrugged helplessly. Much of the world of women was an unfathomable one – and he was *perfectly* comfortable with that *status quo*. He knew more than a lot of husbands – Clea had very few female relatives so when she complained about anything, *he* was usually her first audience. "This time of year is harsh enough, but I hear Mrs. Watson isn't doing well. Some sort of malingering condition picked up when she was living abroad." Their host eschewed stronger drink for a glass of water. "He and his wife plan to celebrate the end of her confinement close to Christmas, and if one more well-meaning person suggests 'Noel' or 'Noelle' as a name, he hopes the Yard will be lenient to his case in view of the circumstances. Consider yourself warned."

Gregson snorted, and managed to swallow his food just in time. "I daresay he'll be ready to get out of the house soon enough."

Lestrade chose to overlook Gregson's superior attitude. He didn't have children of his own, and wasn't likely to. As Lestrade hadn't ever planned on breaking out of his own bachelor ascetics before meeting Clea, he could be magnanimous.

Hopkins, though . . . It didn't take a genius to notice Hopkins always grew quiet and a little bit withdrawn when the subject of children came up. It wasn't Lestrade's business, but the man had been wearing an engagement-ring for well over a year.

"Wasn't the doctor going to come over and work with us over a month ago?" Hopkins asked quietly.

"It's closer to two months now." Lestrade admitted. "We both agreed he needed to see his wife off to a healthier climate before he started working with this sort of case." Corpses and carbolic acid wouldn't help Mrs. Watson's condition one whit. Lestrade did not mention that this was the longest Mrs. Watson had gone on carrying the child its parents had hoped for so long. The truly sad thing was it was through no fault of either parent. Circumstances had been fiendishly against them in the past.

And there's no justice to it at all. If any one couple deserves to be parents, it would be the Watsons.

"I wish Dr. Roanoke hadn't been so ill himself." Gregson was saying. "He and Watson are the best at examining the dead for what they have to say. There are times when I was ready to believe in spiritual mediums, the way that old man could wring the secrets out." He leaned back slightly, dipping a heel of bread into the sauce poured over his portion of rabbit. Without the civilizing influence of women, it stood fair to reason that plates would be mopped clean tonight. While it had been years since the older men had walked the beat, twenty miles a day without a meal in between, they *still* had the horror of letting food of any kind sit still. This did not sit well in higher society functions, where letting food remain on the plate was a sign of good manners. "That old dog knows plenty of new tricks. Remember his spectrum tests on those bloodstains last year?"

"Professional work," Hopkins agreed. His intelligent face creased in memory and interest. "I wish he had more than a say on who his successor will be."

"Someone younger with better connections." Lestrade answered bluntly. "It *won't* be Watson."

"What we need," Gregson began slowly, "is to find *something* on this mess. Time's passing, and the trail's getting colder." His large hands tapped against his plate thoughtfully. "As ridiculous as it seems, I feel as though this pathetic case of con artistry has deeper roots."

"I think it must," Hopkins agreed. "There has to be a great deal of organization involved for this gang to take this sort of advantage of the bereaved. And there has to be some very cold-minded people out there to even make their livelihood on this sort of thing."

"There's no shortage of *those*," Lestrade said practically. "Things have changed drastically since . . . May," he said carefully. "I don't like it, but Mr. Holmes was the type of assistance we needed. There's no one to replace him." He noticed Hopkins give a tiny flinch, like a bramble slapping his face, but politely ignored it. "Without him . . . I don't like to think of how much harder we've been working."

"Bad enough we had to fight to get approval to let him in on those cases in the late seventies . . . What was it, '79?" Gregson chewed thoughtfully. "Almost 1880."

"Right at the lip." Lestrade poured cups of thick water-cider for everyone. "He only seemed to get better and more infuriating with each succeeding year." The older men snickered in posthumous respect for an unusual ally. "Thank *God* for Dr. Watson," the smaller man said fervently.

"*Yes.*" Gregson toasted the poor man.

Hopkins had been playing with his fork, a sure sign he was thinking hard. Some men smoked when in a brown study. Some men twitched. Hopkins was fine so long as he had something to do with his fingers. "Lestrade, did you find out anything on that strange man who worked at both those funeral homes?"

"*Blake?*" Lestrade paused and shuddered. "You're being a bit polite in your description, aren't you? Strange doesn't quite cover it." He turned to Gregson. "Strange fish."

"The man who started out as a cutter for the Army Medical Corps?" Gregson remembered. "You've said that before."

"I think he's missing something." Hopkins tapped his temple significantly. "But no one had any fault with his technique."

"You're right about that," Lestrade said darkly. "As quick as Saucy Jack, [2] if much neater, thank goodness." He managed to eat a bit more, which was admirable considering the topic. "I couldn't find out much except that he was originally posted in Afghanistan at several hospitals. Second son. Low prospects. He has a brother who is a bank teller at the First Bank of the Thames. Their father is a bit higher up, a clerk who specializes in appraising private assets for loans and foreclosures."

"Sounds remarkably dull."

"It's even *more* dull when you get them talking about it."

"Still . . . *missing jewelry?* That was one of the problems with the Rookstool case . . . A soldier who died in Afghanistan . . . his body goes to one of the funeral homes that employ George Blake, who has a brother and a father in a bank. Family connexions with the value of assets . . . Jewelry qualifies as assets." Hopkins gnawed on his lip in thought.

"I know, but I couldn't see anything that overtly tied the Bank with the funeral homes." Lestrade confessed. "If there's something in the paperwork, it's good and buried." Since it was his own house, he willfully committed to the sin of leaning his arm on the table. "Feel free. You might see something I'm missing." He shook his head. "All I found was a secret marriage on part of the son that was a teller."

"Bigamy?" Gregson guessed.

"Nothing so simple. Turns out most banks will fire any of their tellers if they marry before they reach one-hundred-fifty a year. They feel that since one-fifty are the minimum to survive on, they'd be *encouraging* him to steal."

"Ha. As if three-percent interest on a bank account isn't." Gregson sniffed. "So he married, no doubt because the lady was tired of waiting, but the bank wasn't supposed to know about it."

"You have it."

"Now how exactly did you handle that?"

Lestrade lifted his dark eyebrows. "How do you think I handled it? I told him he should listen to his conscience, and I would afford him the time with which to do so. By odd co-incidence, it happens to be *my* bank all this is coming from!" He shrugged. "Give us a few more days on the man, and I'm certain he'll be nervous enough to give us some help."

Hopkins laughed very softly. "This is like building up a house made of playing cards," he said. "I feel like one wrong move will collapse the whole thing. But there's something out of true about this whole situation."

28

"Bricks without clay – isn't that what Holmes used to say?"

"He didn't *say* it – he *snarled* it." Lestrade corrected him. "And more often than not, in my face." He tilted back in his chair, arms folded neatly over his chest. "You're the ring-master of our three-ring circus, Gregson. What do you think of all this?"

Gregson was a moment in responding. "We need Dr. Watson," he said at last. "I don't have to remind any of you gentlemen our reasons why we shouldn't be dropping this case where an outside party could pick it up.

"Things started to show they were sour back in '83 and'84, when some of the Professor's sweet little friends accidentally revealed themselves on the Thames Warehouse scandal. I think that was when some people actually sat up and paid notice of us – the Yard in general, and you and me in particular. Wasn't just the Home Office and the Foreign Office. It was also the people that make their livings out of things we arrest people for.

"Then things went *full* sour when you and I were all but *banned* from getting on the Ripper case, Lestrade. Thought that was bad enough, but it was all just building. Hopkins at least had the comfort of being so new on the job everyone thought he was unfinished in his patterns. Makes a man hard to recruit for either side if you don't quite know what he's on about. I suppose it was his working with Mr. Holmes that gave him some bit of protection there . . . ." Gregson sighed and, for the first time, looked a little older and thinner. "Then . . . that nightmare this April and May when Mr. Holmes had to die in order to make some people sit up and admit there was such a thing as an organized criminal network. Took his dying, and nearly Lestrade, as well as two constables – Hopkins just *barely* missed being a cripple for life!" Dissatisfaction wrenched his mouth.

"We need to work on this case between the cracks," he said. "We do no more than what's expected of us, help each other if it means getting our desks cleared off, but we know what we're to be working on in our spare time. We don't set so much as a single piece of paper down on the Home Secretary's desk until we have the whole thing to show for it. I'm serious." His glare at Hopkins was mixed with worry. "You're a smart one, Hopkins. Be careful that those smarts don't get knocked out of you. Constables are good assistants, and mostly they don't ask questions."

Dinner was over. Lestrade wordlessly pushed forward a small box of cigars and a match-box. He rose to pull out a bottle of something clear and distilled while the others began their period of reflective smoking.

"And you, Lestrade." Gregson didn't look at his host as he spoke, concentrating on trimming the cigar-end with his little knife. "Stay close to Dr. Watson. Make up a story if you have to. People think you're pals with him anyway. They won't think it's anything unusual if you start spending more time with him."

"Because it's either Watson or Roanoke on this case?" Hopkins wondered uneasily, as if he suspected what Gregson would say.

"Partly. That's partly it. The bigger part is, Watson knows to his sorrow what it means when there's something secret running underneath the government. Any time you have a bank involved, there's that risk." He touched a match to his cigar and puffed quietly while his pale face grew glummer by degrees.

"And there's the fact that Colonel Moriarty seems to have included me in his private little war with Dr. Watson," Lestrade supplied quietly. "He's been too quiet for too long. Nothing since we called his bluff over the bloody sword."

"He's waiting.' Gregson said flatly. "He's a Moriarty. If he's anything at all like his unmourned brother, he can wait as long as it takes to get what he wants done. And don't forget he was in Afghanistan too – just like Watson. Just like this Blake character. Just like this poor bastard of a corpse Rookstool."

"I haven't forgotten." Lestrade said just as quietly. "How much longer can you gentlemen stay?"

"I've nowhere to go," Gregson puffed. "My Elise won't be back until the weekend."

"I'm fine," Hopkins added. "What are you thinking, Lestrade?"

"That there's two quires [3] of foolscap in my office, and a free-standing chalkboard. I suggest we head up there and start drafting our plans."

NOTES

1. Upper chest coughs led too often to bronchitis, which in turn to pneumonia. In the days before antibiotics, this was often fatal.
2. Jack the Ripper.
3. A *quire* is a set of twenty-four uniform sheets of paper.

Chapter III – Sleepless and Unsettled

"**H**ere we go, dear."

Mary Watson *née* Morstan was a paragon of womanly virtue. Her husband knew it, but this admiration was refreshed in the way she faced the latest brunt of medicine with patience.

"I used to *enjoy* mustard," she said wistfully.

Her husband had to laugh. There was no choice. Inside the patient resignation of her regime was a tiny spark of good humoured-mischief. "Perhaps you will again."

"Well I shouldn't complain that I'm being coddled." Mary sat up in bed, looking far more rested than of late, but they both knew her lungs were still touch and go. She sighed with just a touch of the dramatic, pulling her forearm over her eyes in a swooning motion. "Have at you, sir."

John laughed silently, appreciating that she could still smile, despite the weeks of foul remedies.

It was only a matter of moments before the warm, wet cloth of mustard plaster was placed on her chest.

"Why is it that lung infections usually start in the *left* lung?" Mary wondered drowsily. It was almost obscenely comfortable to lie under blankets in the tiny tea room, surrounded by her indoor plants and pale late-year sunlight while her husband placed glowingly warm compresses on her skin.

"I would venture because the left lung is smaller." John told her.

"Really." Mary's sleepy eyes opened with interest. "They never mentioned that in our art lessons."

"It's true." With his sleeves rolled up to a point below the elbow (and almost-ironed those rolls looked), down to his waistcoat, he was very much the charming and devastatingly handsome man of her first acquaintance.

"Why is it so? That's asymmetrical!"

"It makes room for the heart." John explained.

"I had no idea." Mary had to think about that for a moment.

"We're really not all that symmetrical when you think about it." John quickly removed the traces of warm mustard-plaster from his hands before they could start a blister and dried them on a hand-towel. He enjoyed the green light of the tea room as much as she did, and the couple sat together for a moment, content in each other's presence now that John had a rare break in his schedule from the eternal influx of autumn colds and ails. "Our liver favours one side. As does our appendix. Sometimes there's an extra rib, or extra vertebrae in the spine. The stomach rests on the left side. We tend to develop one hand over the other."

"This is all true, but still. It's amazing to think of a lung smaller than the other."

"It's even more pronounced in some animals." John told her. "One of my friends in the Army had been from the States. He said the rattlesnake had only one lung. The other vanished long ago. I know that most snakes have mostly one long lung, and a very small one on the left side," he explained ruefully: "We killed enough of them to protect the camp-site."

"But why would there be an asymmetry in the first place?" Mary wondered. "It goes against the logic of engineering, when one thinks about it!"

"Curious, aren't you?" John smiled with deep fondness and he paused to think a moment. "It would have to be because of the heart," he said at last. "The heart is the most vital organ in the body."

"I thought the brain was."

"The heart can function without the aid of the brain – for the most part." John answered thoughtfully. "The fact is, it's a special organ that operates as a pump does. The old blood enters one side – blue and low in oxygen. But when it leaves the heart it is freshly oxygenated and bright red. So you see, the heart, which literally is the organ all others are based against, is not symmetrical. It cannot be. It is designed quite beautifully for what it does."

"I wonder why, then, that engineers and mechanics do not design their inventions along the lines of models that work, as opposed to coming up with something that has little resemblance to the original examples."

"There you have me, dearest. I suppose they could be thinking that following the lines of a living thing would be awkward – there is the medical credo that triangles are never found in nature, but I guarantee you, nor are there perfect squares or circles!"

"What about blood cells?"

"They're not perfect circles. They're flattened and a bit elongated, like an egg. I hope I'm not boring you."

"John, you could never be boring. I am currently bored out of my under-stimulated skull, but that is because you've banned me from sewing."

"I must, Mary. You have to bend over slightly to stitch and – "

" – compresses the chest muscles against the lungs. Yes, I know. You needn't tell me twice." But Mary was smiling. "I only hope you are taking care of yourself."

32

"The consequence barely needs discussing." The last time Mary had felt her husband was taking needless liberties with his health and well-being, she had firmly banned him from billiards for a week. As far as John was concerned, the week had been terrible.

"I think it's ready," Mary said after a few minutes of a comfortable silence.

"Here we are then . . . ." John carefully removed the plaster. A breath of coolness made her throat feel as though she faced a spring breeze. She sighed.

"Ready for a cup of tea?" he asked, as if she hadn't looked forward to this moment for half the evening.

"Absolutely!"

"Very good. What will it be?"

"Hawthorne-berry."

"*Excellent* choice, my dear." He bent his head. She felt the brush of his mustache against her forehead and he was headed to bell-cord for the maid.

"*What* exactly is wrong with Hopkins?"

Gregson didn't pretend ignorance. Lestrade sounded half at the end of his patience. He sighed and accepted another cigar as they watched their younger cohort step lightly down the street to a waiting cab.

"Trouble at home, partly," he said heavily. "You know his folks didn't want him to join the Metro."

Lestrade snorted. "That's hardly news. Did *any* of our folks want us to?"

"I'd say it goes deeper than parental disapproval. Hopkins' people are just a wee bit wealthier than ours are. They had *expectations* for the boy. At least you and I were the youngest sons. *Nobody* really cares what we do with our lives, so long as we don't embarrass them by changing religions or throw a rock at Prince Albert – much as he'd deserve it . . . It's not like we'd inherit their legacies after all." Gregson took the offered glass of whisky. His voice was matter-of-fact, and far more awful than any bitterness or anger.

Lestrade didn't have to say anything. Gregson wouldn't have had the freedom to marry Elise had he been the pampered first-born. She was perfectly lovely with one unfortunate birth defect that a great deal of money *would* have cured. But she hadn't any such wealth, and Gregson hadn't given a shil and a spit for it. Such were the luxuries of the overlooked son.

"Let me guess. He was supposed to get the job nicely picked out for him by a relative or patron?" Lestrade picked up one of Martin's playing cards off the desk and slapped it to his forehead, eyes closed as if he were psychically channeling the *Secrets Arcanum*.

"Oh, very good. Nice to know you're pursuing an alternative source of income when you leave the Force." Gregson toasted him, just slightly tipsy. "Hopkins, poor sod, wants to marry a perfectly sweet girl who has been waiting for him almost two years now. Her parents approve. It's just that *his* parents don't."

"He's been wearing that engagement ring long enough."

"He's going to have to choose before much longer: His lady or his parents." Gregson was unusually sympathetic as the man finally found his cab and whipped off to his home. "They went through a lot of sacrifices. Left the Cambridgeshire luxuries to come here for the advantages of society . . . got *all* their daughters married off to fine families. They should count themselves lucky on *that* minor miracle. Mind you, they're ignoring his younger brother, who's better suited for the family business in transcribing and book-keeping. It's 'Our Stanley' they want to be at their side thick and thin, and too bad if he chokes on their parental affections."

"You think he has what it takes to survive without his familial approval?" Lestrade figured Gregson would know.

Gregson was slow in his response. "He's capable of a lot more than he knows." He watched the swirl of liquid in his glass. "But if he keeps trying to do too much and putting it all on his own shoulders, he'll collapse under his own sense of failure . . . ." Gregson set his mouth. "He's probably the best man we had when it came to understanding Holmes's methods. Mebbe because his mind's still young and strong, and he had a much better education than we did."

"Ha. It goes without saying that most people had a better education than I did." Lestrade spoke in the same sort of voice Gregson had just used when referring to being the forgotten son.

"I don't think Hopkins was ready for Holmes's death." Gregson winced slightly as he spoke. "I feel a wretch for saying it. But those two were just getting into a good working relationship before all this rot happened in April and May."

Lestrade had a rare flash of prescience. "You're saying Mr. Holmes was a good influence on him."

"Very. It's not like his uncle – Hopkins' father is long dead in the grave – sees him as more than an extension of his own ambitions. And his mother just goes along with what her brother says. Holmes *listened* to him, and you could see the man's brains literally stretch overnight when they got together on their first case. I think Holmes liked him too. Said he had the sense to call him on a 'real' case. He's scrounged up a copy of every deathless, mind-blisteringly dull monograph the man's ever written. Probably reads a little bit of them every night."

"I see." Lestrade did. Society was a cramping, choking entity with myriad rules designed to hold everything together on thin cobwebs. What kept a man from falling through the wires was the strength of his own relationships and friendships. Men needed to be relied on and trusted as much as they needed to trust someone. Hopkins clearly hadn't enough sensible people in his life outside of the tight family circles.

Gregson, close to Lestrade's age and far luckier with his career, was still staring at the empty spot in the darkening street where Hopkins had melted away.

Lestrade thought he looked a little lonely.

Gregson blinked, slowly. "I'm sorry, did you say something?"

"I said," Lestrade said patiently, "perhaps you'd like to use the guest bedroom."

"I haven't drunk that much." Gregson protested.

"Didn't say you did." Lestrade jerked his thumb over his shoulder. Gregson looked. Perched on wall behind the small writing-desk was a clear weather-glass. Sea-green water was slowly pressing its way from rising pressures. "I'm thinking that it might not be raining rotting rats and all that other lovely stuff, but it's going to come hard and fast, and I *don't* like the thought of you meeting your Maker by a dislodged sheet of roofing-slate." He finished by a telling glance out the window. "The cabbies have torn off, and you won't be getting a ride home. I hope Hopkins makes it."

"He ought to." Gregson felt a little embarassed. "You don't have to be so generous, you know. This is your best chance to become the Yard's Best by default."

Lestrade snorted, and a definite gleam of the devil shone in those large dark eyes. "I'm not winning anything by default, Euclid. I'm winning because I am the best."

Gregson grinned, back on familiar ground. "Then we'd best both get our beauty sleep."

"You go on ahead." Lestrade's voice took on a false lightness as he pulled spare blankets down from the cupboards. "I don't think I'll get much sleep tonight."

Gregson felt his eyebrow lift. "Not feeling well?"

"Not really." Lestrade hesitated, and openly came to a decision. "Foot always hurts in this weather . . . ."

Gregson wasn't certain that was the full truth. Lestrade hadn't looked like he'd slept decently in a long time, and a sudden storm front wouldn't be the explanation. "Try another toddy then," he offered.

"Perhaps I should."

But Gregson had the feeling that Lestrade wasn't completely paying attention to him, that his mind was going elsewhere.

It wasn't his place, he knew. They were co-workers, fellow policemen, but their relationship was prickly and awkward, both men knowing full well they had wasted years in their rivalry, but they were still unable to give up the unease. There really was only room for one when it came to promotion, and both of them needed it. It was too soon in their shaky truce to mention things like nightmares or troubles of the mind.

Well, that should end once Watson got involved. Of all the men on the Yard, Watson seemed the most . . . *comfortable* with Lestrade – if that wasn't the wrong word. And Lord knew, Watson could be discreet, but if he knew someone needed to take care of themselves, he wouldn't hesitate to say so.

Chapter IV – What War Feels Like

Lestrade wasn't surprised to see the boys were settled in bed and sound asleep. He was surprised to see his wife had followed suit. As it was just short of nine, he wondered if anything was amiss.

Clea stirred. She was a light sleeper, and he wouldn't be able to move in without waking her anyway.

"*Ma-mel?*" He brushed blue-black hair from her cheek. "Are you feeling well?"

"Truthfully, no," Clea confessed. Her voice was faint in the darkness. "It came on a-sudden. I just feel . . . very tired and warm."

"That kitchen isn't proof of drafts," he murmured. "Get you some rest. I'll take the settee tonight."

"All right. I'd ask a kiss in payment, but no sense risking giving you this . . . whatever it is."

"London's full of sickness right now," he continued, stroking her hair, thinking to himself that Dr. Watson must be nearly frantic, what with seeing too many of that sickness every day, and with an expectant wife, weak in the lungs, in the rooms upstairs from his practice.

"Mmm. Will likely blow over with the weather," Clea suggested. She was sliding back into sleep as he rose and sought out another blanket in the chest.

The rain grew stiff and sharp. Tiny clicks rattled against the windows, like urchins kicking cinders on the glass. Lestrade caught himself stoking the fire for the third time and reminded himself the coal budget was a fixed sum. He settled back with the blanket, staring into the low flames without a word. It was warm within, but the sheer bitterness of the outside ensured he took no comfort from the fire.

A low rustle, and Gregson was standing in the doorway. Both men traded a knowing look and Gregson wordlessly took the other side of the settee.

"This must be what war feels like," Lestrade said at last in the low quiet.

"It must." Gregson wrapped his own blanket about his shoulders.

"We're just policemen, Gregson. What in the world can we do?"

"What we always do." Gregson shrugged. "We take care of our own, and that's London first, England after."

"Simple." Lestrade snorted. He paused to rub at his eyes. "Are we doing the right thing, bringing Watson into this?"

"You're still worried about that."

"I'm concerned, of course. You know the kind of man Watson is. Just because he's a perfect soldier doesn't mean he should be used as one."

"We are at war," Gregson reminded him. "And do you think for one moment that Watson would thank us for *not* giving him the chance to make London a bit safer for his family? Sherlock Holmes died for that dream. He won't do any less. You know that."

"I know that. But . . . ." At a loss to explain, Lestrade shook his head and blew out his breath. "I know. But if anything happens to him . . . Who will see to his family?"

Gregson was stone-silent for a moment. "I hadn't thought about that," he admitted. "Doesn't Mrs. Watson still have the Agra pearls?"

"Probably. Can't imagine his telling her what to do with them. Can't imagine the likes of her selling them because she wants the latest fashion." Lestrade snorted at the very thought. "They're probably like us. Holding on to what they've got in case times get truly bad."

"And with that baby on the way . . . ." Gregson managed a very tiny chuckle. "Did you join the naming pool?"

"Certainly not. I have my scruples."

"Come on. You just risked a shill."

"Didn't feel like risking a shill. Besides, I'm quite convinced Watson will not saddle any of his progeny with a name like '*Sherlock*' . . . ."

Gregson chuckled a bit louder at that. "Well, there are plenty of unfortunate names to saddle a youngster with. Most likely it'll be after blood-kin somewhere."

"Most likely." Lestrade sighed, leaning his head back for a minute. "We sound as bad as a bunch of old women, gossiping about a man who isn't even here."

"I'm sure he'd do the same for us." Gregson shrugged.

"I should get those blocks up from the boys." Lestrade muttered. "They're too old to be using them."

"You aren't going to save them for any future brothers or sisters?"

Lestrade hesitated just a moment too long. "I suppose we'll worry about the lack of blocks should that moment come."

Gregson read between the lines. Either there would be no more children, or Lestrade believed there would not be. As he had none at all, he was hardly the type to sermonize.

"Well, every child needs a good set of blocks."

"Police children more than most," Lestrade snorted. "If Watson continues to assist us, we're honour-bound to give him a set for his son or daughter."

"I don't follow you."

"Before Martin knew better, he had a bit of confusion over the letters on the divisional badges. Inevitably, he had his own version of the alphabet going." Lestrade lifted an eyebrow. "You never heard about that? Clea caught him standing over Nicholas' crib, prompting, '*A is for Whitehall, B is for Chelsea, C is for Mayfair and Soho . . . .*'"

Gregson slapped his hand over his mouth. "A policeman's son is a different sort," he managed.

"I wouldn't mind if he followed my steps, but I'd just as soon he found something less dangerous." Lestrade warned.

"Says the man who has smugglers in his tree."

"We have established I'm the black sheep."

"So am I, for that matter. Wasting a two-pence education in the law enforcement." Gregson sniffed. "You know something strange? Most of us aren't oldest sons. I think Stanley's one of the few."

"Can't be that uncommon."

"No, think about it. Watson's a second son. Mr. Holmes was. You're a third son, I'm a third son, Jones and Brown and that youngster Forbes are third sons. Everything goes to the first-born, you know. It's the remainders that must scrabble out for themselves."

"And in our wisdom, we chose the Metro," Lestrade said dryly.

"A lot of us are like Watson – tried service elsewhere first. Now he helps us in other ways. Never really knew where to pin Holmes, though. I daresay even his own family could share that problem."

"We've been doing a lot of thinking about him, haven't we?" Lestrade leaned his cheek-bone into his hand. "It was almost this time last year that he and Patterson began collaborating."

"And it all went to Hades three-and-a-half months later." Gregson agreed. "And now he's dead . . . and Patterson's all but fallen off the map. Wonder where he is now?"

"I don't know and I don't care," Lestrade spat. "He can be mucking stables for Wessex for all I care. That was a bloody stupid mistake he pulled. And I was even more one for letting him have his way."

"Lestrade." Gregson sighed. "Don't take this the wrong way, but it isn't like you had any say over what Patterson was going to do."

"I know what I ought to have done. I ought to have quoted verse and chapter a few pages out of our manuals. He had too much independent freedom in that raid against Moriarty's gang. And now look. Holmes is dead because a foolish Inspector underestimated the raid."

"Patterson had a personal stake in bringing Moriarty down. That stake was far more personal than any of us knew," Gregson reminded him. "God alone knows what that was, but perhaps it was because he'd been swimming in the muck for so long . . . he was willing to do anything to stop the leader."

"Leader. Who is left to take his place?" Lestrade shook his head. "It can't be a coincidence that this Colonel Moriarty is plaguing Watson. He as much accused him of causing trouble from the start."

"It's always the relatives closest to the Crown that cause the worst trouble." Gregson reminded him. "And you have to wonder what sort of trouble this is, that Watson wouldn't get his closest friend involved."

"Watson was always more aware of Holmes's mortality than Holmes was." Lestrade sighed. "He shouldn't have died. He was brilliant, but he was still *just an amateur*. It wasn't his business to stick his neck out like that. That's our job."

"Business or not, it's what he did." Gregson pointed out. "I agree with you whole-heartedly there. It wasn't his job. But I suppose he felt that if he didn't do it, no one else would."

"We would have," Lestrade persisted, the stubborn little man as grim and dogged as ever.

"I know. But did he? Did he even notice us?" Gregson asked the air quietly. "Watson said matching his brains against Moriarty's was the most important moment of his life."

"Some life if it led to his death," Lestrade answered bitterly.

The gust of wind came up without warning. It was less wind and more fury, picking up grains of stinging sand and shell and tossing them in the old man's face. He cursed in phlegmatic French, leveling several imprecations upon the gods of the wind.

Sharp grains clung about his face. When he blinked, they fell out of his lashes and sprinkled his coat, only to be picked up and flung back again with the next wind.

The old man's anfractuous route was time-consuming along the wind-swept coast. The etesian north winds had struck within schedule, but when one was as nomadic as himself, it was difficult to be prepared for everything.

With relief he climbed up the narrow path to the stone library. With a breath pulled from deep in his lungs he pressed the door after him, using his back.

The lean little library-clerk at the front desk – dwarfed by the majesty of the cathedral-like architecture – looked up and smiled, passing on a greeting in whispering French. It was returned with a measure more strength.

"I have the delivery you have been . . . expecting?" The man ventured in his shy attempt at English. For good measure he held up the fat envelope, sealed and ribboned.

"*Merci* – !" A rattling cough comprised of silicates interrupted the bulk of the thanks. The old man took the package with a final sigh and huddled his way to a private corner where he was known to prefer reading in uninterrupted peace.

Alone at last, the old man ceased to look quite so very old. He wiped at his face with a linen cloth, trying again to gain some success over the irritating sands caught in the tiniest bit of his skin. There was no wonder, he mused darkly, that the Vernets never spent more than sporadic holidays here and *never* in the winter. The sheer misery of existence from day to day was enough to drive nobler men than himself into dark thoughts and even darker actions.

Once, a local had told him the local courts granted lighter sentences to those who committed violence under the presence of such winds. At the time, he'd thought it a case of Gallic romanticism, an indulgence of emotions that contrasted to his cool Anglo-Saxon intellect.

He now understood the reasoning for such laws. The human equation was turning out to be far more fluid and complex than he'd ever imagined. That a demographic could change from one country to another, so strenuously . . . Well, that was food for a new thought.

Watson had understood that in a way. He'd spoken of how Englishmen in tropic climes had committed actions they would never have fathomed were they back home. Musgrave had spoken of his hot-blooded Welsh servants . . . .

Perhaps environment was more a factor than he'd thought.

He wasn't going to wholecloth embrace a philosophy before he'd finished spinning it, though. One had Gregson, who was as Saxon as a Viking, yet he could be hot-tempered and rash. Or Lestrade, who had a mood that was as far from Gallic heat as the imagination *could* get.

But back to Watson . . . .

The old man smiled to himself, wistful and hopeful. For a man who'd lived abroad so very much, there was more English starch in the man's spine than any twenty people he could think of. The British ideal was supposed to be resolute in all actions, and yet Watson was the only purely resolute man he'd ever known. He'd always been that way, even as a shaken, ill veteran without two strong legs to stand on.

Did he ever regret any of his actions? There were days when that question loomed like a vulture blocking the sun. Could he?

Or were his actions so firm on the narrow paths of life that he never had to step out of true?

It took courage to move swiftly. He was still pondering the correctness of his own impulses.

The smile faded like the sun behind clouds. Long fingers twitched around the heavy wax seal. It was a false emblem, one created and used for special communications the Foreign Office used to disguise real information under the false front of dry estate taxes.

One moment of choice, and eight months of running. A long-term consequence to an instinctive move.

Surely it could not last much longer. Moran was a hunter, but he was not overly patient by nature. Surely he would move soon.

It was the small things that revealed his enemies. Moriarty would have never fallen, were it not for that one little slip he'd made last winter. All Moran had to do was make a similar move.

And then he would move faster than he'd ever done in his life.

Chapter V – Nothing New Under the Sun with Crime

Hopkins met Gregson at the office, none the worse for his quick departure. "How are you, Inspector?" he asked equably enough.

"Better than *Lestrade* is," Gregson answered. "His wife's starting to get ill. He'll show up for the evening . . . ." He waited until they were out of the casual range of eavesdroppers in the hustle-bustle of the Yard. "For now, we're going to pull Lestrade out of this a bit, give him updates and the like, but you and I are going to concentrate on what we can learn about this funeral nonsense. Lestrade's better than we are when it comes to getting information out of people. We'll leave that to him." By reputation alone, most suspects preferred to confess everything rather than endure Lestrade's obstinate form of questioning.

Hopkins nodded his agreement. "It makes sense." He glanced at the backs of his hands nervously. "Tobias," he added under his breath, "I'm not a superstitious man, but . . . ." He stopped talking for a moment. "I don't *like* what's happening. What we've learned so far is . . . well, this is *corruption*. If we *aren't* in full possession of the facts, the Yard will look like the biggest fools that ever stood in clamshells, and if we *are* in full possession of the facts, the case will blow open a . . . a *very* sensitive subject." The dead were sacred. The dead were to be mourned under intricate ritual, and the living would sacrifice on their behalf, but to take advantage of both the dead and the mourning . . . it went against the grain all the way to the bones of the young Inspector.

"And when people sink so low, you haven't any idea where they'll stop. What if they move to murder to cover their trail?" Gregson finished for him. "Crime's been organized before in London. I'm certain it will be again. We're talking about at least a fine old tradition since Queen Elizabeth . . . ." He shrugged, cool and analytical at an unsettling prospect.

All that changed a moment later when a young clerk ran up and pressed a wire into his hands. "Compliments of the season, sir," the boy quickly touched his capbrim. "Dr. Watson to Scotland Yard."

"And I'm the closest one standing in the door, eh?" Gregson grunted with a gruff smile. "Don't spend it on gin, now." He pressed the first coin his fingers found in his pocket into the messenger's hand and flicked the envelope open.

Hopkins shifted his weight from side to side, watching as the other man read the contents. His blonde eyebrows shot up once, and a growing smile spread over his mouth before the eyebrows shot up again.

"Well." Gregson looked up. "It was about time we had some good news." He passed over the missive to Hopkins.

Hopkins took it, and needed but a second to absorb the contents. He grinned, and then a low whistle was his reaction.

"That's rather a large baby," he said as if he knew something about the subject. (Gregson's eyebrows shot up a third time.) "But . . . *Oh, dash it!*"

"What?"

"I don't think *anyone* in the pool picked the name 'Arthur'."

Gregson laughed. "If not, we'll find something noble to do with the pot!" He plucked the paper out of Hopkins' hand and thrust it into the face of Bradstreet as he passed by en route to Bow Street. The stout man stopped as quickly as a train, barrel chest sucking his breath in to avoid getting paper slapped into his nose.

"Already?" The Runner wondered. He shook his head, gravely disapproving as the other men gaped at him. "Children these days," he mourned. "Can't wait for Christmas, can they?"

The kitchen was blessedly quiet, emptied of an incredible amount of generosity for the celebration upstairs. Finally, the last of the refreshments had been served and existed in proof as crumbs on dulled trays. A single apple lolled on its side, glued to a tiny pool of soft toffee. It was so ripe its skin gleamed red as a rose against the metal.

John Watson wearily regarded the small apple, smiled – his face felt sore from seven days of smiling – and picked it up. It disengaged with reluctance and he bit into the fruit. Flavours mingled in his mouth, all pleasant. In the warmth of the kitchen, *his own kitchen*, he was tired and content.

Above his head, one could not precisely discern the celebrations, but he could sense them in the occasional pressure of the boards between the floors. He chewed, glancing upward, still smiling because he knew without needing proof that Mary was part of the happiness.

She deserved it.

While he would like very much to return upstairs, he knew that this rare moment was *Mary's*, and she had been so lonely these past few months. A woman's confinement was never good for her sense of self-worth. Someone like herself was in need of something to do, people to nurture, people to fuss and love over. Quite often he thought of his luminous wife as the lighthouse to which birds flocked.

Lighthouses, however, shone better in the darkness, and it was rare when all of Mary's decent friends could get together – the ones in John's book that were more than fair-weather ladies and social courtesans. (Holmes had had more florid, stronger words for the sort that Watson didn't even want to *think* about this close to his wife.) He had no doubt they were all having a perfectly marvelous time with the lady of the house and their little host . . . .

Someone tapped on the tradesman's entrance. John straightened in the act of digging for a knife and flipped the iron clasp off the door. "Good evening to you after all, Inspector."

The Inspector was flushed from the cool weather, but his dark eyes (lined of late), were gleaming as he held up a soogin sack. "I have been ordered," he said in his soft voice – that is, soft until he had to use it otherwise – to pass on the compliments of the season, no matter *what else* happens to me, and to inform you that once all is well in my own household, the Mrs. Lestrade fully intends to answer the good Mrs. Watson's invitation."

Watson threw back his head in a laugh. "You mean she managed all *that* around her laryngitis?" One hand on the door-frame, he leaned to the side and used his apple as a baton. "Or is she resorting to hand-signals of a most evolved kind?"

Lestrade shuddered like a cat in damp. "Don't give her any ideas, even from afar!" he warned. As Watson stepped aside, he stepped in, passing the bag over. The kitchen was a warm relief after the outside. Watson caught his grimace of the factory coal-smoke on his neat clothing. "No, she's using up Martin's precious chalks and slate-board. I'm sure they'll both celebrate her return to voice with all due pomp." He pulled his bowler off and slapped it on the wall-hook in one smooth jerk at Watson's direction. "Nicholas, of course, will celebrate his mother's voice for his own reasons."

"And what reasons would that be, Lestrade?" Watson felt a smile coming on. Without the distractions of other people, he felt he was starting to understand the little man a bit better. He certainly respected the man's unnerving stamina. As a former athlete before his wounding, Watson could not help but recognize endurance.

"He wants her to take him to the Museum for the stuffed sharks – *ghastly things* – and she naturally refuses until she's all well again." Lestrade spoke very properly, but the gleam in his eyes said he was well out of the affair, and glad of it.

"Do let her know we're most thankful." Watson had finally looked inside the bag, much to Lestrade's amusement. He blinked and looked back. "Err, this is a surprise."

45

It was Lestrade's turn to laugh. "It isn't for Mrs. Watson, John!" The detective managed to stay sober enough to talk around his mirth. "Good Heavens. I know we old coppers are supposed to be a *copper-plated* sort, but giving a new mother a bottle of – Well, it's for you. My Clea's reserving her actual gift to mother and child for when she can visit in person."

"Well, *thank* you then." Watson peered at the bottle. Another faint chuckle of sound floated downward. The men automatically glanced upwards. Then they looked at each other.

Ten minutes later they were lounging up against the old reworked stone fireplace, coats off and sleeves rolled up in concession to the warmth coming out of the iron stove so carefully set inside its maw. The whisky chilled at their feet while John carefully quartered small winter apples with his knife.

"So how is Arthur Watson taking the world?" Lestrade asked, murmuring thank you while taking an offered plate.

"He's doing marvelous. Sleeps steady, wakes up when he has a reason to, good weight, and I'm *hoping* there's a glimpse of his mother's eyes." Watson had found the cook's wooden bread-plate, and dropped it, loaded with bread and cheese and the last bit of hard sausage, between them. "It's too soon to tell, I know, but . . . ." He shrugged. "Every Watson in the world has brown eyes." It was a mixture of wonder and complaint. *"Every one."*

Lestrade shrugged too. "So long as they're working, eh?"

"Too true. And he's perfectly healthy. It was hard on Mary to hold herself back for so long, but it had to be done."

"You were looking fagged enough at the end," Lestrade pointed out. "It isn't easy, for all the priests seem to think so."

"Of course."

Another trickle of sound. Lestrade frowned at the ceiling in slight puzzlement.

"I think they're in a guessing game right now," Watson explained.

"So glad we're out of that," Lestrade answered fervently. "I think I do enough guessing in my line of work."

Watson passed over the mustard-pot for the sausage. "And you? Your wife had no warning with this. That's a bit unusual."

"Clea herself is unusual." Lestrade tried to make light, but he was concerned underneath his smile.

"How did it happen?"

"I have no idea." Lestrade shook his head. "A week ago we were dressing hares for supper, and I noticed she wasn't working quite as . . . well, swiftly as she normal does. Not that I'm being provincal or anything, but Clea can peel a rabbit faster than I can draw a breath. But I had company over, and Clea likes to take her meals with the boys when I'm working." Lestrade accepted an offer of some white cheese, still frowning at the memory. "I hadn't noticed she'd gone to bed early."

"Laryngitis isn't just caused by strain and overwork," Watson cautioned. "It could also be from an infection caught from this wretched weather."

"This year's about as bad as it's been," Lestrade agreed in a low voice. "We lost two of our best Constables out of Stepney. Nearly died of pneumonia, and I don't know if one's ever going to get his health back." Because Watson was the sort to feel for everyone, Lestrade added, "He's set up well enough, but he'll miss the walking. Most of us coppers do. I know that doesn't make much sense to most people, but . . . one gets attached to those twenty miles a day."

"Soldiers feel the same way about their regimentation," Watson said knowingly. "It becomes a part of one's life." He found a clean place for the platter. "I've lost a few patients, I regret." The doctor's strong face lost some of its usual gentleness to sorrow. "But as to the Mrs. Lestrade . . . Anstruther says she's very strong, and is already improving."

"Oh, yes . . . she's physically improving . . . but as far as her mental state . . . ." Lestrade scowled. "She's even taken up *knitting*, God help us!"

Watson managed not to laugh at his guest's disgruntlement. "So. How is the Yard?"

"*Quiet*, thank Heaven." Lestrade rarely got to use those words. "I think part of it was the wretched fog. It forced people inside for so long they lost some of their inclination to get into mischief."

"*That* I can believe." Watson put his back to the warm stones. A contented sigh escaped his lips as the heat soaked through his shirt and waistcoat. In that moment, John Watson looked as close to being at peace as Lestrade had ever seen him.

Not that the man had been at peace so much . . . The Yard had not been able to ignore the way the man matched Sherlock Holmes in the fact that neither of them looked anything less than haunted. Holmes, of course, was haunted by the very weight of his intellect. With Watson, it was clearly the past. The police who had served for the Queen before their badges had always been quietly deferential to the doctor – a fact no one else could fail to notice. "*The Queen's Major*," Constable Addey said once, touching his hand to his brim even though Watson was nowhere hear. Snow had been a veteran, though his scars were the invisible sort. It gave him what strength he needed to patrol the worst of London without a *shred* of concern for himself.

Twelve out of a hundred men in the Force were veterans from some sort of war. They noticed Watson without speaking about him. That discretion said much, and warned the others that criticism of the man would not be taken lightly or kindly by certain policemen. Lestrade wondered if Sherlock Holmes had ever noticed how Watson's presence had gently smoothed the way through some of the rougher men.

Lestrade was just glad the man had recovered from his ordeal in the desert. He'd looked like a walking corpse when they first met.

Watson was not as tall or imposing as Sherlock Holmes had been – but then, *he* did not give the impression of being taller than he was. No one would ever inflate the man in their minds . . . unless they were under-estimating. Watson appeared to be content with that – eerily so, for his had a great amount of pride in other things – his work, his wife, his appearance . . . but when it came to being noticed, he could not care less. It was an interesting contrast.

"Well." Lestrade had the instinct to climb out of those woods within his thoughts. He picked up the small bottle and handed it over. "Let us know when you get tired of your humdrum existence in daily practice, Doctor. We're willing to take you on as a police surgeon whenever you wish."

Watson's brown eyes flickered like the lights dancing in the glass bottle. Lestrade could read a mixture of hope and sorrow and that good solid worry every man carried when it came to paying the bills. "I don't wish to impose upon Roanoke."

"Roanoke would like you to take on some of his cases," Lestrade said calmly. "In fact, he would *prefer* it be you."

As usual when a compliment came his way, Watson wasn't certain what to say. "I should give him my thanks, then." He poured out a measure of his drink, and studied it a moment before taking a healthy gulp. Something blinked in his eyes and he blurted without thinking: "Those are large boots to fill!"

Lestrade couldn't help it. He guffawed. A moment later, Watson joined in, slightly sheepish. "Large they are, too." Lestrade grinned and accepted the bottle back. "Half the size of narrowboat oars!" He toasted Watson easily.

Watson's blush was fading, but he was still smiling. "I might as well talk to him," he said slowly. "I hate to say this, but I'm tired of looking for things to write about, and while the payment helps, I dislike waiting for my payments at times!" Since early that year, Watson had arranged for the publishing of six of his recollections of Sherlock Holmes's cases.

"I wondered if writers were always looking about for stories," Lestrade confessed.

"Only in a way," Watson struggled to explain. "Mostly . . . we live life aware that everything is a story to everyone." He sighed. "But do you know what the most aggravating portion of it is? It's encountering things that are . . . well, when truth is stranger than fiction, and so much stranger that one is accused of being utterly fanciful . . . or even addle-witted." Watson snorted, ruffling his nose in his annoyance.

"Oh, I can sympathize." Lestrade said easily. "I've had a few cases like that myself. Not that I wanted them to happen, but one can't discount the evidence of your own eyes."

Watson smiled slightly. "I imagine you've quite a few stories of your own."

"None that would make sense. You were talking fancy . . . There was one case I worked on that I tell you, wouldn't have made sense to anyone."

Watson tilted his head, curious now, like a cat irretrievably drawn to a dragging yarn.

"Not a pleasant story for this sort of night." Lestrade warned. "A multiple murderer and a Hand of Glory are involved."

"That can certainly wait another time." Watson's lips twitched. "But you do know the Christmas season has traditionally been one for telling blood-chilling tales."

"Especially ones with ghosts in them, but there's none in this one. I promise you, when things settle, I'll give you the whole mess – I mean *story*." Lestrade smiled weakly at his *faux pas*. "To me it's a mess. I'll throw you the tangle, and we'll see if even you can make a story out of it."

"A deal it is." They clinked heavy glasses together.

"Has there been any further harassment from the Colonel?"

Watson had not been surprised by this question. The two men were now in that comfortable state where the alcohol must be allowed to burn out of the system. Lestrade had no desire to look like too fine a mark on his way home, and it was utterly comfortable by the hearth.

"No," the doctor said simply. "That in itself means he's either distracted by something . . . and that would have to be a considerably urgent something . . . or that things are progressing the way he wishes."

Lestrade pondered that carefully. There were times when listening to Watson required holding up his sentences and parsing them for clues. "Perhaps there's little he can do this time of year."

Watson snorted slightly. "You may be right. I hadn't thought about that."

Don't tell Mr. Holmes, Lestrade snapped his teeth together just before the joke could escape. He cleared his throat. "I'm glad," he said honestly. "I'd hate to think of you dwelling your thoughts on his like."

49

"I know his mettle." Watson sounded as unperturbed as ever. "He waits for his opponents to exhaust themselves before he moves in." He yawned slightly. "Nothing new under the sun," he said as if to himself.

"I beg your pardon?"

"Oh . . . something Holmes used to say when the subject of Moriarty came up." Watson frowned slightly, musing. "Nothing new under the sun. He said there was already an existing precedent somewhere, no matter how remarkable a case was."

"You mean there would be another version of Mr. Holmes somewhere? I'm afraid that's a bit flabbergasting. Not to mention another Moriarty . . . Who in the world would another Moriarty be?"

"Jonathan Wild." Watson said softly. His brown eyes were faraway, staring through the plaster of the wall. "Holmes always swore that there were no surprises, if one could see the patterns. I had to believe him, for he spent more time studying the criminal than I ever did – or could, for that matter. A poor physician I'd be if I didn't." He smiled at himself. "But his was a mind for drawing parallels . . . and seeking out the differences, no matter how small and insignificant."

"MacDonald said something of that sort to us once," Lestrade said slowly as a memory ticked through his mind. "He said . . . Mr. Holmes had mentioned Mr. Wild in the same breath as the Professor."

Watson nodded just a bit. "Yes."

"That was in . . . '87? '88?"

"1888." Watson breathed out, dissatisfied. "And I assure you, it will be many years and many, many deaths later before I'll be able to publish *that* tale."

"Good enough to wait for?"

Watson did not hesitate. "I am most proud of that writing," he admitted. "Though I wonder how I will look back upon it with the eyes of an older man."

"Don't wait *too* long. I plan to retire within the next thirty years, you know."

Watson barked his laughter.

"How are you, Clea-*bihan*?"

"Tired." Clea whispered, "But shouldn't you be at work?"

"I *am* at work," He smiled, producing a glass. "Your childer, I'll have you know, are up at their grandfather's and having far too much of a good time at his expense. Nicholas is going to learn very quickly not to throw his weight at Martin. Bartram's decided Martin needs a few . . . pointers."

"Sweet Lord!" Clea rasped. "As if I couldn't teach my own son!" She scowled. He shrugged in a *"What can you do with him?"* motion and she gave up, accepting his offer of the soup mug with fatalistic good grace. She managed her way through all of it, but not one teaspoon further, while he read some of the more interesting bits out of the paper.

"Will you be all right if I head to my office?" He pulled the quilts up straight as she settled back down.

"I'll be fine," she breathed. "I'll . . . ring . . . if I need something." She tapped the little brass bell by the bedstead-table.

Freed, if for the moment, Lestrade traded Clea's empty tray for a full one in the kitchen for himself, and made his way back upstairs (avoiding the usual collection of small, swift-footed animals that Mrs. Collins seemed to keep at odd times and even odder hours). It was a detour of a moment to pick up the book checked out of the London Library. It was heavy and blocky and well-used by countless enraptured readers. He set it on his desk with a heavy *thup*.

Jonathan Wild.

Lestrade literally had to stop and gather his courage before he opened the book up: A cigarette before reading something difficult worked when he was deciphering Padriag Dooley's creative language. It ought to work for a milestone of sensationalist literature.

A True and Genuine Account
of the Life and Death of the Late Jonathan Wild
by Daniel Defoe
(Reprinted)

51

Chapter VI – To Devon

The weather was not improving. The closer it grew to Christmas, the less of a holiday spirit the city seemed to have.

It was almost impossible to see outside the ice-glazed ripples on the growler's windows. Lestrade's breath only settled on the other side and added to the frost. The detective shivered deeply inside the depths of his heaviest coat. He suspected he had more layers than the cliffs of Dover. They weren't really helping.

I should have taken the time and found that Jersey Elizabeth knitted last *Christmas*. For a moment, longing thoughts of that dark Shetland wool distracted him from the cold. The price of the larger vehicle depressed him, but the cold wind had made him shiver while winding his whistle, and instead of two blasts for a cheaper hansom, he'd been stuck with the first cab to answer his single, shuddering blast.

A hansom was much colder, but it was faster. He'd been there by now in a hansom . . . He was just beginning to give up on stamping the circulation back into his feet when the horses stopped. He couldn't leave fast enough, though he had to kick the door to dislodge another scrim of ice settled inside the hinges.

Let *no one* say the Diogenes Club was inhospitable. After the ride Lestrade had just had, he would have been content in a saltpetre mine. The doorkeep, a man he recognized from the Commissionaire Corps, waited with the patience of a silent Job for the newcomer to thaw his hands out before signing the register. Lestrade wondered what the man had done to make himself inhospitable enough to qualify for their hiring of his services.

He'd been in the Stranger's Room only twice before, and that to see Mycroft Holmes. Since his brother's funeral, almost no one had seen the large, even more mysterious man. Common consensus was he was expressing his grief in the only way he knew. Lestrade didn't dwell on the subject himself. It was none of his blooming business.

Both times before, Mycroft Holmes had been by the window, watching London go by. There was no point in that today. He was seated in the chair that allowed him full view of the room without having to turn his head. A tray of coffee was before him, and he answered Lestrade's diffident greeting by waving him over.

"I had two cups sent up. You still prefer *café noir*, I take it."

"I'm not likely to pick up a taste for sweets this late in life," Lestrade admitted. "Thank you, Mr. Holmes."

"Not at all. Your visit promises to alleviate some of my boredom."

Well, that *was* possible. Lestrade considered it was equally possible that his need for information was so humdrum for a man of his intellect, it wouldn't even do that. He winced as the cup's heat traveled through his cold-scalded fingers.

"You have been to see Dr. Watson."

Lestrade had once thought that should he ever accustom himself to the ways of the Detective Holmes, nothing would falter him. That was before he'd encountered Mycroft Holmes.

Sitting with Sherlock Holmes was a bit like sharing company with a carnivale barker, who was using his trained eye to pull out all the embarrassing bits about you to the rest of the audience. Lestrade always felt that if there was something to mesmerism, he would have been *exactly* the type to make his subject act like a chicken – just to demonstrate his skill, mind you. Any humiliation was wholly secondary.

With Mycroft Holmes, however . . . .

The man was so damned intelligent it came off him like rays off the sun. And it would be very, very easy to be burned in those rays.

"I visited Dr. Watson just the other night," Lestrade felt the heat of the drink loosen something icy and knotted inside him. "On behalf of his recent good news."

Mycroft Holmes – Lestrade could barely think of him as anything less than "Mr. Mycroft Holmes" – grunted. "I am glad he is prospering."

"I suppose one could put it that way." Lestrade had never backed down from Sherlock Holmes's annoying superior brains, and he would not shy his feelings from his superior brother.

The big man never blinked. "Your visits are seldom enough. How may I be of service?"

"I am searching for a man. You may know of his whereabouts." Lestrade reached into his card-holder and pulled out the one in question. He slid it across the varnished tabletop to Holmes's cream.

Mycroft said nothing for a moment. "I am surprised that you would seek the acquaintance of a man you hold partially responsible for my brother's death."

"He left unfinished work at the Yard, and it falls upon my shoulders to tend it." Lestrade coolly sipped his coffee. It was a fine blend. He wouldn't afford *this* in a month of Sundays.

Those grey eyes, lighter than his brother's, were almost silver. In the proper lighting conditions, they lacked any tint at all, which created a more than unsettling impression of whiteness. When they flickered in thought, that impression increased tenfold.

"I confess to curiosity, Mr. Lestrade."

53

"You truly are hard up for amusement then."

Mycroft chuckled. It was a deep sound, like a rock moving underwater. "You are certain I would know his whereabouts?"

"Mr. Holmes," Lestrade put the cup down, "I do. But even if I didn't, I would still be here. You were in communication with your brother before his death. You have demonstrated knowledge of the operations against Moriarty's gang, and to have that, I believe you would have known something of Mr. Patterson." He shook his head, suddenly tired of people who wanted to string out a conversation longer than they had to . . .

"I assure you, I am doing nothing of the thing."

With intelligence came something close to supernatural awareness. Lestrade sighed inside himself.

"You are leery of intelligent men," the big man pointed out, with a comforting lack of concern. He might have been discussing last year's weather. "The influence of rather sadistic older brothers, no doubt. I am afraid the marks are as tangible as claws on silk."

Lestrade was a moment in collecting his voice. "My history is no secret. I daresay most of London could quote it all to you."

Mycroft Holmes grunted. That faraway look was back in his eyes. "There is always the question of what a person's true talents would have been, were they allowed flourishing. You defeated them with your determination, but it is not the same as battling and winning on their own ground. That was a failing within Sherlock. He could not help but seek out an intellect he could battle."

Yes, and when he couldn't, he taunted us for being stupid. I spent too much of my life hearing it from my brothers to be impressed.

"You know why he did it." Mycroft Holmes again proved his ability to read thoughts.

Lestrade sighed now. "Yes, but I'm not here to speak of the dead, sir. That is . . . a history I am not ready to re-visit."

"Very true." The big man smiled slightly. "I believe I have an address of use to you."

It was warmer in Exeter.

Lestrade was almost exhausted of energy and hope by the time he left the train station. At least the ride had been a bit easier than his first trip from Paddington Station to Dartmoor – and he hadn't had to ride all the way to that wretched Grimpen Mire again. Just the notion made his hair want to grey prematurely.

There was never much to do in a train save think, stare out a window, keep warm, or find something to read. Lestrade had done plenty of *that* with a map of Exeter, and followed it up with a period of stone-cold silence that resembled brooding more than actual thought.

With the map memorized, he sent a wire from the telegraph station so Mrs. Collins could tell Clea he made it safely (at least that far), and turned his steps to a place all but guaranteed to see the former Inspector: A tavern called The King Alfred's Wall. The wall in question looked to be genuine Roman fragment. But then, that was Exeter.

Where the Age of Industry was forcing advancements at breakneck speed, Exeter lacked the coal and iron. As a result, the town was failing by degrees to keep up with the world on its own terms. Lestrade took in the fact that transportation meant refurbishing the canals for the cargo barges, not the railways, and decided it was a pleasant change.

He crossed the canal by the nearest lock and stepped inside the tavern with a breath of relief. Now that he was here, it was only a matter of waiting.

The tavern was neat as a pin, not something he would take for granted. The ground floor was opened by the first floor ringing it with a row of rails and an impressive staircase. Lestrade frowned and realized he was in a re-modeled *dancing school*. The couples would have descended that stair from above, and they would have used the first and second floors like balconies to look down at the dancers below. Lestrade was impressed at the determination required to salvage an old building like this.

Few people were inside at this early hour. He ordered the meal of the day and a water-cider to wash it down with, and went outside in search of a paper-chaunter. By the time he'd returned, everything was ready.

Quarter-to-nine . . . Lestrade snapped his watch and made a show of casually eating. He then spent another hour reading the paper front to back, and then again. He was going through the paper his third and last time when Patterson cleared his throat.

"Well, you certainly took long enough." Lestrade said by way of greeting. If Patterson could ignore his manners, then so could Lestrade. "I saw you in the back as soon as I came in."

The former detective looked harassed. Ill colour tinted his lean face, and there was something that was *too* neat about his coal-black suit and lime-creamed hair and starched collar and cuffs. The man was as perfectly dressed as a paper doll, and he looked just as ready to snap as one if under pressure.

"Would you like to sit down?" Lestrade asked politely. It was a drastic change from the last time they'd traded words . . . traded them like weapons, with all the sense of little boys who agreed to take turns shooting at each other with the same sling-shot. "I'm not aware of the protocols of asking a co-owner if he wants to sit in his own tavern . . . ."

55

Patterson made a chuffing sound. He slid into the chair across from Lestrade. "I'm quite surprised to see you here."

"Believe you me, I was just as surprised to see you'd retired."

"There wasn't any reason to stay on the Force." Patterson said simply.

"If you say so." Lestrade pulled out his smoking tin. "I wouldn't be here if it weren't for pressing business."

"That," Patterson said, "I can believe." He reached for his own tobacco.

The two men lit off the small candle in the table's centre. Lestrade waited a moment, gauging the other man as someone who might be as brittle inside as he appeared. He left it to him to open the floor.

Despite the early hour, Patterson signaled for a glass of wine and sipped half of it down before he did just that. "What sort of pressing business brings you to the thriving hub of Exeter?"

"I found you," Lestrade said slowly and clearly, "because I yet again swallowed my pride and went to Mr. Holmes – the elder and now *only* Mr. Holmes." The smaller man managed to skewer the taller one as if their heights were reversed. "I'm not here to make war. I'm only here for information."

"I can't imagine what information you'd be needing." Patterson's lips were tight. "The case is over. Moriarty's gang was captured save for Moriarty, and Mr. Holmes finished him at his own sacrifice."

"I wasn't there, but I do remember hearing something of the sort." One might have cut a live tree down with Lestrade's voice.

Patterson's hands went stiff over his drink. His mouth reduced into the thinnest of lines and he had the grace to look down. Lestrade leaned back in his chair, pointedly not bringing his reluctant host's attention to the ragged mark left on his temple.

"What I need, you probably have off the top of your head," Lestrade told him.

Patterson risked looking at him. "What do you want?"

"I want the late Professor Moriarty's life. I want his origins, his habits, how he rose to crime if that was ever traced – and I'll settle for conjecture – but if all I have is a single sheet of paper and a list of achievements from crooked cradle to watery grave, so help me I'll take it." Lestrade's dark eyes had narrowed to that black look a guard dog adopted prior to attack. He was just waiting for the right signal.

"No need for that." Patterson said at last. "I have copies. I kept copies of everything."

They walked upstairs to his rooms in silence. Lestrade half-expected him to take his coat and walk to a security-box down the street, but that was dispelled when Patterson stopped at a well-polished door with a plaque: *J.R. Patterson – Investments* looked back at him in a curt block text.

"You have an office in a tavern?" Lestrade lifted an eyebrow.

"Some of the best businessmen have had offices in taverns." Patterson smiled with some genuine humour beneath as he pulled out his key.

"Jonathan Wild being one of the best."

Patterson gouged the metal of the key-plate in his shock. Lestrade kept his grin to the hidden side of his mouth.

"Have a seat," the retired detective gestured to a low settee. There was little furniture in the room, but a great deal of effort had gone into making the place comforting. The palette was all in forest green upholstery and warm butternut walls and furniture. Hepplewhite, well-cared for despite its age.

Where anyone else would have framed images of people on the walls, Patterson chose strange, windswept landscapes of the moors, prehistoric stone relics basking in the full sun. Lestrade wondered what sort of philosophy the man was expressing.

"This should be complete." The thin man emerged from the back room with a bound-up waxed envelope in his hands. "If this is what you're looking for, well . . . ." His gaze slipped away. "You're welcome to it."

Lestrade did not reach for the papers just yet. "Tell me something, Patterson." He ignored the "Mister", treating the other man as if he were still a Yarder. He saw the flinch. "How long did you study this Professor?"

Patterson did not hesitate. "Thirty years."

Patterson did not look old enough for that number, but then, Lestrade looked older than he was.

"Did you ever learn anything about his family?"

Patterson's gaze slid away again. Not in furtive avoidance, but . . . embarrassment? "He came from a good family."

"That's the common street talk. Repeated so many times it must be seen as the truth. What do you know about his family?"

Patterson's breath left his lungs, aggressively. In a similar ferment, he struck the top of his small dining table with the papers. "As dangerous as anyone above us in station," he said bluntly. "Respectability, prestige, the fruits of years' labours . . . Bear you in mind there is no doubt the Moriarty will *work* for his rewards. They have an intersecting record within and without the military. The Professor had the mathematical ability, but his brother the Colonel is reputed to have a similar talent for subterfuge and tactics."

Lestrade was hardly surprised. "Did you ever learn enough of the brother to develop an opinion or . . . assessment?"

Patterson looked uneasy again. He fidgeted, moving to the narrow window, shooting his cuffs as he did so. He did not directly face out the window, but stayed to the side, as if expecting a bullet to come through it.

"It's quite difficult to gather intelligence about someone within a military circle," he said at last. "They're almost a different species, Lestrade. As different from you and me as a Hottentot or an Aborigine or a Chickasaw. They keep to themselves. One must have the assistance of someone within the military to accomplish something . . . and that sort of aid would be seen as an informer – no matter how sympathetic the others are to his cause." He reached for a pipe this time, and packed pale leaf inside the bowl in quick, nervous stamps. "When there is a problem . . . the problem is dealt with according to the particular rules of behavior within the military. They have ranks as intricate as anything in the heart of Westminster, though it may be less confusing, as a man's rank is judged at a glance by the amount of braid, or the epaulet, or the medal on the chest . . . It's a form of government intrigue, Lestrade. So many of that sort has *so many* friends that would just as soon squash any of us like insects – not because we're beneath them in station, or because they hate us . . . but because we're going up against one of theirs. It's as territorial as a pack of wolves."

Lestrade stayed silent, sensing a breaking point in the man.

"I can say only one thing with the confidence of my personal research: The Colonel *knew* his brother's true means of livelihood. He did nothing to stop him, or criticize him . . . and appeared to be close to him." Patterson reached up and touched his mustache one-handed. "Not close in the ways of brotherly affection. Close in the ways that . . . two different hawks would be in the same room. Closely attentive to each other. Perhaps dependent in some way. Feeding together if need be . . . but not . . . affectionate."

"I think I understand what you're saying." Lestrade sighed and rose, sweeping the waxed envelope off the table and into the protection of his coat. "It will take a military man then to truly face the Colonel as an enemy and see to him."

"You won't find one!" Patterson blurted, and stopped, astonished at himself.

"Why wouldn't I? Surely Major Watson wasn't the only honest officer in the Queen's Army."

"Only one man went up against Colonel Moriarty and lived to tell the tale." Patterson was lighting his match with eager strokes now. "Your Major Watson's patron, Colonel Hayter, now of Reigate. And he lives in Reigate, Surrey now, because that was all that was left for him to do when Moriarty finished with him."

"Yes, I've met the good Colonels." Lestrade drawled out the words just slightly, deliberately demonstrating the remnants of his Celtic accent. "Colonel Hayter intimated there was a bit of a history between himself and the Colonel Moriarty."

Patterson snorted like a furious horse. "A history indeed. And he came so close to stopping that man. That's the worst of it." He smoked frantically. "Man's as elegant a woods-colt as his professor brother was. The Professor pretended to be all perfectly normal while he was chalking his sums on his blackboard. His brother the Colonel . . . he does the same with his chess sets. Collects them. Plays with them. Hoards them. Even throws them away when he gets tired of them. But they are quite the same." Patterson set his pipe down like he had his papers. "Enough. I did my part to stop the Professor. He was the worse of the two. I've left that world, Lestrade. It was too much for me." The thin man turned to look at him, and in the poor winter light he had no more colour than one of the requiems in Exeter Cathedral. "I tried, but I tried too hard for too long. I'm done with this."

Lestrade remembered his first significant encounter with Patterson, and how he'd rescued him from an illegal torture den. Seven years ago, in a seedy abbey so terrible that there were times that he still remembered what he'd seen at night.

"I'm not asking you to rejoin the CID," he said at last. Was Patterson younger than himself, or not? His past was a mystery, which suggested his way had been smoothed by the Home Office. And if it was the Home Office, then Patterson had been tapped for this cold work since the start.

He rose to his feet. There had been a time when he'd despised the man, but now he wasn't certain he was looking at a *man*. Patterson suited the figure of a ghost now, and the hard vitality that fueled his irritating bold confidence was gone, burned to ash. He didn't know what he could say to the man that wouldn't be taken as false comfort. Holmes's death must have haunted him as much as it had the rest of the Yard.

"I respect your decision to retire," he said at last, and carefully. Patterson stared through him but not quite at him. "But I suggest that . . . you stay in touch with the Constabulary. For your own safety, mind you. And . . . for your own peace of mind." He held his gaze with his own eyes, not liking the anguish inside them.

The law arrests the guilty. Justice incarcerates them . . . but torture would be to place mirrors in each cell.

"I'm going to spend the night in Exeter, and head back first thing." Lestrade finished. "I have no intention of causing you discomfort, so if you could recommend another establishment?"

59

Patterson twitched, and put his hands together. "No. You should stay here tonight. I can hardly recommend another establishment over my own, can I?"

The attempt at making peace was as tragic as the attempt at humour. Lestrade couldn't say no, for the effort it had cost the man.

And I used to think I'd like to retire to the water and open a pub or something, he thought. In this case, it wasn't helping the policeman who actually had.

Chapter VII – The Ways of Exeter

Lestrade shut the door after Patterson's polite farewell and went straight to his battered gripsack. In minutes, his loaned copy of Defoe's Jonathan Wild and the life of Professor Moriarty were resting side by side on the table by the bed.

He was close.

That feeling came but rarely, perhaps five out of twenty cases. Something was at his grasp and if he could just cipher it . . . .

The small man lit the candle by the bed-stead, blowing out the match in the same motion. It was doubtful he would have recognized himself in the window reflection.

Jonathan Wild.

Professor Moriarty.

He began to make his list.

Patterson mixed himself his third drink of the day and sat with it by the fireplace. Lack of sleep left sooty smears under his eyes as he held the squat glass in his fingers. It was still too early in the day for something to steady his nerves, but the tavern ran itself well enough. He'd focused his considerable energies in choosing employees who could be trusted to know their job and do it with little supervision.

His partner would return from his holiday by the middle of January. All he had to do was keep his composure for that long.

He sighed, not quite lulled by the way the wood crackled in the fireplace. The old hickory burned nearly as warmly as coal, and he found the flame much cleaner. The lack of cleanliness was not something he missed about London.

A faint tap on the door announced the presence of his manager. "I beg your pardon, Mr. Patterson." The young man stood smartly, even though his employer was not turning to look at him. "But the Christmas Waits are here asking for contributions for last night's caroling."

Patterson heard himself laugh quietly. "Now there's an unpleasant chore, Stevens." he noted. "Walking up and down Exeter in the worst hours of the night, singing every poor soul out of their beds, and then to come back the next day to ask for some pittance to cover their holiday work."

Stevens winced with a smile of his own. "They do sing well enough, sir. I'll grant them that. I can't think of the number of Christmas carolers that got me out of bed by their lack of harmony . . . I would have paid them not to sing, I think."

Patterson snorted lightly and rose to his feet, reaching in his pocket for the usual handful of coins gentlemen kept. "This should work it out well enough." He hesitated a moment and dropped another scatter of change down. "Tell them that's also for the next time they come to sing. An advance payment, as it were."

Alone, the retired detective returned to his spot, resting his feet wearily upon the ottoman. He was tired, he thought. No, this went deeper than tired. He felt old. Worn thin.

Battling an abnormal giant could do that to a man – if he survived. Patterson was alive, but there were times when he was unsure of his status. What did life mean if there was so little of it left? It was a question best left to the philosophers.

Lestrade had been reluctantly caught back up in Defoe's storytelling while listing parallels against Moriarty. He ended the matter by rising, slapping the book shut. Walking back and forth the small room helped him focus a bit more, and he came to a quick decision, returning the waxed envelope to the inside of his jacket and shrugging it back on.

Exeter was growing less unpleasant by the minute, but the wind coming off the coast reminded him of the salt winds of Plymouth. Weather was shifting – and when did it not this time of year? The little man tilted his head up, seeking the birds. He found them, riding the high currents. They used their wings to steer, but did not flap. Well, that just told you what the force was . . . Lestrade decided it was a good thing he'd taken the time to find his Jersey after all. He'd need it tonight.

"Lestrade? Inspector Lestrade?"

He was already turning with a smile on his face. "Montgomery? Is that you?"

Inspector Montgomery was beaming above a dark green muffler. No doubt his wife had pinned the holly sprig on its tips. Cadaverously thin and inhumanly strong, he looked more suited to the undertaker industry than he was with law enforcement. Still, even he could get a touch of colour to his sharp-boned cheeks this time of year.

The man did more drinking on duty than was smart, but he could hold it like a Highlander.

"Geoffrey Lestrade, as I live and breathe . . . ." The bony man hitched forward on the narrow street, his long legs crossing the entire length in three strides. Behind him a man Lestrade could barely see was struggling to keep up. Lestrade well remembered himself doing that on a few cases. "Did they transfer you over here too?"

62

"Not likely. I haven't been good enough for that sort of punishment." Lestrade slapped his gloved hand inside Montgomery's. "Still leaving the new Inspectors in your wake, I see."

Montgomery grinned, his large, chisel-like teeth just as startling as the rest of him. "I'm just glad there isn't a limit to the maximum height," he passed the old joke. "Geoffrey, meet Inspector Loseth, recently from the tropical isle of Streat."

Lestrade blinked. "It can't be very tropical right now, can it?" Streat was a little-known, peat-bogged and rocky isle in the North Sea.

"Not very," Loseth chuckled. He was young enough to give Lestrade a severe flash of nostalgia. "I think they've sent me down here to soften me up."

"Are you working?" Montgomery asked. "Time for a drink?"

Lestrade rolled his eyes with a smile. "I was looking for a place to eat, actually. Any ideas?"

Faster than Lestrade could blink, he was seated at a murky establishment before a dish of Captain's Chicken while Montgomery explained more than he really ought about the quality of the local brews.

Eager to change that subject – Montgomery would yet get himself discharged from his duties over his drink – Lestrade turned to the youngest member of the group. "If I may, what brings you all the way down here? I would think the Isle of Streat is quite a change."

"Nothing but peaty bogs, lots of duck-hunting, and windswept lands." Loseth grinned as he forked up his own dish. "One rather pitiful castle . . . six or seven if one counts the ruins. Still, the duck-hunting is as good as it can get."

"I would say . . . a lifer, then?"

"Completely."

"Could you tell me how it came about its name?" Lestrade was cautious with the chicken. He wasn't shy with spice, but this was lively with curry and something else he couldn't quite identify.

"The whole isle is long and narrow, and almost as straight as a Roman Road, which used to be called Streats. That's how we get the word 'street,'" Loseth explained. "In a way, it's a bit of a joke." He shrugged, smiling at himself for having such origins. "The Isle still keeps to a bit of the old Viking laws, and you might say I was sent down here to make good on my education." At their guest's blank look he lifted his glass of weak beer. "Of late, there've been some interesting artifacts getting dug up from the peat. Sacrificial victims, it looks like. They're well preserved, and the old family that has the castle is thinking of turning their ancestral home into a museum."

"That's rather generous of them." Montgomery grinned. "But I would imagine it would get a crumbling old heap off their hands too."

"That may be their strongest motivation!" Loseth laughed out loud. "It's a fright, and no mistake. But if there's a museum, they'll need someone full-time to deal with the law enforcement."

The conversation moved to other matters, such as the way crime seemed to change shape as much as a lump of clay, and how it seemed that Channel smugglers were picking up their pitch in ferrying duty-free goods over the water. Loseth was fascinated by the topic, and regrettably, Montgomery made Lestrade out to be some sort of expert. Lestrade was kept hopping, mentally, and he returned to his room in a much better mood.

It felt as though only a few minutes later he had his summary of both criminal masterminds . . . .

Both had settled in London during a period of social turmoil. Moriarty had been of the age to carry an ambiguous attitude to the law anyway. Times had been harsh, to say the least, with some of the most violent riots in living memory, executions and deportations, farm workers hovering just above starvation as mechanization took away their means to work. Coppers had been called Peelers back then, for the Metro's Police Act had been passed only a few years previously.

That really puts things in an odd perspective. The detective caught himself tapping his pencil against the table-top. *Moriarty was born before photography. Before the abolition of slavery, the Poor Laws . . . Good God, he was born close to the creation of the Peelers . . . .*

Policemen knew of upheavals as times when crime existed at its worst levels. For the first time, Lestrade had a stunning insight: Clever and foresightful criminals would see such times as rich hunting-grounds of opportunity. An economic boon for themselves.

Moriarty had never been caught on *anything.* Wild in contrast had been arrested *many* times, and each time he ran afoul of the law, he appeared to gain more and more from his experience. Introduced into existing gangs and networks, Wild had soon supplanted them with his own powers.

Moriarty . . . someone had let Moriarty in. No doubt they regretted *that* deeply. Nothing was actually written, but those rumors of scandal had cost him his University chair. Patterson had initially attempted to ferret out the truth of that as his means of defeating the man, but just because one's enemies wound up dead didn't prove one had anything to do with them. It just caused suspicion . . . .

Lestrade rubbed at his forehead. Too much lack of sleep was starting to catch up with him. The fresh air of outside felt like a memory now. He rose on a half-whim and opened the window a bit, thinking.

Wild and Moriarty had both used their time wisely. If anything, Moriarty had scrupulously avoided Wild's frequent arrests. Both had been popular with criminals and lawmen alike. MacDonald insisted that even when he knew the man was crooked, he couldn't stop treating him like a benefactor in school. Watson gave a very different accounting of the man, but then, that was the difference between the man the world saw and the man that truly existed.

Both men drew profit from the turmoil of British soldiers returning from war. It was enough to turn a strong stomach.

Lestrade stopped and rose to dig his smoking-case out of his jacket pocket, thinking as he did so. The stories weren't pretty. Wild had made the most comfortable living possible by exploiting the flaws in the system. He used criminals to steal goods, and then returned them to the owner on the pretense of his men finding the articles on his authority. On occasion, something incriminating was found and Wild would employ blackmail for substantial rewards. The poor person was forever in Wild's power after that, as Wild had no guilt about using them if they were needed later.

Moriarty's success was in his ability to *create* profitable crimes. Lestrade was seeing him as a sort of demonic telegraph-operator, receiving requests for business and fulfilling his clients' illegal desires for a steep cut. What was it . . . fifteen percent? It was like going to a bank of crime! As the planning was all on his side, his personal risk was minimal. The profit margin was not.

Possibly the worst part was Wild's men were utterly *terrified* of him. Moriarty had dealt with all disappointments in one way: Death. Wild dealt with death too, but in a more blood-curdling way: He turned his own men in to the authorities and pocketed the reward as they were sent off to their own execution. Forty pounds was *still* enough money to sell someone over . . . .

Moriarty had put out a respectable face. So did Wild. Wild was self-proclaimed a moral, upstanding citizen and a worker tireless in his efforts to clean up England and Ireland. Money and favours had poured on him, just as Moriarty seemed not to have hurt for comforts.

Perhaps brazenly, Wild would also sell stories of his daring exploits as a thief-taker to eager newspapers. Lestrade wondered if that trick would perform in this less credulous day and age.

If the public hadn't been growing suspicious about corruption, Wild might have continued his work uninterrupted for decades. As it was, Wild had not been cautious. It was a gap in comparison between himself and

Moriarty, who would have had the world believe he was nothing more than a simple mathematics professor.

(Here Lestrade made a note that Wild's unfortunate mentor had called his gang, "Mathematicians.') Facing his execution, Wild botched his suicide with laudanum and went in a stupor to the gallows to public approval: *"Wherever he came, there was nothing but hollowing and huzzas, as if it had been upon a triumph."*

Lestrade shivered to think of it. He was tired. His imagination was wanting to exist again. He buried it under a rising sense of awe at Dr. Watson. He didn't know if he should be astonished or incredulous, because either Watson *was* as stupid as half of London *thought* he was, or he was under the delusion that Lestrade was smarter than *he* really was.

Lestrade tapped his pencil almost angrily, agitated by the inescapable truth before him.

Watson had implied by lack of embellishment that Holmes had been the expert on Jonathan Wild. Very well. Wild had been a criminal, one of the most famous London had ever seen. Lestrade could well understand that.

But for Watson, who adored the yellow-backed novels, to be unaware of something *Daniel Defoe* had written? The author of *Robinson Crusoe?* And if *that* wouldn't be enough poppycock and rot . . . there was the sad ending to Wild himself: Bodysnatchers had stolen his corpse right after burial and promptly sold it to the Royal College of Surgeons.

Watson was as ethical a doctor that ever took an oath. Past experience told Lestrade that Watson would not be the least bit ignorant about a case of body-thieving.

Again, he returned the waxed envelope to his jacket. Definitely too tired to pursue this further. He could always pick this back up on the train tomorrow morning . . .

Lestrade kicked off his shoes, thinking to nap on top of the covers in the warm room, but as soon as he was on his back the ceiling spun into orbit. *Oh, no.* He managed to get to the lavatory down the hall with a narrow margin for error. That unidentifiable part of dinner was suddenly identified. *Food poisoning in Exeter.* There was probably a joke in this somewhere.

If someone makes one comment about my walking out here shoeless, so help me . . . He leaned on the rail heavily, feeling the sweat drip off his face. Downstairs the passers-by moved back and forth on their agendas. Smells of cooking food wafted up, and he clenched his jaw against a phantom urge to test his stomach again.

"Inspector?" Patterson was poking his moody head out of his door. "Are you well? You don't look well."

"No." Lestrade spoke through his teeth. He would function if it killed him. Clea always swore he wouldn't even accept getting killed unless the angels gave him a promissory note in advance, signed by both patron saints of the Yard, and witnessed by Saint Anthony. "Something I ate didn't . . . agree."

Patterson was alarmed. "Did you eat here?" He shook his head. "Of course not. Where did you eat today?"

"Some little place off High Street. Captain's Chicken."

"Oh, Good God. That is not the most honest establishment." Patterson paled slightly and moved to give him a hand. "Every so many weeks it seems someone's getting re-acquainted with their meal there. Was anyone with you?"

"Local boys . . . Montgomery . . . and the new boy . . . Loth . . . Loseth . . . ." He swayed slightly. The patterns on the hall-carpet were horrifying in their sudden desire to leap off the fibres and start dancing in circles. Without warning, the vertical stripes of the wall-panels turned to a dizzying herringbone.

"Neither of those men have been in Exeter long enough to know any better!" Patterson helped steer Lestrade to his room. "I'll run up some melomel. Do you think you can keep it down?"

Lestrade gulped. "I'll give it a try."

"I'll get a basin too." Patterson kicked the door open and helped the other man stretch out. He went to the window and carefully adjusted the opening so a faint but steady draught of cool air could wash over his face but not his chest. "Do you wish the lights on?"

The rest of the evening passed in that short-lived misery known as food poisoning. Lestrade was perfectly immobilized for several hours, unable to move while his spine re-lived old memories of getting pounded by his wife's youngest brother.

Gradually, the pain edged off and some of his mobility returned. He was in a foul mood. The pain had been too great to think, so he couldn't even keep his mind occupied. The honey-based wine stabilized the worst of his stomach, but his muscles were sore from locking up. He wondered if Montgomery had even been affected. Chances were nothing could have pierced the line of defenses in all that personal pickling from his private flask.

He took pride in the victory of washing his face in the bowl of water left by the fireplace and went promptly back to lie down. In the growing darkness the single candle was burning low. He closed his eyes with growing relief.

A moment later he froze.

Something was scrabbling softly outside his door.

Chapter VIII – Coincidence?

Outside the cracked window, Christmas Waits were singing at the top of their lungs something about Christian charity. Lestrade barely heard. The rest of his attention was rooted to a clear-cut case of illegal entry in his room.

A stiff sheet of parchment paper slid underneath the door and stopped. Metal rattled in the keyhole as someone inched the key out. It fell with a soft pat of heavy brass against the paper.

Lestrade waited as the paper slid back under the gap in the door, taking the key with it.

Now the burglar would wait, making certain his slight noises hadn't been detected. Lestrade did not move, but his lips mentally set tight. A few hours ago he would have still been paralysed with bad food. Now he was sweating for a different reason.

The key slid easily into the lock. No hesitation there. Whoever did this was experienced.

The door opened without a sound. The burglar was pulling up on the hinges, taking the weight of the door off the metal bits that could possibly squeak. The hallway was black – far too black. The lights were off too.

A moment. Lestrade heard breathing in the quiet of the room, and to his surprise he heard the tiny snick of the door swinging shut again. The burglar rested his ear to the wood, listening for any suspicious sounds *outside*.

Lestrade thought that was passing the notion of strange, but it made *his* upcoming job all the easier.

The small candle was down to a puddle of wax. It guttered in the faint breeze. It was a man a little larger than Lestrade. He watched from the curtain of his eyelashes as the intruder satisfied himself, and then stepped into the very edge of the light.

Inspector Loseth paused over the dying candle and coolly pulled a stub out of his own pocket. Lestrade did not care for the feral concentration in the young man's face. In the pinpoint of light against every hollow and slope of his face, he looked furtive and frightening. Nordic blue eyes reflected pale disks in his suddenly deep sockets and, to Lestrade's growing surprise, the man did no more than satisfy himself that Lestrade was asleep on the bed. He then turned to the small wardrobe resting against the wall and began going through the pockets of Lestrade's coat.

And that was quite enough.

The islander whirled at the sound of the bedsprings moving, his face twisting in shock. A moment later an angry Lestrade was shoving him into the wardrobe, pistol pressing into his collarbone.

"I can see Montgomery forgot to tell you," Lestrade snarled, their faces almost touching in the dark. "I have special permission to carry an iron with me *at all times*." The tip dug deeper into Loseth's suddenly white skin. "A thank you for my dealing with some unpleasant folks for the CID. They can't promote me. Special benefits are cheaper."

"I'm not going to do you any harm," Loseth rasped dryly.

"I can *see* that." Lestrade answered evenly. "I suppose you carry that barker in your pocket for the duck-hunting back on Streat?"

"I swear to you, Lestrade. I was just wanting to look at those papers."

"What papers?"

"You know!" Loseth whined. "You're not supposed to be awake! I wasn't going to bother you!"

Lestrade's aching body would run out of strength very soon. He made a decision and latched onto the other's collar. Loseth gasped as he was spun back into the room. Lestrade pistoled him in the back of the head and dropped him to his knees. The Derbies were on him in a heartbeat. The revolver clattered to the table by the candle.

Lestrade paused only to yank his whistle from underneath his necktie and pull on it.

Patterson was slamming the door down not fifteen seconds later.

"Once a policeman, eh Patterson?" Lestrade wondered dryly. The retired detective was pale as paste, his hair askew and ruffled in his pyjamas. Both hands were wrapped around a rifle that looked to date from the First Afghan War. Behind him three or four members of the tavern were holding lanterns and weapons. Lestrade wondered if Gregson would believe any of this.

"You may need this."

Lestrade lifted a very heavy head to look at the glass in Patterson's hand. He took it. It was easier than refusing.

Patterson ignored the fact that the other man wasn't drinking it. "Whatever is so interesting about that man's gun? Other than the fact that he might have used it on you?"

"Look at the patina." Lestrade turned it over. Patterson did with a frown, puzzled and not understanding. "That whole weapon's been frequently washed in tea." He stood stiffly (his back was absolutely killing him), and ran his finger over the metal. "Perhaps you've seen your maids and chars do the same thing to your ironwork."

"I know nothing else gets rid of the city-grease," Patterson admitted. "But why go through the trouble of putting a gun in tea? You'd have to re-oil the whole thing."

"Tea hinders rust," Lestrade explained. "You'll see the trick often among the rural areas, where men and women are working long hours in unpleasant conditions. The Gipsies and Didikkos do this a great deal." He frowned himself as he took back the weapon. "I give my iron a tea-bath as often as I think about it. Can't afford rust to ruin a weapon when you're out in the bloomin' Grimpen Mire, or some place even worse."

"This is interesting, but why do you look so annoyed about it?"

"This isn't a well-known trick, Patterson, nor is it worth everyone's time. It's *tedious*. It's for people who are investing in a rather . . . uncertain career." Loseth, despite his youth, was clearly an old hand at some dark activities. "It makes me wonder what else that boy was up to before he came down here – and while I'd like to say it's a stretch to call his being here a coincidence . . . he did imply he'd been hoping to look at your papers for a long time."

"I'm going to have to interrogate the staff again." Patterson sighed. "How anyone even knew you had them . . . ."

"I don't suppose it was a poor conjecture for him to catch on I had waxed papers in my coat while I was talking to him, and also I was here to speak with you."

"Just in case, I think I'm going to start purchasing rent on the building across the street. I've often thought a man with a spyglass looking into my study could cause a world of harm, yet I can't actually move that safe from where it is, nor can I pick up the window and move it three feet to the left." Patterson was deeply, *deeply* annoyed. It could not have been a good thing for his pride to realize he'd been retired less than a year before his mistakes rivaled the rawest recruit.

In the privacy of Patterson's suite-like rooms, it felt like a different world. The men quietly listened to the Waits as they moved to the "Boar's Head Carol" in the streets. "Inspector Montgomery's furious, as he has a right." He sighed. "Do you believe in coincidence?"

"Sometimes." Lestrade stifled a yawn. Now that the rush of danger had passed, he felt as though he'd tried to box several brothers-in-law at once. In a moving train. "What does coincidence have to do with the fact that I manage to stumble into the one defective Inspector in all of Devon?"

"Remember what I said earlier about how Montgomery and Loseth haven't been in Exeter long enough to know not to eat at that fleatrap?" Patterson turned, nodding as Montgomery himself entered. "That case of food poisoning purged you of most the chloral hydrate Loseth slipped in your dish." Lestrade gulped down his yawn, suddenly wide awake. "I found the rest of the drops in his pockets."

"I'll *kill* that little pebblehead," Montgomery beat Lestrade to the vow. "That son of a . . . ." Large, knobby fists took turns smashing into his hat.

"As spicy as that chicken was, it's a wonder he didn't make it opium." Lestrade shook his head.

"Not practical." Patterson said softly. "Everyone knows you react badly to opium. Even a newcomer off a small island in the North Sea." The lean man's face was shadowed in the hard light of the gas jets as he spoke. Lestrade thought that though he looked pale and drawn, he still had more life to him than the haunted shadow of that morning.

That morning was a hundred years ago . . . .

"Chloral would make it look like you'd merely fallen asleep, and there wouldn't be any particular side effects. A basic dose takes an hour to induce sleep. I daresay its effects were fighting against that . . . over-ripe dish." Patterson locked his hands behind his back and paced slowly, the heels of his shoes pounding into the carpet. Lestrade and Montgomery watched him.

"Why was he wanting to see these papers so badly?" Montgomery stabbed the waxed envelope with a stalk-like forefinger. "It's just the life story of a dead man!"

"I would venture that there are still some remnants of the Professor's gang that would like to know how much we knew of their fallen leader," Patterson said calmly. "It's a decent tactic. They couldn't have gotten it out of my safe. Even Mr. Sherlock Holmes couldn't crack it – and I had him try it." A sigh escaped his cold lips and he stopped to pull out his pipe. "It should be interesting to see what kind of story he'll try to fabricate, Inspector."

Montgomery sniffed. "I'd agree, but I've heard it all before." He shot a worried look at Lestrade. "Will you be all right, Geoffrey?" He was satisfied with the nod. "I'm going to take him in then. And for that matter, I think I'll leave the food to that little establishment to the Ministry of Health. I'm not certain it's food poisoning if it prevents a crime."

Lestrade tried to chuckle, but he hurt all over. *All over*. Patterson caught his wince as he reached up to huddle inside himself.

"Stay in my rooms tonight." Patterson shut the door after Montgomery, still packing tobacco. "The settee's unusually comfortable, which is why I bought the thing in the first place."

"Not a bad investment," Lestrade agreed thickly. He rose to the water carafe and gulped a glass down with haste. "And now that Montgomery's gone," he swallowed, "What's all that tommyrot about my sensitivity to opium being common knowledge?"

"It is common knowledge among Moriarty's people," Patterson said simply.

Lestrade groaned softly and put his head in his hands as he fell back into the settee. "Quimper," Patterson heard him mumble into his palms.

"Well, he nominated you," Patterson pointed out reasonably. "There were a good twenty-five people subjected to that experimental blend, just because the Professor was hired to create a drug that reveals paranoia and deep-set fears."

"Three of those are dead now," Lestrade said as if to himself. "Straight, Patterson: What do you think this means?"

"I think it means someone is reaching for Moriarty's crown." Patterson puffed frantically.

"Well, at least it isn't Quimper," Lestrade said in an ugly voice.

"No. Quimper enjoyed his personal freedoms far too much to sacrifice them for the responsibilities of power," Patterson murmured. "I don't know where he is, though."

"I don't think anyone does, or if he's even alive or dead. I haven't seen him since . . . May Day."

"Fitting, that." Patterson noted. "If he ever left the Continent to come back here, we would have known."

Lestrade laughed without a sound. "I can believe that."

The two men were silent, having run out of things to say for the moment. The song of the Waits melted against the crackling of the fire.

"I still can't believe you retired."

"I made mistakes." Patterson answered just as simply.

"I hope you've spoken to your Church about that overweening pride of yours. Last I checked, only ministers and saints were permitted the luxury of infallibility." Lestrade rarely used that particular tone of voice. Bradstreet compared it to being skinned alive with a badly sharpened railway spike.

Patterson failed to flinch, which suggested to some degree just how battle-worn he truly was. "Mistakes cost lives," he said at last. "Sherlock Holmes is dead. There will never be another one." With a weary breath he put his hands in his pockets, his back against the warm fire-board. "You nearly died, too."

Lestrade stared into the flames. "I was ready for that risk, Patterson."

"Risking our lives for barely enough wage to subsist on – it's what we do. We ask for no pity nor an apology. We chose to be policemen. But

72

we're not supposed to live when one of the people we've sworn to protect dies." Patterson's bitter eyes were as sharp upon Lestrade as Lestrade's voice had been upon him a moment earlier. "Don't tell me you're the same man since April," he said evenly. "You're not. You look like you haven't slept since spring."

"Nightmares will do that to you." Lestrade chose to be honest. It invariably unsettled his opponents.

"You think I don't know what you're thinking?" Patterson wanted to know. There was no blame in his voice, only another addition to the load of self-incrimination he'd been living under. "Mr. Holmes made a difference."

"You aren't going *too* far, are you?" Lestrade said sarcastically. He rose to his feet wearily. "I've taken this from better men than you, Patterson. I *won't* take it from a Surrey chicken." He joined Patterson at the fireboard, both men staring at each other.

"Did I know what Sherlock Holmes was? His family were squires, you mouth. *Squires*. Did anyone of rank ever do anything for us before?" Lestrade sighed at a thousand unpleasant memories. "Besides get in our way and interfere at every opportunity? No. He was rude to us. He seemed to think we could have gone to school and gotten the same sort of education as he had, and he *never* missed a chance to call me an imbecile, but he had his own lights, and he stuck to them. He always reminded me of one of those old thief-takers from the past, come back to a modern era. He looked for problems, and he solved them. I still don't know how he did it nine out of ten times, but I'm a workman. I can't solve anything in my head and expect a Jury to believe me."

Patterson suddenly laughed. "Yes, I suppose that's why Mr. Holmes could do what he did. He was a *gentlemen*. Gentlemen are permitted the ability to think."

Lestrade snorted too. The two men were suddenly united in the common ground of being a Yarder working with Sherlock Holmes. In a way, part of the pride came from being able to survive the worst parts of the dead man's personality.

"He was . . . ahead of his time," Patterson finally said in a voice soft with respect. "Some of the methods he used, I'm beginning to see elsewhere, in France. But . . . ." He sighed and shook his head. "I had to retire before I even had the time to study . . . to improve my own methods, and I'm a bachelor without any ties or responsibilities."

Something went click in Lestrade's mind. "Well, perhaps *you* should think about becoming a private consulting detective. That ought to leave you some time to keep up your studies."

Patterson snorted in scorn, but there was a surprised look in his eye. "Well," he said at last. "I don't know what to tell you, save it appears Moriarty's gang is trying to do something about itself."

"And Loseth was one of them." Lestrade couldn't believe he was still on his feet. Once he took that settee, it would be all over. "Or in their employ. Either way it's the same."

"We'll speak to him in the morning." Patterson stared down at his empty pipe ruefully. "He probably imagines I know everything about him."

Lestrade had to smile at the thought. Loseth had not been calm or controlled at the sight of Patterson. "I look forward to it."

But in the morning, Lestrade was simply too exhausted to rise in time. He was in the middle of insisting (in a grudging mood) that Patterson go anyway when Inspector Montgomery showed up yet again.

One look at the giant's bony white face and Lestrade groaned out loud. Patterson stared from one man to the other, not knowing what it meant.

"Mr. Loseth is dead." Montgomery said heavily. "He hung himself in his own bars between the changing of the shifts."

"How like a Moriarty touch," Patterson said bitterly. "How very like."

Yes, Lestrade thought. And it was high time to start acting as if the Professor was back from the grave. Because a lot of people were suddenly in danger all over again, and that included Dr. Watson.

Chapter IX – Growing Darkness

Mary Watson watched, proud and victim to a slight anxiety as John lifted Arthur up. Sleeping peacefully, the baby never stirred as his father lowered him into the weighing-scale in his practice room.

"One whole pound." John murmured with a smile as wide as his face permitted. "There's not a thing wrong with an infant growing like that."

"You do that quite well," Mary whispered back.

"I've been practicing on the patients' children." John confided. "And it helps to warm the scale first." At this pronouncement, Mary buried her smile in her hand, lest she wake Arthur up. Buried in soft muslins and a cape in concession to the chilly time of year, the infant was perfectly snug. "But it *really* helps if they're asleep.

"Now," John transferred Arthur back to his bassinette and bent slightly to give his wife a kiss, "what time were you expecting me, dear?"

"Supper should be ready for you at eight," Mary pointed to the mantel clock. "According to *that* clock, and *not* the hall clock."

"Thank you for that distinction." Still chuckling, John checked his personal watch against the clock in question, and snapped the lid shut.

"I wonder why you haven't had it fixed," Mary mused.

"I think it reassures the patients if they come in and believe they're a few minutes earlier than they thought," John said thoughtfully. "At any case, I shan't be long. It's only a quick walk to the chemist's after the meeting." He paused to drop a final kiss on her forehead. "If I'm to have *most* of Mr. Gordon's order filled out, I should have everything lined up tonight for tomorrow's work."

Watson turned quickly and shut the door after him. A puff of wind smelling of the Serpentine and horse-dung made his nose wrinkle. He tucked himself in and hurried his steps to the corner chemist's.

Inspector Montgomery set his glass down with a bang against the scraped coping of the Game Chicken's bar. "One more," he said gruffly.

The barkeep nodded, used to the formulae, and pulled up the wine bottle. "We'll be getting a new run of the Oban single malt this coming Thursday, Mr. Montgomery."

"Really, George?" The giant stood upright for a moment, which put the top of his head perilously close the rafters. It was one of the reasons why he was quick to doff his hat whenever he stepped indoors. He was tired of paying for the hatter's repairs.

"Yes, sir. So fresh I'm certain the crates will still carry a smell of the Western Highlands." George grinned and his gaze passed to the signal of a distant customer. With a nod he began fixing up an absinthe.

Montgomery nursed at his wine again, feeling how the weight seemed to slump upon his shoulders. It was a problem with being so tall, he thought. You had more of the Earth pressing at you. When he was younger it had been amusing to see the expressions on the faces of the toughs as they thought anyone with his bony physique could barely hold a toothpick. He was stronger than he looked, like that American president. Nearly killed a man in a fight once, the story went. But the older he got, the more he felt the downward tug in his bones and joints and every tendon. Drinking helped.

Finding out one's new partner and protégé was on the hook for criminal activity would also lead any man to drink.

He watched as George set up the curved absinthe glass and poured a single shot of greenish thick liqueur in the bottom. He nodded, satisfied, and then rested the ornately carved, slotted spoon on top. One sugar cube rested delicately in the centre. George preferred the Spanish *absente*, which he said was lighter and sweeter than the usual French form, with something called a "citrusy overtone". Montgomery didn't understand it, really, but it sounded interesting.

The barkeep had set up his art, and was now prepared. A stream of melted ice-water slowly poured over the sugar cube. Clouds formed in the drink as the level rose.

"The secret of a good drink," George confided. "Just straight absinthe is boring, if you want to know the truth. The cold water pulls out all the herbs and spices, the anise, the wormwood, the fennel . . . it just isn't the same otherwise."

Montgomery nodded, his attention hypnotized by the great care George committed to a single drink.

"Would you like one, sir?" George offered.

Montgomery was tempted, but not too far. "I'm a man of my habits, sir." He lifted his nearly empty glass in his hand and finished it. "I have not yet grown tired of the grape."

George chuckled lightly in his throat and poured him one last glass for the journey home. Montgomery picked up the new bottle he'd purchased for the morning and tucked it under his arm, where it promptly vanished in the folds of his gigantic coat.

The giant wrapped his red muffler about his long neck as he ducked under the doorway. Long and ungainly when sober, he was not improved with drink. Used to the spectacle, the flow of Exeter's evening population easily made allowances for his passing.

The wind was picking up from the River Exe. Still warmer than most parts of the island right now, but when that wind was there . . . Montgomery shuddered and pointed himself back to his small flat by the depot. His long legs carried him slowly but swiftly across the narrow roads and canal bridges. The Christmas Waits scattered across his way like little chickens and he chuckled. *Little chickens outside the Game Chicken . . .* The chuckle turned into a slightly drunken laugh. It echoed strangely in the fast-vanishing daylight.

He should pay his respects to poor Patterson, he thought to himself. The man needed some sort of cheering-up after everything that had happened. Man's nerves were shot as it were. With that less than clear thought, the tall man stopped as if suddenly hesitant, and swiveled around on his heel to make his steps to The King Alfred's Wall. Funny name for a tavern. That was a Roman wall it was built against, but he supposed it was a decent story somewhere.

Exeter attempted to be a well-lit town, but there were many roads, narrow paths, alleys and mews to traverse. Most people carried a lamp with them when they were taking the hundreds of possible short-cuts from one place to the next. Montgomery usually scorned that, trusting the surety of his own feet, but he tripped slightly on something that clinked and he rethought that position.

Be a pity if you fall now, the Inspector thought. The Burgandy wasn't even opened yet. With that thought, he tripped again, this time on a dry beef-bone. A small dog growled from behind a large crack in the wall.

"Off wi' you," the giant mumbled, and stopped to wipe his face. The walls were a bit on the narrow, weren't they. He lifted his head, seeking re-orientation through the scraps of sky poking through the straight black lines of the buildings. He was in someone's mews, deserted by the feel and the stale smell of very old horse-dung.

Mews were not safe, even for a policeman. Perhaps especially for a policeman. Montgomery slowly turned to go back the way he came, but the gang of toughs that had so patiently followed him since the tavern was blocking the alley.

"You'll find the department almost runs itself." Roanoke's long fingers spidered over the bowl of his pipe – a pipe almost as decrepit as the one Holmes had favoured. Dr. Watson found himself distracted by the knowledge that there was more than one person like that in London.

Not that Roanoke would be a Holmes. Yet, there was something about the old man, something about his sawed-off patience and a compassion masked in the widest wall of thorns, that drew parallels.

"If I may, what are the usual working hours?"

"Regular workday, but if you need to adjust, just let someone know first. We need more men, and we all perform a useful function." Roanoke lit his pipe, and the smoke proved him partial to a very light, fresh blend at odds with the mummified pipe it burned in.

"I should be able to start next week," Watson said after a moment's thought. "I should make certain Anstruther and my usual helpmeets can adjust to the two to three days you'll have need of me."

"Well, we can't make you rich," Roanoke pointed out, "but the pay's regular and in that, reliable. And we run a clean ship here. Most of your 'patients' won't have died of natural causes or disease." He sucked thoughtfully, collapsing his cheeks inward. "You might find some interesting cases, though. Frankly, I guarantee it."

Watson held his reaction to that inside. He was growing tired of "interesting" cases, as too many times they gave him feelings of most unwelcome *déjà vu*.

"Make sure you carry a weapon with you if you work late at night." Roanoke's rusty voice paused him in the doorway. "Word gets out. There's all kind of dregs who imagine there's something good in a Police Surgeon's bag . . . something to sell or take for themselves."

Watson swallowed hard, and nodded. "Understood," he said softly.

The first man was the boldest – that was the rule for the wolf pack, and that was the rule for gangs that built their strength on bravado and muscle. His hand lifted and something gleamed in what little light remained in the growing darkness.

Montgomery cried out despite himself. The giant staggered backwards as cold air whistled through the cut in his heavy coat. The uneven earth of the mews went against him at his heels and he wobbled, close to falling.

They all paused as the tall man put his back to the dirty wall, huddled in on himself as he lowered his head to peer at them. Their faces were as dirty as their clothes. Factory workers home for the holiday, blending in with the night itself.

"Slow down, sir," a thin, whining voice cajoled with a disrespect that offended the Inspector through his drunken haze. "We're not wantin' to make it hard for yourself. No, we aren't." Their accents were anything but what came natural to Exeter.

"You're all going to find yourself behind bars before dawn, you insolent little bugs." Montgomery rarely made note of his great height, but it came in handy in the past. "I'm not too old to send you all up."

Low chuckles. He'd said something not worthy of even a return taunt. Montgomery saw how they paused, grinning at each other in the trade of a silent joke before they swarmed upon him.

"Have your order ready, Dr. Watson."

Still distracted by his own thoughts, Watson paid the full sum plus a fifty-percent advancement for his next order on the spot. He picked up the carefully wrapped box of brown paper and double-tied string with both hands and sought the little handle cunningly fashioned out of the knots. "Thank you, Addington. You've been most helpful on short notice."

"This whole time of year is short notice," Addington pointed out with a slight twist of his mouth. He wound up laughing at himself. "Don't mind my Scrooge, doctor. It's just the sight of all this snow coming back." He nodded with a resigned smile to the fat flakes striking against his window-glass. The look of a man who'd made a bet against Mother Nature, and was trying to be a good sport about losing. Another slew of flakes shattered like sea-jellies as he spoke. "Good to see you again. Keep yourself dry and warm, Doctor."

"As always." Watson grinned, tapping his finger to his hatbrim to the man across the counter, inspiring a final laugh as he returned to the streets of night-time London.

Montgomery was a giant, but some giants are quick. And in the darkness they hadn't realized what he was carrying.

An arm nearly a yard in length moved like lightning. Glass burst wetly against the slimy bricks, close enough for one man to clutch at his face with a cry. When the arm returned it was to slice open another's face with the broken end of the bottle.

Montgomery never bothered to fight like a smaller man. It would have been like flying in the face of God. He merely waded into the flock while they were still confused. Partly because of the drink in his system and the heat of battle, he forgot to use his police whistle.

Watson paused to switch the parcel in his hands. The dragging weight pulled at his shoulder. With relief he leaned on his walking stick and peered at the end of the street for a welcoming cab. The resolution to walk had ended three minutes into the swiftly gathering storm.

The writer in him could not be unaffected at the way the city was transforming before his eyes. The street-lamps caught each swirling flake until an illusion of buzzing clouds of silent white insects filled the streets.

The bells were ringing. He shook himself, ashamed to have let his wits gather wool. Mary was expecting him in less than three-quarters of the hour. He puffed a cloud of his own into the night, and stepped off into the white street.

Into a walking dream.

They shuffled their way to him in the silence of the snow, lit with star-shapes cut out of lanterns hammered out of food-tins and bailed in soft wire. They hopped on uneven feet, crouched like hunchbacks, danced in circles, flapped wings made of cloth and feathers and paper wrapped around their limbs, and peered at him through animal-masks and painted faces. Warped sticks and polished tree-roots waved in orchestral rhythm among the falling flakes. Rags and paper cut-outs and flowers made of sea-shells swayed with each step.

Golden bells dangled from dowsing-rod fruitwood painted silver and leafed with green paper. Silver branches of birch whistled in the air by a man in a birch-bark cap. Rags of silk fluttered in unfelt breezes. A giant bird-man perched and fluttered, tilting his head to see from around the lengths of his long black beak. A bear-man growled, false blood painting his muzzle and the wooden shield in his hand. A smaller man with the skin of a wolf over his head scurried circles around the parade. A third had the tusks of a boar depending from the sides of his cheeks. A tall youth dressed as a fine bearded gentleman on one side. His other was a smooth-faced woman with gold hoops at his ear. The man's side bore a walking stick. The woman's a *pince-nez*.

The Obby Oss danced to the tune of old policeman's rattles, candlelight tossing hellfire from the eyesockets of the bleached horse's skull. The painted sheet that implied his body was marked with woad and weald and Saxon Green. The human feet dancing beneath the sheet's hem were shod in iron shoes.

And the Oss was chanting:

> *"Good Master and Mistress*
> *As you sit by your fires,*
> *Remember the ploughboys*
> *Running through your mud and mire."*

The Oss tossed its head. The parade chanted back, low and deep-throated:

> *"The mire it is cold and deep.*
> *Travel us near and far,*
> *The mire it is deep and cold,*
> *Travel us far and near.*
> *Thank you for your Christmas Joy*

And a mug of your wassail-beer."

Watson would have pinched himself to see legend come to life – or he would have conceded to the better valour of his grandmother's stories and run for cover. But never in his life had he expected to witness a Medieval Mummer Play crossing Paddington.

The Oss stamped its feet. Sparks shot off the iron shoes nailed to the dancer's soles against the cobblestones. Bells and ribbons swayed against their shins.

They were passing him now, the leaders of the group. The Turk and Crusader strode past side by side, faces set proudly as their mails gleamed in the shaky light of the streets. A sword hammered in someone's smithy gleamed black iron in heavy gloved fists. Watson stared. He was entitled. The Turk carried a blade he recognized from Afghanistan. A bronze star glittered on the Turk's chest and the doctor broke into a broad grin. A fellow veteran was in the play.

> *"In I come, the Turkish Knight,*
> *Just come from Afghanistan*
> *England for to fight*
> *I'll fight thee King George*
> *George of courage bold*
> *Let the blood ne'er run so hot*
> *For sure I'll draw it cold."*

Exeter:

"Inspector! My God!"

Constable Withers was not likely to forget the sight that fell before his lantern. The tall, bony frame of the new man lurched forward in the light, holding one arm and covered in spatters of blood top to toe.

Bloodshot-bright blue eyes blinked owlishly in the beam and the giant slowly lifted one hand to block the glare. "Withers?" He mumbled. "Is that you, Withers?"

"Yes, sir, it's me – Withers . . . ." Withers gulped hard and nearly dropped his lantern in his haste to reach the Inspector's side. He recollected his duties just in time and shook out his police whistle. Montgomery leaned full-length against the boards of a false-front store as the Constable winded for help. "Are you all right, sir?"

"Hmm?" Montgomery blinked again as if unprepared for the question. "Oh, I suppose so." He puffed air through his red nose. "I lost my Burgundy," he said sadly. "It was a good bottle of Burgundy."

81

Withers' logical premise was that the Inspector had finally overdrunk his limit, and dropped his carry-home, cutting himself on the glass. It wasn't blood after all, but wine. He turned in relief as Jones and Chessman came running. "Give us a hand!" He exclaimed. "The Inspector's gone and gotten hurt!"

"I beg your pardon?" Montgomery asked in a voice thick with indignation and exhaustion. "I was set upon in the mews." He sniffed loudly. "Had to break the bottle," he added softly.

"Robbers? Hold on, sir. Jones, see to him. Chessman, come this way." Withers scooped up his lantern and ducked into the dark passage from which Montgomery had just emerged. His feet splashed in something wet. Behind him, Chessman choked.

"My God!" Chessman's better eye took in more details than Withers wanted to see with his lamp. "Oh, my God!" He put his glove to his mouth and breathed through his nose.

"Steady, Chess." Withers said it without thinking, a trained response. He hesitated over his next step. "Don't . . . try not to step in it," he whispered. One last look was enough. "Come on," he backed away. "We've got to get more help. Get to The King Alfred. Patterson's got the space for wounded."

"Those men aren't *wounded*, Withers." Chessman hissed as they beat a retreat back to the street.

Chapter X – So Unprepared

"King George, King George, what has thou done?
Thou hast been the ruin of me
By the killing of my son.
O Where is a doctor to be found,
To heal the Turk my son,
Who bleeds upon this ground?"

London:

The Obby Oss danced with feral impartial observation as the mummers swayed, dipped, and murmured. Father Christmas mourned the death of his son the Turk. Transfixed as a child before a carnivale, Watson watched as the parade acted out the Mummer's Play as they went down the street. By stages the quack doctor produced his credentials and brought the Turk back to life, one step on the road at a time.

He was still watching when he was again alone on the street.

Mary will not believe this . . .

Mary. The doctor shook himself, shocked at his lack of attention. *St. Mary's Bells* . . . It was almost eight. He was behind the time by the half-hour!

"*Foolish man,*" he said to himself, and hurried to his home, fast as his limping gait would allow.

Lestrade all but fell into the main office of Scotland Yard. It was hard to say what looked worse about him. The pallor of the cold on his face, or the high spots of red on his cheeks.

"You look *terrible,*" Gregson informed him, as if he didn't have the sense to know.

Lestrade spared him a scathing look. "I can always trust you not to sugar-coat it, Euclid."

"You loathe sugar." Gregson would ever be willing to use a man's words against him. "What's the Mrs. Lestrade going to do when she sees you like this?" The little man instantly groaned into his gloves. "So what does the other locomotive look like?"

"I," Lestrade said through his teeth, "haven't the time for this, Gregson. I'm trying to find Dr. Watson, and it would be a very *very* good idea if I could *find him right now.*"

"He was at a meeting with Dr. Roanoke most of the day," Hopkins came up behind. "Outlining his duties."

"So he *is* joining us? *There's* a piece of good news." Lestrade suddenly slumped against a filing cabinet, drained dry.

"What's wrong?" Gregson folded powerful arms across his chest. "You haven't looked this bad since the fight in the Crimping Den."

"Where do you want me to start, Gregson? My meeting with His Lordship Mycroft Holmes, or my going to Exeter on his recommendation to find Patterson, or my finding Patterson operating a funny little tavern that used to be a dancing school? Or my running into old Monty – remember him, Hopkins? Or how he and his protégé took me to dinner in a place that gave me food poisoning?" Lestrade paused for breath. "Which didn't turn out *too* badly, as it led me to purging the chloral hydrate Inspector Loseth slipped on me in an effort to steal the papers off my person that Patterson had given me – "

Hopkins and Gregson had quite forgotten to move, blink, and possibly breathe. Lestrade had his advantage, and he took it.

"It was *almost* worth it for the look on the little crook's face when he broke into my rented rooms, thinking I'd be dead to the world. I popped him and blew for Patterson, who showed up with a rifle older than the Chief Inspector, and Monty showed up angry enough to pinch hobnails with his tonsils."

Gregson cleared his throat. "Monty, eh?" He cleared his throat again. "Is he still drinking?"

"When did he *stop*?" Lestrade deflated his lungs as he sank into a chair. "He had one glass in my presence. That's *all* you want to know?" Lestrade shook his head wearily. "Someone's wanting these ridiculous papers, and it could be the Colonel. I've been trying to find Dr. Watson but the snow slowed the railways down to a crawl, and then when I went to his practice, his wife said she'd be *here*, and now you say he's left?"

"Calm down, Lestrade." Gregson lifted a large hand. "He should be back at his home by now – surely. It's just a matter of going back there." Gregson turned to signal a constable, belatedly catching that the smaller man was pushing himself up to make his way out the door again. "Hang it, Lestrade, you're going back right *now*?"

"No time like the present," Lestrade sighed. "And I'm already behind schedule."

"Stop." Gregson leaned over the filing cabinet and grabbed Lestrade by the collar. "Hopkins is going with you."

"Me?"

"Him?"

"It's high time Hopkins got to know your methods of doing things, Lestrade."

"I'm going to *Kensington*, Gregson, not darkest Africa!" Lestrade bellowed.

"See? When he's like this, just don't quarrel with him. Don't give an inch, but don't quarrel with him. Fightin's just another source of sustenance for him." Gregson tossed Hopkins his coat. "And do your best to keep up. You know how it is with little people."

Hopkins had the good sense to keep his mouth shut. Lestrade was past him in years and under him in height (by three whole inches), but no one doubted who'd be the winner if it came to fisticuffs.

Lestrade also kept his mouth shut. He was conserving his flagging energy for getting to Kensington in what Hopkins thought was record time.

"Not a single bloody cab," Hopkins panted when they crossed the next street. He startled himself at talking. Lestrade grunted, ignoring the now-blinding curtain of snow as it whirled down into their faces.

"Horses hate it when they can't see, Hopkins," he said almost casually. "That rule about covering their eyes to get them out of a burning barn doesn't *always* work." He paused, stopping so quickly in his tracks Hopkins nearly ran straight into his shoulder-blades. "And they aren't sure-footed in this sort of whiting. That makes men and horses more edgy than anything. Cabbies aren't going to risk their livelihood with a lamed horse."

Hopkins paused, leaning on his knees as he caught his breath. Lestrade seemed to have gotten his wind back – unbelievable as it sounded. He took a step underneath the lamp-light. Snow made lace of his thick lashes and thin brows. His sharp dark eyes glittering with some sort of metallic thought Hopkins couldn't follow.

"What the devil's a *parade* doing out here?" the younger man saw him whisper. He paused, puzzled and annoyed because something had happened in London without his knowledge, and he didn't care for it. "No permits for an assembly . . . ." He scuffed the loose snow at their feet. A bell still sewn to a sad little red satin ribbon went rolling into the white storm.

Hopkins didn't know what exactly happened then. All he saw was Lestrade's large eyes grow larger, into bottomless pools of a strong emotion that boded ill. He turned to look at his companion, grey-peppered snow already collecting a quarter-inch on his bowler-brim and shoulders.

"Hopkins, run as quick as you can. We're taking the short-ways to Dr. Watson's practice. I'm not going to wait for you. Don't bother to wait for me."

And he took off with a speed that belied his twisted foot.

Hopkins could only follow. He soon came to the conclusion that Lestrade's fearsome reputation extended from the Yard and into the ranks of crime, for no one appeared to accost them as they sped through some of the worst alleys, mews, snicketts, and back-building gardens west of Aldgate. Hopkins wasn't even certain where they were when his difficult guide stopped for a second time –

– and jumped backwards, into the alleyway to signal Hopkins into silence.

Hopkins heaved his breath, staring fruitlessly into the swirling darkness of the alleyway. He bent his head to the shorter man's and whispered (he hoped) into his ear: "What is it?"

"Lamps are out." Lestrade said coldly. "They were burning when I went to see Mrs. Watson not a half-hour ago."

Hopkins felt a glacier sweep away his ribs. He completely froze, incapable of movement from some unspeakable horror. Menace lurked in every pool of darkness before them.

Snowfall had never sounded so threatening.

Lestrade put his back up against the frozen wall. Hopkins saw him set his mouth into a razor line as a decision came to him. "Get your whistle out," he said softly, and began pulling off his gloves.

Hopkins was still telling himself *Lestrade wasn't that nervy* when Lestrade pulled his cupped hands to his mouth. That eerie whistle vibrated in his teeth and the air of London. Just as quickly Lestrade yanked his policeman's whistle from nowhere and blew on it hard as he could. And illusion of two policemen, not one. Hopkins caught on and followed suit a second later.

Constables were half-imprisoned with their heavy boots and wool, but they could move when they had to. Muffled shouts floated up in the ghostly light of the snowy lamps half-a street down the way. A shrill eleven-shill whistle answered.

The darkness disgorged swearing figures into the street from the alleyway directly across from them.

And that was exactly what Lestrade had been waiting for. Hopkins died his thousandth death of the night when the older man threw himself into the knot of four large, ugly men who were no doubt armed.

"*Stop!*" It was incredible a voice like that could come from Lestrade. "Halt! You are under arrest *right now, sir!*" The last was said as Lestrade struck a man twice his size down with his truncheon. Hopkins wasn't surprised when the man went down and stopped moving, facedown in the snow.

Carpe diem. Hopkins leaped into the mess too, blowing madly on his whistle. Lestrade was the one who could carry the iron, he thought darkly. Why wasn't he *using* it?

Mary Morstan Watson was a child of the colonies. She didn't *need* to think. When the whistle sounded practically outside their door, her first thought was for Arthur. Before the maid had finished her exclamations she had entered the nursery and swept the baby up in her arms. He chirped in his shock at being risen, but he subsided just as quickly to find himself in his mother's arms, pressed close beneath her chin.

She backed away, for his crib was facing the outside window, and pressed herself against the hall-wall's plaster and wainscot, still holding him close. He was distressed, but her long experience with children taught her it was his own reaction to the unknown – and to his mother. Once he sensed his mother was calm, he would calm too.

And so, Mary was calm.

Had John seen her in that moment in the shadows of the hall, he would have been admiring but not surprised. No one, not even his late friend, needed tell him the tiny woman he married was in possession of fire and steel.

She had, after all, faced the end of her play-years in India, transportation from the hot climes to Edinburgh, and the bitter loss of her father only three years before her future husband even returned to the island in the wake of war.

Across the hallway, the maid was thrusting her fists into her apron-pockets and quivering like an aspen in the breeze.

Perhaps we were hasty in dismissing Ivy, she thought. Ivy had been halfway to useless in chores, but her head had been steady for emergencies, like burst pipe and ragamuffins throwing a stone through the windows . . . .

"Theresa," Mary snapped softly. "Do get in control of yourself." Her voice, deep for a woman, had the effect it desired. Theresa stood upright, and though her face was pale, her resolve was steady as she saw how her employer held her drowsy babe in her arms.

"Shall I take young Arthur, Madam?" she asked, and Mary could only be impressed at the speed in which the girl had caught on to the importance of things.

"No, not for now, Theresa." Mary turned her head to look down the stairs to the ground floor where. Outside in the snow, an indubitable fight was taking place.

In front of Hopkins' eyes (he would make judgment later in the warmth of his own office), Inspector Lestrade paused in winding his whistle to strike out with his truncheon. A second man fell at his feet to join the first – and on the first, truth to tell.

"You can stop now, Hardwynn!" the small man snarled. "I arrest you in the Queen's name for the harassment of a veteran of her Majesty's Army – to wit, Major John H. Watson, formerly of Princess Charlotte of Wales' Regiment of the Berkshires!"

It was one thing to bluff before a single member of authority. It was quite another to scorn the accreditation behind it. Hardwynn broke and started running. Hopkins looked up in time from slapping the derbies on his own man and thought, *"Too bad,"* but Lestrade wasn't finished.

Lestrade was still scowling with nothing but severe indignation, as if the man's fugitive state was a deliberate act against him, and threw his truncheon. It went end over end and struck the heavy end into the lower spine. Hardwynn collapsed as neatly as a marionette without strings.

Lestrade merely snorted at the display. "Amateurs," he said under his breath before catching Hopkins' expression. "Mother of Paul, Stanley. Hasn't Gregson *taught* you that trick?"

Hopkins could only shake his head from side to side, *No.*

"Gregson," Lestrade muttered. "Lazy intellectual, square-built sod . . . ." He sighed and stomped through the snow (now shin deep) and nipped his truncheon up. His Derbies went on the groaning Hardwynn.

"Good Heavens!"

Hopkins for once, beat Lestrade to it. Dr. Watson, the reason for their mad pelt across the snowy streets, was limping heavily to his practice, stout stick in his hand and looking as though he was quite ready to use it on someone. "What is happening, gentlemen?" he demanded with a pale face and robust voice.

Lestrade was standing (one boot on the back of Hardwynne) and fishing for a quick cigarette as a minor army of constables swept onto the scene. Had it only been a few seconds of rout and flight and pursuit? Logic said so, but it was still unbelievable to Hopkins.

"Hello, Doctor," Lestrade smiled with a weary twist to his lips. "Just taking care of a bit of . . . mess by your place." He suddenly put his hands inside his coat pockets as if they were frozen in the swirling winds. "Might I trouble you for the temporary loan of a desk in order to write some notes?"

Watson was no fool. He took in the fact that the men being cleaned up with no little annoyance on part of the constables were long-standing acquaintances with the Metro (the invectives were muffled, true, but his ears were sharp).

Hopkins watched in growing amazement as the veteran lowered his stick to the purpose it was intended for, and nodded as if it were summer and tea-time.

He looks disappointed to have missed out on it, the young Inspector thought. Unaware of what a man truly felt when his hearth, home, and family was threatened, he was doing well to recognize that much.

"Certainly I can, Inspectors," Watson said firmly.

Chapter XI – Out of Retirement

The Yard had limited experience with Dr. Watson's wife (outside of the flabbergasted admiration that he'd found a helpmeet). But when Mary Watson descended the stairs and merely pressed her hand inside her husband's before asking the Inspectors if they'd like to join them for supper . . . Well, the admiration grew like mushrooms that night.

"We couldn't impose," Hopkins began.

Lestrade quietly kicked him.

"I never know who John will bring home with him." Mrs. Watson's deep blue eyes twinkled with something that looked like just a tiny spark of mischief, or that smug knowing so many women kept. "I always cook extra, and there's an excellent pork roast with potatoes waiting."

"Dr. Watson, forgive my being blunt, but if you hadn't been delayed by that parade, we wouldn't have beaten you to those fine gentlemen who were seeking to cause you so much trouble."

Watson faced the information with a nod, not surprised. No doubt the tactics had already occurred to him. "I suppose it was a lucky thing that my romantic nature got the better of me for a moment," he admitted with just the barest hint of a smile behind his mustache. "But I'd never seen anything like that before in London. In the outlying towns of my youth – yes, but not in years, and never here."

"It was an illegal assembly. No permits had been written for it, but I suppose no one'll check their papers." Lestrade managed to sound disgruntled as he accepted a small aperitif from his host.

Hopkins grinned. "Not everyone has the entire book of procedures memorized like you do, Lestrade. But since we're parsing possibilities here . . . ." He lifted his eyebrows. "How did you know to run to the doctor's so fast? All I saw was a scrap of ribbon and a mummer's bell tied to it."

"It wasn't the ribbon or the bell. Everything started to fall together at that moment." Lestrade sighed. "My being accosted the same day I got to Exeter. Loseth's suicide . . . It occurred to me that a ciphered wire could beat me to London, especially if the snows were slowing the lines the way they did." He shrugged slightly, still disgruntled. "If they couldn't get the papers off my person, and the Colonel was involved, it stood to reason Dr. Watson might be facing some trouble. Things went from important to urgent in short order."

"I believe I even recognized the man that Constable Perkins collared," Watson admitted. In the warmth of his sitting room, Mary and

Arthur upstairs for bed, he had dropped the persona of quiet doctor and was now a quiet, calm soldier.

Hopkins for one would have preferred him to be a bit more emotional, but he suspected Watson was reserving his energies for later . . . He fully expected there to be a later.

"Yes . . . ." Lestrade rubbed at his eyes. "Johnny Jump-up. Used to be a Snakesman, but when he got too big to fit through his victims' small windows, he graduated to ground and first floor breaking-and-entering. Starting to get on in years for that profession, and I'm surprised to see him in a little gang like this." His lips were tight with his unhappiness at the way things were going. "That was the lowest of the low, as far as crime is concerned. They were barely competent in their heydays. I don't know why anyone would hire them to give you a hard time." Watson was quiet, which caused a suspicion to emerge in Lestrade. "Would the Colonel have done this?" He asked pointedly.

"The Colonel," Watson answered slowly, with bleak eyes, "back in the desert . . . he was rumored to rid himself of less than competent soldiers and even officers and our native assistants by pitting them against better opponents."

"You mean he could have arranged this to get some of his less reliable people out of the way?" Hopkins whistled. "That's cold as frog blood, man!"

"And if they actually succeeded, it *would* have been killing two birds with one stone." Watson rose and went to the fireplace for his matches. "If I may be so bold, this was nothing more than an idle experiment."

"So you think it was the Colonel."

"No less than you do." Watson said flatly. "He's giving us something to take our time and energies while he waits for his preferred moment to strike. How better than to make him work for us?"

"He really is a cold one," Hopkins muttered. "How does he get loyalty from his men if he isn't loyal too?"

Lestrade sighed, finally shaking his head. "Looks like we're even doing him a favour, getting his least competent men off the street."

New Scotland Yard:

"I *swear* I will find some way to get even with him . . . ."

Inspector Bradstreet grinned over Gregson's desk as the tow-haired man rifled through a bottomless expanse of papers. "Now what did Lestrade do, Tobias?"

"Managed to apprehend a cluster of termites right off Dr. Watson's practice," Gregson muttered. "While he sits and talks, I have to make sense

91

of all this paperwork . . . ." He muttered some more while he found a clip and a new file. "Take a look at this little beauty he brought back from Patterson's." He held out the waxed envelope that had been the source of so much annoyance to the little detective.

"Blessed Henry Fielding's ghost," Bradstreet invoked the sacred founder of the Bow Street Runners. "What is this, '*The Unlamented Life and Times of Professor Moriarty*'?"

"There's something off about this account," Gregson said thoughtfully. "Bits of it reads like some sort of appalling history . . . like a court recorder deciding to break in to romantic fiction. Lestrade said there were some disturbing patterns in this, and I'm inclined to agree."

Bradstreet sniffed. A dark sound. "Patterson is about as fanciful as a Dowager Duchess. If there's something off about his accounts . . . I'd worry."

"I'm already worried." Gregson pointed out. "Suicide rates are going up among the officers. We're getting the backlash off that new 'Jack the Ripper' scare, and tram drivers are *still* pouting over the use of passenger tickets – as if it's *our* fault – ." Gregson took a deep breath. "It's hard to solve cases when you're working against London itself," he said softly.

"Self-pity doesn't become you, Gregson." Bradstreet said rudely. "We've come a long way. You think what our predecessors went through . . . Arresting children as young as ten for thieving and watching them hang for it. The pirates at Wapping. Lord, the illegal provision for bodies back only ten years before I was born! Forgery was still a capital offence. No Police Courts Act. No Ormond Street Hospital to take sick children to when you'd found them freezing in the gutter – "

"Shut it, Bradstreet, I see the light." Gregson lifted both hands in a sour *pax* gesture. "I see the light." He reached for his horrid little pipe. "Go get Murcher, would you? I have a mind to chat with our Mr. Johnny Jump-Up."

"How are you, dearest?"

John smiled and came up from behind his wife to wrap his arms about her. Outside the window, winter filled up the streets. "I am fine, sweetheart." He paused to press a kiss in her yellow hair. Mary smiled, watching the unsung heroes of the city replace the shattered globes in the street-lamps on their street. "I am sorry to frighten you."

"You did nothing of the sort," Mary answered with a bit of starch to her low voice. "It was almost like the old days for you, wasn't it?" She put the back of her head directly against his collar-bone. "A strange, criminal act, a fight . . . Are you going to write about it?"

"Not tonight."

She couldn't have been more astonished.

He was smiling as she turned around to look at him. "Not tonight," he repeated. "I'd much rather have a quiet night with the two of you."

"It may not be very quiet, John." Mary cautioned. "Arthur's slept a great deal. He'll be waking up in the early hours."

"I don't mind." John spoke with such confidence that Mary could not help but lift her eyebrows at him.

"John, your son kicks as though he's already on the rugby field."

"Well, excellent. But I have a remedy for that affliction."

"This wouldn't involve some horrid sleeping-draught for a child, would it?"

"Dearest, you wound me." John went to his bureau and rummaged in the top drawer to pull out two large horse-blanket pins. What it was doing with his prized neck-ties, she hadn't a notion. "Just bring our future player for Blackheath here and I'll demonstrate a successful Northumbrian trick. My old nanny swore it was the only way I kept from kicking myself right out of the cradle . . . ."

Lestrade sighed, glad to see the broom propped outside the tradesman's entrance to his building, and made use of it before he stepped inside. It took longer than he liked. As fast as he freed his low-cut boots from the snow, more flakes fell down to replace them.

"Hang it," he growled, tired and *quite* ready for the sight of his own fire-place, his own chair, and the sight of his own wife, *thank you*.

He keyed open the door and stamped the rest of the snow off onto the sisal mat. Snow clung almost to his knees. Just lovely. He could easily imagine the complications the storm was going to give everyone at work tomorrow.

The large stoves were low. He gave the door a quick peek and threw enough lumps in to last until Mrs. Collins rose up for her morning's magic. Hanging his wet coat on the hall-hook, he stepped up to their rooms as quietly as possible.

All to no good with Clea. She was standing at the top of the stair, smiling down.

"You look better," he smiled back up. "How's the throat?"

"I'm on the mend," she said softly. "How was your trip?"

"It was quite an adventure," he paused to kiss her forehead. "I'll tell you all about it once I've gotten the tangle straightened out."

"I'm glad you made it in. There's talk it will snow like this another foot."

"Probably a mistake in the meterological reports somewhere . . . We're getting weather from some other place due to a slip of the pen or type-key."

"Aren't you the wag." They moved side by side to the sitting room. "We have a guest," she said quietly as he yanked his nearly useless shoes off with a groan.

"A guest?" Lestrade froze while removing a disgusting wet stocking. "Who?"

"An old compatriot of yours," Clea poured him a small drink. "He's asleep in the spare bedroom. I wasn't going to let him out on a night such as this."

"Well, who is it?"

"He left his badge on the table." Clea answered without answering.

Lestrade craned his neck and felt his mouth drop open. It was Patterson's CID badge.

"Is it all right, dear?" Clea was asking. "He was willing to leave , but just the thought of someone going out in that . . . ."

"I . . . Yes, it's fine, Clea. It's . . . fine." Lestrade let his head fall back against the settee. "I'm merely . . . surprised, is all." He swirled the liquor and threw it back in a gulp. "It looks like he's come out of retirement."

Chapter XII – Coded Messages and Hidden Meanings

"**A**s you can see, the Vernet family is well-represented here . . . ."

The guide was so perfect he was scarce to be believed. With his smooth, polished French that spoke of no single dialect or accent or regionalism, and his unstoppable poise, he could be any Frenchman. Indeed, it was that impression the Louvre cultivated.

The old gentleman in the back of his group (women and bored idlers) was either hard of hearing or slightly absent-minded. He never looked at the guide directly, but once in a while his grey gaze would lift and strike, proving he was aware of much. The guide was not fooled by this seeming lack of constant attention. Many people listened better without their eyes to distract them.

The guide began of course, with Claude Vernet, the founder of the Vernet legacy, a skilled painter at fourteen. At adulthood, he was the greatest seascape painter in the world, who had incorporated the human figure into his natural surroundings in a way never before equaled. Claude of course led to the son Carle, pupil of the famous Lépicié. A child of Bordeux, Vernet's love of horses led to his breaking tradition and portraying them as they truly appeared, not in the style that was considered popular. This simple act had inspired a minor revolution . . . a revolution that despite sniffs and criticisms, was nowhere near the bloodiness of the Revolution.

All Vernets made for interesting storytelling, even *grand-pere* Claude's father the furniture-painter. (The Louvre included one of his sedan-chairs as an example of how with proper cultivation, the artistic mastery can only hope to grow and develop). But *Claude* had a suitably tragic note that was popular with the women and paying artists: His own daughter had been executed during the Revolution, and grandson Émile had been born within the very walls of the Louvre. Stilled after his sister's death, Carle re-emerged slowly, with a vastly different approach to his pieces.

It was the son, Émile, who continued the legacy of creating Vernet traditions. Perhaps immune to the prestige of art after being born in such a place, this Vernet chose historical truth over Romanticism.

"*I am a painter of History, sire,*" the guide quoted Vernet's words to Napoleon. "*I do not violate the truth.*"

95

His tour ended, as always, with applause. The tips were left discreetly.

Another group. Another bit of money. The guide was gratified at the poor weather, which had lasted long enough to inspire folks to go outside out of sheer desperation.

Only the old man remained, and he was leaning forward on his battered walking stick. One in a while he would begin to lift his hand as if to comfort an injured part before he stopped himself. The guide had seen that mannerism before, in many veterans.

"I beg your pardon, sir, but may I help you in any way?"

The old man smiled a bit, his grey eyes gleaming. "I was wondering if the Louvre changes so much . . . I am old, but this is my first visit."

"That I could not say, for I have worked here only a few years."

"So! The Vernets – do they ever return, to see the works of their forefathers?"

"There are not so many of them left, I regret to say. One hears of an off-shoot or two once in a while, for they are such an interesting people, it is no wonder they were attracted to other interesting people."

The old man chuckled. "Too true." He paused a bit, and leaned heavily. "Forgive my awkwardness. I am just come from Avignon."

"Ah, windy Avignon."

"*Avenie ventosa, sine vento venenosa, cum vento fastidiosa,*" the old man quoted softly.

"Pest-ridden when there is no wind, wind-pestered when there is." The guide bowed. "You have my admiration to be sure. How is the mistral now?"

"The perfect *mange-fange*," he was told. *The perfect mud-eater.*

"You are a student of the four winds, yes?"

"I have been called such." Yellowed teeth grinned. "But there are actually *eight* winds: The mistral of fame. The *tramontane –* " A skinny, tobacco-browned finger traced the eight points of the compass in clockwise with each name: "The *gregale*. The *levanter*. The *sirocco*. The *ostro*. The *libeccio*. And finally: The *poniente*."

"Perhaps you would find this a diverting topic." The guide pulled out a newspaper, neatly folded into one-sixteenth its spread size. "I was reading it just this morning. There are some curious notions about the weather these days."

"I do not presume to promise my understanding," the old man's hand took the paper with a soft crackle. "But I am student enough of the world to retain my curiosity."

But he did not open the paper. Not then, nor even when he boarded the first carriage that would take him his rooms by an acceptable hour.

The old woman ran a reputable inn despite her being stone-deaf. It may have added to her popularity, for this close to the Rue Austerlitz, intrigue flew like spring swallows, and even the children, sons and daughters of diplomats and embassy workers, drank double-entrées and hidden messages as easily as they drank foreign languages.

Sigerson watched them from his third-storey rooms as they played, *patios* filling the air like their snowballs. What would have been a terrific burden of snow in London had changed under the capricious winds and glazed Paris in frosted glass. Never as dirty as London, it resembled Hans Christian Anderson's palace of the Snow Queen.

Staff kept the seasons at bay by trimming the branches off her trees and forcing them in water. It took weeks, but flowers would emerge. Yellow forsythia and pale cherry were the preferences of the establishment.

He appreciated the gesture while feeling out of sorts at an indoor incongruity. *Winter was not a symbol for emerging life,* he thought. *There is no such thing. In the bitter winter weather, there is only dormant life.*

Restless, he set his glass down, wishing there were something better to occupy his attention. The constant flow of foreigners and foreign diplomats using what seemed to be *the entire establishment* for their illicit affairs was tedious and dull. He was weary of disguises. The plaster that twisted his features inevitably burned after a time. The longer he wandered, the more of a struggle to keep his nails trimmed. Tinting creams and rubber and putties made his face strange and unfamiliar. His hair never stayed the same short length he preferred for cleanliness.

Back in Baker Street, he could always take it off unhindered and unguarded. Here there was no such moment as a relaxed one.

He'd missed the sounds of his own people in the empty mountains. Now that he was among them, he remembered the dangers of not being lonely.

He had been invisible, in the way the land off the edge of the map was invisible. Now he was forced to be invisible by becoming someone else. Someone unworthy of note. Yet another boring scholar on vacation in a large city.

The Louvre was not the same when he had to visit its halls in disguise. When he had been Sherlock Holmes, he had enjoyed walking in its halls, and sampling the music of the theatre, the opera, and even the German compositions wafting out of the street from the Rue.

The music felt thin – *stolen* somehow, without the honesty of *his* face to watch the musicians.

His violin was in Baker Street. He could not join in unless he did so with a beggar's instrument. Even then, it would be too great a risk. So he pretended to smile when a piece was massacred, and threw empty praises at their technique.

He had not played since March. *Another* March was less than a quarter-year away.

I would pick up my bow now, *and play better than any of them.* He had no doubt of his belief. When he was alone, his fingers sought the movements over the strings, and he would play the arm-rest of his chair, hearing the music in his psychic ear.

When he had been Sherlock Holmes, disguises had been amusing, enlightening, and even rewarding. He could pull on another being as easily as a jumper, and he could remove it just as quickly when his task was over with. They were exercises for a skill. One to improve his career and possibly save his life someday.

But not now. Here disguises were forever, and now . . . *Sherlock Holmes* was gone. He was *Sigerson.* He was M. Lafayette. He was a wandering Belgian. He was a prim and bewildered cleric. He was a loose-jointed American seeking his pre-Civil War family roots. He was a harsh-tongued intellectual addicted to the newspaper and the laudanum. He was *not* a private consulting detective attached to agony columns and cocaine.

Sherlock Holmes was gone. Unlike the dissolution of Tibet, this was a willful sacrifice. One might best call it suicide.

Newspapers were a poor distraction.

He sank to the edge of the bed and pulled at his pipe without thinking. How much of Mycroft's funds had been spent on tobacco? More than food, surely. More than drink, absolutely.

Long fingers traced over the black lines on white. Less than thirty hours' travel between himself and Watson. Yet he was facing news almost two weeks late.

Watson had once said Holmes never sent a letter when a wire would suffice. Why would he not prefer a wire? An old argument between them, and perhaps never to be resolved.

He smiled at the newsprint. A healthy baby boy. Arthur after his mother's father. Middle name not listed. No doubt it was a personal matter, as it was for many people.

He knew few people who should bother with being parents. The Watsons were in that small category.

He lifted the paper then, until the single candle was burning on the other side of the page. Tiny pin-pricks, no larger than atoms to the casual eye, glowed back at him. It was a matter of skill to line up each letter resting beneath the pricks to spell out the next message.

When he finished absorbing it, his brows were lifted high and frozen. Were things going so badly with Watson that he had to resort to *working for the Yard*?

He was dissatisfied. He was *not* content with such news. A suspicion that Mycroft had been sending him placebos of data, harmless items that would not make him pine for home – that was discounted now!

What would make Watson join the Yard? It wasn't as though the pay was stellar . . . .

He rose and paced out his agitation while he waited for the coals to gather in the bottom of his pipe. Smoke followed in his wake, thick and oily in the thin winter atmosphere. His active imagination had already conjured up myriad possibilities to explain his Boswell's apparent defection. Lack of funds figured prominently.

Reluctantly, that was discarded. Watson had been improvident in the past, it was true. But he was the man who knew his limits. It had taken him a long time to adapt his behaviors from the military man on leave.

Watson could expend his wound pension on the horses in the hopes of a good win as quickly as he could on purchasing a hot meal for a former veteran. At least once, Holmes had found him at a bakery, buying up every day-old loaf they had in stock for the sake of some Boer cripples at Hyde Park.

There had been no explanation for his behavior – that would have been too much like the need to make an excuse for the proud man. Yet, there had been a single, illuminating sentence in a letter to Holmes while he was abroad that explained it all:

> *Lomax and I went to the Gardens again. The poor man needs surcease from his bereavement, and yet it is difficult to convince him he needs this time for himself. To indulge in his grief feels selfish to him, as it does for many younger sons. I can only accept that he is willing to sacrifice his own health for the sake of others, as the proverbial last-born is raised to sacrifice himself for the sake of the eldest . . . .*

Watson might well have been speaking of himself. He hadn't even known it.

Irritation mixed well with his worry for Watson. He pressed his lips tightly and sent a dart of smoke against the window glass, where it coiled and settled against the chill. He watched its condensation and sent another breath out.

A good marriage. A long-awaited son. Solid practice. He was writing a nearly fantastical amount of work to the periodicals now. Old copies of previous prints had made their way even to France, where he found himself reading and re-reading the accounts among the coffee-lounges. "A Scandal in Bohemia" had graced the pages first. How the Parisians had laughed at the description of the King! Less barbaric and more agrarian, they felt the only forgivable vulgarity was in the size of one's engagement-diamond. It had been difficult to listen to their cheerful banter and pretend he knew nothing of their topic. Soon enough, the battered *Strand* made its way to his hands.

In a much less famous paper, Watson had followed his side-trade with a small article about a man's humorous attempts to speak precise English around those who had their own unique view on what English was. Obviously any references to certain intellectuals were purely incidental . . . . "The Red-Headed League" had made him laugh with recollection, as only Watson could make him laugh. It had also chilled him, for it had briefly placed him far back into the previous year, when John Clay and his ties to deeper crimes had not yet consolidated.

Watson had produced three more small but enlivening articles on the people who sought their livelihoods in the Thames. As the river was part-and-parcel London itself, they had been well-received. Rather than take the usual dull tone of an unemotional professor, Watson had made it a comedy of errors in getting lost in his search for a good piece of fish for supper. The crowning touch had been observing a Constable with a Yorkshire accent thick enough to cut treacle, trying to tell a bewildered crowd of Cockneys they were breaking the law with an illegal assembly.

Every day he struggled not to write to Watson. That day the urge had been particularly powerful.

"A Case of Identity" had followed, poignant and subtly tragic. Was the title a double play on words? Watson had buried their client's true name and description and circumstance so skillfully it was doubtful she recognized herself in the story. Perhaps she would think there had been another poor deceived woman in England, one much less attractive than herself. *No one* would ever know the name of the girl.

His deception is of the honest sort. That the country-folk use when they are trying to convey a message without conjuring unwanted emotions. No talent for outright falsehoods. He paints a small truth with ornamentation until it is as unrecognizable as it can be . . .

"The Boscombe Valley Mystery" was next, and he had smiled to remember the case. Watson had sensibly glossed-over the more complicated details of the matter, for they had been of little importance compared to the solving of the case itself. *Why* Lestrade had called him on it was a mystery to this day, for even *he* could have eventually discerned the truth . . . at least he hoped so. *I wonder how many people tried to find the Boscombe Valley District on the map and came up frustrated?* The thought was a charming one . . . Watson's sense of mischief at play, creating a plausible but fictitious locale for the murder.

"The Five Orange Pips" . . . not satisfying, but chilling, and a necessary moment to convince the readers that there were ways of reaching higher courts than the ones of man.

"The Man With the Twisted Lip" had been the last one of the year and he'd waited for the other *patrons* to finish their reading and verbal dissection intermittent hours before it was his turn. What a gamut! At least it had shown some unexpected fortitude with Inspector Bradstreet. A more narrow-minded and regulatory man would have insisted on persecuting that wretch for false premises, or deceiving the public, lying about his identity . . . It was most likely their communal dislike for leechlike newspapers that he had let the matter slide quietly and discreetly.

And to this day, he would be impressed and amused that the poetic beggar he'd once tossed five pence to had been a man as good with disguise as himself.

How much does a writer make? Enough to survive on? Watson had talent, but talent was rarely rewarded for its own sake. He wondered if it was all going to his literary agent, or to some other expense.

For Watson to be working with the Yard as a medical consultant and Police Surgeon . . . .

He was returning to that dead theory of poverty. Disgusted at himself, he tossed his pipe down. Watson could not be so close to debt that finances would bring him to this end. What, then, would be his motivation?

Minutes ticked. The snow-war continued on the street.

He returned to his pipe and refreshed it.

Were Watson's moods *returning*?

That was less attractive and more likely than poverty. It was so much less attractive, it was no wonder he was searching to prove Watson needed the work for the money.

Watson would appear to have everything he ever needed and wanted at this point in life. A successful practice, a burgeoning career as a writer, a wife and son.

Was Afghanistan's influence returning to him?

Grey eyes narrowed thoughtfully. He searched in his mind, slowly and cautiously, for records of the past buried in his brain-attic.

Chapter XIII

"What do you mean, *Montgomery* was attacked?" Lestrade nearly dropped the coffee-urn on his guest. "People *know better!*"

Patterson shook his head wildly, caught between a smile and a grimace. He reached for his hot cup in open gratitude. "You and I may know better," he reminded the smaller man. "As does a large portion of Saffron Hill, but it's possible that just as Montgomery and Loseth didn't know Exeter, the reverse was also true."

Lestrade slumped backwards into his chair, his thin optimism bludgeoned by reality. It was a grim topic of conversation against the brilliant white sunlight reflecting through the windows. "They took one look at his blurry drunken shamble and thought he was easy pickings, didn't they?" he muttered.

"As it was, it was looking grim for his chances to live outside of the salt-box.[1] Those five men were sliced to ribbons and the court was *not* happy to be hauled to duty right at the closing hour." Patterson sipped his coffee calmly. Despite the dark smears under his eyes, his movements were as controlled as if he'd had a peaceful night's sleep.

"Ribbons," Lestrade repeated. He closed his eyes for a moment. "He has a temper, but one usually doesn't know that until they prod him too far."

"And by then it's too late." Patterson agreed. Despite the attempt at levity, he was not looking completely at ease.

The bodies must have been in a state, Lestrade thought. "What happened?"

"I suggested to the magistrate office that it was no co-incidence that the men all had extensive records in violence. *Three* of them were actually suspects for some murders in the past. They fled before they could be arrested. Once I hinted to them that Exeter would naturally take the credit for identifying these loose ends, the atmosphere warmed considerably."

"I can imagine," Lestrade said with feeling. It took a case involving murder or a suspicion of murder to bring the London police into an outside area. There were inevitable resentments on both sides. Lestrade did his best to be amicable to the boroughs as a result. Lucky Bradstreet. Bow Street Runners might not be able to go anywhere they wanted, but they were *respected*.

"Exeter's always been an interesting place for crime," Patterson admitted. "Not that there was ever that much of it, but . . . I suppose its

102

geography and transport-lines deceive the ungodly that it would be a simple thing to hide there."

"Lord Above, Patterson. If this keeps up, they'll transfer Monty to some spot in the depths of Surrey." Riddled with pre-existing and deeply entrenched members of the constabulary, it would be no tame place for a man fresh off the Metro.

"I had everyone's distinguishing features recorded." Patterson made a *tsk* sound. "Montgomery was too drunk to think of sounding his whistle. If he had, some of his attackers would be alive for questioning now."

"You have to wonder what Mrs. Montgomery is thinking about this." Lestrade blinked. The woman was a phlegmatic sort, but intolerant of any disruptions to her schedule – such as her husband coming home late for dinner. No excuses. *"Five men?"*

"The fifth man had time for a confession before he bled to death." Patterson adjusted. "They were hired by 'some swell' to 'get him quiet' before he talked to anyone."

"Talked to who? And about *what*? Loseth?" Lestrade felt the urge to bang his head on the newly painted walls.

"I don't know, but that was my guess. Unfortunately for that theory, Montgomery told me Loseth never told him anything of interest save the occasional complaint about living on the Isle of Streat, and even that was dull."

"Monty would call free tickets to the London Zoo dull." Lestrade sniffed. "That's just how he is."

"At any rate, *someone* feared Loseth had been indiscreet somewhere. And it's possible he did, but how are we to know?" Patterson shrugged. "It won't be easy to trace him. Not at all."

Lestrade nodded his understanding. If there was anything more close-mouthed and insular than an island culture, he'd yet to hear of it. "That rather makes my night much less interesting in comparison, but I'm not calling it a coincidence."

"I'm not so certain," Patterson cautioned. "An attack of low-class ruffians of poor reputation, even among their own people, on the same night? There are many factors."

"In a city of millions, it would be easy to call it coincidence, but not when there's an attack in a much-smaller city at the same time. The ties between Dr. Watson and Montgomery are thin, true, but they are there." Lestrade poured another cup. He was going to need a lot of it, just to get out into the road this morning. "Hardwynne . . . the man I nabbed last night – the man barely has the sense to tie his own shoes. His mother was exposed to glazing-lead before his birth. There just aren't a lot of things he can do . . . He's been arrested I don't know how many times for the

103

most ridiculous crimes. His major talent is being gull enough to do whatever someone tells him to do, so he goes off and distracts the police, leaving the rest of the gang to do what they actually want." Still annoyed by the memory, Lestrade sipped his drink carefully. "What are you going to do now?"

Patterson merely shrugged. Just beneath the gap between his cuff and his wrist-line Lestrade could see old scars glimmering. "I'll go through the usual channels, see if they'll welcome me back." He rested his empty cup back on the saucer with a faint clink. "And then I suppose I'll say the vacation is over."

Lestrade felt a thorn of guilt. He hadn't expected Patterson to turn over a new leaf so completely. He also didn't know how far this would go.

Kensington Practice, Upstairs Rooms:

" . . . and then he pinned *Arthur's diapers to the bed!*"

Clea's tender throat nearly seized up with the laugh that threatened to burst out. The two women shared a delighted little laugh at the unexpected brilliance of husbands.

"It's strange how there are things you'd *never* expect a man to have in his brain." Clea shook her head, still smiling as Mary poured out the fresh cups of tea. "It sounds like a good solution!"

"Arthur didn't even notice . . . perhaps a half-hour later he was a bit puzzled at his immobility, but that was the end of it. He seems to have a sweet personality when it comes to life. I know it's too soon to tell . . . ." Mary passed the sugar bowl. "Does Mr. Lestrade have his own tricks?"

"He's often surprised me, and I'll stand by that." Clea Cheatham Lestrade chuckled. When she married her husband, she lost the social standing to be an equal to the likes of the Watsons, but she was a natural rule-breaker and perfectly satisfied with her decision. "But it's mostly in his attitude," Clea added. "He's indulgent with children. Seems to prefer their company, actually." For all that, they appeared to give him the hardest time. Even Clea's toddling nephews had the instinctive knowledge that they could use Geoffrey as a human punching-bag. When Clea had half-heartedly protested the treatment, Geoffrey had merely lifted an eyebrow. "I'm used to this from Cheathams, Clea."

"It's all very *Celt*," Mary smiled knowingly. "John is like that, though his manners forbid his being less than perfect with his fellow man. Children know, somehow . . . Their parents bring their children to him every time for his ability to reassure their fears."

Several more minutes passed in pleasant conversation. Clea was not immune to the blandishments of children, and Arthur was a born charmer.

Awake, the baby was content to watch the world as it played about him with his curious dark eyes. Mary had quickly proven her intelligence and experience with babies by sitting the child upright in a padded chair where he could watch the women talking.

"I'm afraid I took that lesson from my own nanny. She said I was so plump all she need do was sit me in a chair and I could not move!" The young mother smiled, sweet and slightly self-deprecating. No false modesty in this one. "It took me a bit of time to learn to play with my toys, even my blocks."

"Well, young Arthur should enjoy playing with *those* blocks. Before you know it, he'll be old enough to stack them."

"Thank you. It was such a thoughtful gift." Mary's bright blue eyes looked again to the wooden toys inside the box. Geoffrey, Mrs. Lestrade had assured her, had been put to work painting the rooms over the weekend and while he was at it, used the odds-and-ends to re-colour the blocks. "Your entire family's been most thoughtful to us."

"Not at all." Clea said seriously. "This is a trying time for everyone. I can't imagine what you must have gone through the other night."

Mary only looked resigned. "I should like a quiet Christmas."

Clea leaned over and rested her hand over the other woman's. Mary was taller than she, naturally. Most people were. "I daresay you shall," she promised. The Watsons deserved that . . . and so much more. It wasn't fair that they endure so much for so long, and the world was not writ along the lines of "fair" but still . . . .

"*Taddiz!*"

Lestrade braced himself for the double blow of sons pelting down the steps of their grandfather's house but to no avail. The cobblestones were hard on his spine through the padding of snowdrift.

"Martin, Nicholas," he gasped weakly. "You're lucky there's a snowpack to protect your old *Tad* . . . otherwise you'd be hitting the workforce early to support him."

"How's *Mamm*?" Nicholas piped up. His sweet voice was wholly at odds with his build – which would soon rival something of history's Little John (a role he was increasingly asked to perform in the school plays). Lestrade was resigned at the knowledge that he would be two-hundred-per-cent Cheatham when he finished growing. *Just have to take on another job to keep him fed properly* . . . .

"Your mother is ready to see you, you imp. She misses you, though I can't imagine why," Lestrade panted. He suddenly flipped the boy into a lump of snow that sheltered the boxwoods about the Cheatham house. Nicholas naturally crowed to be so treated. He popped out in a minute and went back for more of the same. Martin, smaller, older, and rather a bit more contemplative, stood quickly off to observe with a smile that was close to a smirk.

Through it all, their Uncle Bartram observed from behind a black beard and a definite smirk. He was the youngest of Clea's family after Clea, but he was now the *largest*. His square head swiveled on his thick bull's neck as he observed the boys mistreat their father.

"That a kicker-move I just saw, Lestrade?" he wanted to know.

Lestrade scowled. "*I am not a wrestler*, Bartram. How many times do I have to make that clear?" He climbed back on his feet, brushing lumps of snow off his coat.

"Until I believe it."

"Why *don't* you believe it, for Heaven's sake?" The detective barely avoided swearing in front of the children.

"You were raised in Devon. Devons are kicker-wrestlers."

"I lived in Devon for less than Martin's lifespan. So help me, you keep pestering and I *will* break your other shin . . . ." Lestrade abruptly stooped and swung Martin up by his heels. "How much for the little one?" he asked while Martin shrieked.

"*That* one? I'll pay good money to have him off my hands . . . ." Bartram snorted. "*Feyther*'s expecting you," he announced. "An' I'm to give them one last lesson in Lancashire wrestling before you take them back."

"Next time, you'd best wait for Clea's presence. She wants to make certain you're doing it right."

"Huh!" Bartram snorted like a draft horse. "Wants to make certain I stick to legal moves, you mean."

"Well, that too . . . ."

"No imagination, that girl . . . ." Bartram grumbled. "Lads! Downstairs to the mat. Last time."

"You wanted to speak with me, sir?" Lestrade paused to lean a bit closer to the large fireplace. His wife's father was just emerging from the breakfast room, sunlight glinting brilliant prisms against his snowy hair.

"Merely to ask how my daughter is," the old wrestler's blind eyes were always inward and thoughtful looking. "We also received a letter in the post to you . . . perhaps it was accidental that it was placed to this address."

"A letter to . . . ?" Lestrade didn't understand.

"It is on the mantel."

Which he was tall enough to reach, thank goodness . . . Lestrade often thought the reason why the Cheathams hadn't moved out of Little Venice was because this was the only house built to their large proportions. He found the paper and pulled it down.

Charles was blind, not stupid. "Not bad news, I hope," he said gently.

"Well . . . I didn't expect my grandfather to send me word *here*," Lestrade said slowly. He fished out his small knife and split the gum open. "I suppose he mistrusts a post to my address."

"I reckon," Charles said wryly, "that a man who lived as a smuggler might have a bit of difficulty with trusting."

Lestrade read quickly. "He was visiting 'friends' as he put it, up in the northwest, and that . . . ." He paused to clear his throat. "Well. He says business is good – I hate to think what that means, and I'm glad he isn't more forthcoming – and that he'll be down for a visit when the seas clear."

"I can't imagine what he would call a clear sea," Charles confessed. "It will be good to see him. Remind him he is always welcome here." He leaned into his usual spot by the fire with a contented sigh. "Good to know there's no bad news."

Lestrade politely agreed. Mr. Cheatham didn't need to know that his grandfather, the redoubtable old man, only saved his skills in correspondence for bad news. Something was up . . . but hanged if Lestrade knew what it was just yet.

West Country . . . that included Lancashire, the Cheatham's ancestral home. Charles even maintained a small estate there, just big enough for open-field hunting.

Lestrade went through the motions of a pleasant visit with his father-in-law as his sons went through that grueling form of Cheatham affection known as "wrestling tips". He was thinking, though, as they spoke of other things.

It never paid to ignore the actions of old Potier. Lestrade adored the old rascal, but he kept to a code of behavior that was strictly to his own moral codes, and Lestrade was a policeman. Their lives guaranteed a limited contact.

Something was up, and it must involve Clea's family somehow . . . or Potier wouldn't have addressed that letter to Little Venice.

This on top of what's going on with Dr. Watson, he thought as Charles Cheatham passed the teapot. *It's just as well he's a paragon of resourcefulness . . . He has to be.*

The thoughts lingered with him as they cabbed their way back home, Martin and Nicholas occupying themselves in a guessing game that thoroughly absorbed their energies while their father leaned back and rested.

Sherlock Holmes would have had a *very* short career indeed without Watson's influence. A short, brutally ended career. You couldn't buy a

107

dogsbody like Watson, for it had been a partnership in all ways, each man answering the other's weak spots. Lestrade recognized it, for he and Bradstreet had enjoyed a similar unity before circumstances pulled them back to their separate spheres. To this day, he still missed having Roger with him on a hard case.

Watson was not a genius on the order of Holmes, but he was smart, tough, broadly educated, resourceful, and if he ever repeated a mistake, it was London's greatest secret. The nightmare of April might have passed with the barest mention of his friend's sacrificial death . . . but Watson wouldn't forget.

Nor is he letting London forget either . . . Lestrade tapped his thigh, mouth set as Martin trumped Nicholas for the latest round. *Six published cases of Mr. Holmes . . . that's one every other two months, it is. On top of the two novels . . .*

The little man suddenly felt his eyes fly open at a disturbing thought: *Is Dr. Watson issuing a challenge to somebody with those stories?*

Chapter XIV – The Lines of Rivalry

"**A** challenge? No."

Lestrade was about to sag against the wall with relief at Watson's words. The ride from home to the man's practice had lasted a hundred years. *I'll be going to Bedlam if I start seeing conspiracies everywhere*, he thought.

Then he caught what the other man was saying:

"But I suppose my writings *could* be seen as a challenge."

Dr. Watson looked merely thoughtful, completely unaware of the reaction from his sole audience. "After all, they are determined to bury him."

It occurred to Lestrade, and not for the first time, that more than one of poor Mrs. Hudson's lodgers had contained a private compass for trouble. "Dr. Watson?" the little detective queried with extreme hesitation. "What do you mean by that?"

"I mean," the larger man glimpsed a crowd of passers-by on the other side of the window and calmly drew the drapes. In the chill winter he busied himself with strengthening the lamplight in his consulting room. Lestrade watched silently, hat still in his hand.

"There," Watson said to himself, and brushed his hands off as he reached for his small smoking case. "Have one, if you please." Lestrade complied. "I haven't another client for at least half-an-hour," the doctor explained. "Very well. What I mean is this: I do not believe it a coincidence that my friend's death meant so little to the press."

"To be truthful, we were puzzled at that as well." Lestrade admitted. "But as you may know, the papers are an entity we try not to anger. And we do not understand their reasons for doing much."

Watson smiled slightly. "You don't like the newspapers so much, do you, Inspector?"

"I didn't say that," Lestrade said, and grimaced. He'd spoken too quickly.

Watson's smile grew.

Lestrade sighed. "No. No, I do not like them. Have you any idea how often they've ruined the chances for a jury because they came to their own emotionally charged conclusions about a murder? You can ask them to withhold their stories as politely as you can. It won't matter. They must sell their stories, and to do that, they have to make it so people want to catch on the gossip. And then the prosecutor or the defense, sometimes both, must work harder than ever to submit an impartial case."

"I agree it is the written word at its worst, besides blackmailing," Watson said ruefully. He picked up a discarded tea-cup and sipped it slowly. "Publishing is a thorny world." His lip twisted to one side. "Holmes always felt that the media was a useful tool, to be manipulated if one were careful. I couldn't tell you how many cases he observed simply through the daily reading of the Agony Columns." At Lestrade's grimace of horror, the doctor chuckled, low in his throat.

"My experience at the gallery showing told me as much," Lestrade confessed. "All these years, I've been blissfully ignorant about how the arts function." Watson quarreling language with those overstuffed ottomans caused him to laugh. "I may benefit from a bit of education," Lestrade said at last. He wished for a smoke, but wouldn't ask. If Mary was well, Watson would have already offered him tobacco. "So, you aren't publishing your stories to challenge the likes of . . . the Colonel?"

"Nor anyone else," Watson said firmly. "I would not . . . abuse his memory in such a way. I am publishing because he gave me his permission to reveal his methods after his death. I accept that . . . ." He swallowed and brushed his mustache. "It is like any chosen career. One must be careful of making enemies. "

"It seems that one cannot be true to oneself without creating enemies, Dr. Watson."

"*There's* a poignant observation, Lestrade," Watson said with a touch of weariness to his voice. "For my part, there are the usual rivalries and resentments . . . One must keep silent and not defend one's own work for fear of making things worse."

"You mean you've been criticized for your work?" Lestrade wanted to know. "Well, it's clear I'm not an expert in the field, for I don't know why that would be. You write well, but you aren't confusing the way a lot of those overly educated people write. If it's more confusing than the old version of the Bible, I don't have the head for it."

Watson's lips struggled not to smile. "Well, thank you very much," he said with feeling. "I appreciate it."

"Why exactly would there be any resentment against you?" Always a potential motive for murder. Lestrade found himself wondering if he had to keep more than one eye on Watson in the near future.

"No more than the usual reasons," was the surprising answer. "One's style is constantly compared to others, both living and dead. Too many similarities can be seen as a homage, if one is well-liked . . . but if not, then you see sheer viciousness." Watson leaned his back to the wall-paper, thumbs hooked into his front-pockets, elbows hanging loosely.

"Mentors like to take at least part of the credit for a protégé's success. At the same time, they own to none of the scorn . . . and I have seen gifted writers lose their talents when drowned under the stifling influence of those they look up to. I wanted none of that. My inspirations are dead. I have no one living to imitate . . . and I wished to avoid the groups and halls of insulated writers." He made a defeatist sound, still wry. "I belong to no writers' clubs. Merely that of my profession as a doctor. Once in a while I join up with a reading-group or something of a similar nature . . . but *nothing more*, Lestrade. I want nothing to do with the arguments and favoritism in those established groups. I work independently."

"You work well, if I must say, Doctor." Lestrade still didn't know how the man had the time to do what he did, unless he simply went without sleep.

"Thank you." Watson released one hand to pick up his teacup. The remnants had to be dreadful by now, and cold. Lestrade blandly pretended he didn't notice when the doctor glanced to the ceiling where his wife kept their rooms, and quickly poured the liquid into the large clump of greenery. "Ferns are English," he confided in a low voice. "They like tea too."

"That would explain their size . . . I didn't think those were ferns at all." Lestrade eyed the octopus-like mass sprawling out of the pot in a vegetative escape attempt.

"Where was I . . . ?" Watson blew out his breath and reached for a pack of very slender cigarettes. He offered his guest one first, absently courteous. "I am an independent writer, Lestrade. Because I avoid the social circles that inevitably surface, and keep to my own paths . . . I suppose my reputation is seen as . . . ungentlemanly."

Lestrade snorted his opinion of that. "If you aren't a gentleman, no one is."

Watson glowed just a bit at the praise. "At any rate, Inspector, I am an amateur writer and what little success I enjoy from my un-chaperoned skills are seen as a challenge to some individuals who insist on established methods and an extensive relationship with literary creches and circles.

"I write for the larger audience. Not the limited monographs, or the scientific journals – those are few and far between for the effort I must put into them." He shrugged. "There is a . . . prestige in writing learned pieces for prestigious and respectable formats, Lestrade. Don't mistake me. There is a part of me that would like nothing better than to sit down and write for a solid year and see my name among the great monographers, scientists, and researchers." His smile lit, warm and wry. "But the effort is gigantic, and the recognition is fragile and confined to small groups."

Not to mention, the pay would be a factor too.

Lestrade knew gentlemen did not discuss wages. It was crass and a sign of *unforgivably* low-breeding in the extreme. But if a monetary reward was seen as a form of support and approval . . . well, writing for periodicals like *The Strand* made more sense.

Lestrade couldn't imagine anyone being to the point where they didn't need just a little bit more money. Well, there was Holmes, of course. He'd worked with Royalty and Heads of State. Watson had as much intimated that his friend could have retired on his earnings if Moriarty hadn't erupted.

"You out-write your peers, then?"

"I have. I may not be on the lines of Kipling," Watson grinned at the absurd notion, "but I am content with my writing. Demonstrating Holmes's methods was long a desire of mine, and I believe I am accomplishing that. I am also," he pitched his voice suddenly lower, "accomplishing a few other goals with my other projects."

14 Paddington Street

"All right, Martin . . . add the lime now."

Martin Lestrade wrinkled his nose but dutifully added the two quarts of hydrated lime to the large pail of five gallons of milk about to go bad. Despite his size, he dealt with the forty pounds of weight easily. At his side, Nicholas stood ready with the gallon of boiled linseed oil (a mere eight pounds, Nicholas was using it as a weight to test his arm muscles).

"Your turn, Nicholas." Their father mixed as they poured, slowly and patiently. It really should have been given an hour to sit and think, but the weather above their heads was fast turning strange. "What colour will it be this time?"

"Brick red." Nicholas said without hesitation. "Mrs. Collins loves red. She told me."

"All right . . . drop it in. Martin, you get the cheesecloth. If we're going to use it now we need to strain it out."

"Can we paint this ourselves, *Tad*?" Martin pressed. His eyes were growing even darker with age, until they seemed less blue and more bottomless. On overcast days like this, they were almost like his father's. "We'll be careful."

"You want a job, then? Is that it?" Lestrade smiled as he pushed up his hatbrim. Behind Martin, Nicholas was nodding vigorously.

"Very well, then, but you're just painting up the facings, and that only where Mrs. Collins says to, correct?" A volley of reassurances met his stern instruction. "Go speak to her – and watch you don't get the paint on your clothes! Your loving mother will lovingly hide all three of us."

He watched them take off, young, lively, and healthy despite living in London. Their mother's good meals and visits to their grandfather's country estate was likely the cause of that.

His ears sharpened at the ring of the Italian bell on the other side of the pergola connecting the courtyard to the open street. "Hmmph," he said to himself, and automatically looked himself over for any stains, smears, or blotches. Cool wind picked up, whipping his osnaburg shirt.

Constable Murcher's battered face looked back at him from the other side of the iron gate. An all-night beat. His soot-smeared face was bloodshot and worn lean with fatigue. "Sir?" he asked diffidently. "Inspector, sir, not wanting to bother you when you'll be getting on duty in an hour . . . ."

"Not at all, Constable." Lestrade lifted the latch from the other side and let the big man step inside, a bit out of the press of dusty air. The fierce snowmelt was adding to the sudden dank chill of the air. Tonight the hard-ups would be huddled over every scrap of warmth in London. "What is it?"

"Well, there's a strange sort of murder over at the station." Murcher cleared his throat. "Rather . . . strange."

"The station? The Yard station or the rail-station?"

"Paddington Station, sir." Murcher cleared his throat again. "Inspector Gregson felt you should see to it."

Lestrade waited patiently for a clarification that did not happen. "Did he say why?"

"Well, sir, there's a card in the man's pocket, addressed to Dr. Watson. Name of Colonel ur . . . Hayter . . . Thought that since you've met him, it might . . . Well, it might spare the doctor for now."

"Oh, good Lord." Lestrade said without thinking. *Colonel Hayter is dead?* Lestrade thought of that tall, exuberant veteran, strong as a tree-stump, and felt a cold ball under his ribs. *Murdered?*

A strange sort of murder?

What did that mean?

Chapter XV – Hayter's Cards

Paddington Station

The little man stood as still as stone before the other policemen, a part of a silent circle in long coats and hands in pockets. Inside the circle the dead man was prone, right hand sprawled carelessly outward in an L-shape. Still and quiet as the hands of a broken clock, they were the numbers on the facing.

Detective Tobias Gregson was the first to speak, clearing his throat first as he always did when his burden of thoughts forced him to voice something. About them the low rumble of railyard traffic shuddered past, rattling the bones within their shoes.

"I can't say I've heard nor seen anything like this." He cleared his throat again. "I don't mind telling you, I'm at a loss . . . Did McCrumb give his report?"

"Aye," old Singer said gruffly around his mustache. "Opened up a standing wardrobe loaded onto the freight-wagon from the train . . . the body fell right out, bounced off the rim of wagon . . . was so board-stiff it flipped over and landed on its back like it is now. He managed to say that much, before Burns took him back to the station."

"I would think they stopped for a bracer or two on the way."

The little man's comment surprised the other five men – but they held the silence in quietly. Lestrade was not a man to casually speak.

Finally, the Inspector sighed. "It's going to be difficult to see to this. Who do we have before Watson comes in today?"

Gregson understood his question, and apprehension tinkered in his face. "Dr. Pennywraith."

If anything, the hush around the foggy street grew even thicker as the name was absorbed.

"Gregson – "

"Yes?"

"See to it that Pennywraith tends to this first thing. If I so much as hear of a rumor of a sense of an inappropriate sense of priority, I . . . ." The Inspector's face froze for a moment, unable to sort out the worst threat from years of imagination. "I'm going to ask some questions of an expert. I'll meet you at the station."

He turned on his heel and began walking away, knowing what he would hear:

"What expert? We haven't had a bloody expert since Holmes fell off the damn waterfall."

"Easy, Singer." Gregson cautioned. "Holmes was a good man."

Lestrade threaded his way through a London that grew ever busier in fits and starts, even though the clouds remained. Almost as regular as clockwork were the endless swarms of children, mostly boys, running on their errands. Lestrade noted them without conscious thought. Most of them were born in the gutter and would end up worse, and yet there was nothing to do but do what one could and hope for the best. How many of them had fathers, brothers, uncles, and friends already in Newgate, exiled, or hung? Hundreds. And yet there was no personal malice in the taunts and jibes thrown at him. It was as if they understood everyone in London fulfilled a function, and his was to take up those who had fallen in his power.

Lestrade entered the better streets with no more relief and actually a sense of guilt. He was all the closer to Dr. Watson's practice, and closer to giving a very unpleasant report.

For all that Holmes was a baffling genius, the man he called his Boswell was one too. The Yard understood him no better, though the doctor was the easier of the two to like. He was the more human, while Holmes had been so cerebral as to be unreachable. A mental Old Man of the Mountain, and every bit as cantankerous as that folklore character could be.

London was still empty without Holmes, and it was growing emptier. A city of millions and one man had made such a presence in the crowd . . . The detective clutched his hat on instinct as a gust of wind blew up, closed his eyes against the grit flying into his face.

Holmes is dead and I don't know where Dr. Watson even stands.

He stopped for a moment, waiting for the wind to pass him. Papers skirled about his feet with the grime. (He would find it all inside his shoes that night.) The hard-ups ran by, backs to the wind and chasing playbills from the previous night's performance of Handel. A stray dog trotted after them, ribs showing but not quite on the brink of starvation yet. It smelled as though it was eking out a type of living by the tannery.

Holmes would be delighted in this sort of challenge. Of all the things that was the most infuriating, annoying, and choking about the man . . . it was his need to *think*. For a friend of Watson to be in need . . . Well, that would have been extra butter.

Lestrade's carefully stifled imagination had chosen the worst possible time to break free of his mind when Bradstreet told him of Holmes's end in Switzerland. He had not actually believed Holmes was dead until

Watson stepped down from the train with that terrible expression on his aged face.

Mary Watson had flown to her husband's side, and praise God for that. Lestrade was still plagued with guilt at the memory. No one had known what to say – their own helplessness had crippled them. They were reduced to lifting their bulls-eye lanterns in a salute, silent because words would have betrayed their inadequacy. Watson's face had literally wobbled as the presence of his wife brought him back.

I cannot keep plaguing him with these things . . . Colonel Moriarty . . . his term of service . . . his family . . . Only yesterday I was asking about his writing!

Holmes had fallen, but Watson was still on the edge of that abyss. Mary had pulled him back, but would he still fall?

Part-time work as a police surgeon couldn't make up for what he's feeling. And now he has to worry about Moriarty's family targeting him . . . What if this murder is part of it? If someone even suggests it could be another coincidence, I'll . . . .

He kicked a loose cobblestone out of his way. This news was not going to be received well. No, it wasn't. And Watson would see right off just how disturbed he was.

Holmes's vision had been of the cleverest sort, able to derive a universe of information from a single detail. Watson, however . . . he had a panoramic eye that bade him see every player at once. Watson noted the larger view, as if he was sitting in the front row of a stage. His observations, Lestrade realized later, were designed in a way that would not intrude upon another person's privacy. The stoic Watson could not bear the idea of seeing too clearly, yet he understood the need of Holmes to do that very thing, and admired his strength to do so, even though he understood Holmes's abilities were sharpened by his refusal to let others get close.

The all-work maid was polishing the plaque on the door with a carelessness Lestrade found slightly mad. Employment was hard enough to find in this world. Was the girl so directionless she could ruin a task so simple? It wasn't as if she could blame the softness of a spring day – Christmas hadn't even struck yet. London was often violent or sullen or both, and today it oppressed with the threat of more snow. Lestrade was grateful for his re-soled shoes. The streets and walks were littered with countless remains of coughs and hacks.

Lestrade chose to ignore the girl as a lazybones and stepped beside her to ring the bell. True to his suspicion, she paused but did not stop her lackadaisical polishing to announce him. His lips set tight with a displeasure that he knew was none of his business.

116

A rustle from inside the brick frame, and Watson himself answered the door. Lestrade hoped his slight start had not shown.

"Lestrade?" The doctor's eyes lit with his usual spark of the old warmth Lestrade recalled. "Inspector, what brings you back again so soon – ?" He flinched as the wind (probably the same one, doubled back to plague Lestrade again), blew up. "Never mind that for now, do come in – It's good to see you, even if you're here to join the ranks of the influenza victims! I had three since your visit yesterday." Watson took the Inspector's hat to the rack and turned as his wife just emerged. "Mary! Is the tea ready?"

"I was just about to inform you." Mrs. Watson smiled, all gleaming hair and skin. "Inspector, will you be staying? Something hot would be the best precaution with this epidemic."

Lestrade began smiling – the first one of the day. "In truth my business with your husband can wait over a cup."

"Oh, no need to wait." Mary smiled up as her husband produced her walking-cape. "I was taking Arthur to see my friends in the country." Watson smiled too, giving her a gentle squeeze on the shoulder. "I set the tray in the consulting room. I daresay it reeks the least of polish."

Watson chuckled softly. "Give Katie my best as always."

"You know I shall."

Matched as close as ringneck doves, Lestrade thought. Their affection was as close and warm as a quilt against the cold winds.

The cab-man rolled up as summoned, and Lestrade watched as Watson casually passed on the luggage to the man, threw in an extra coin, and paused for one last wave as his wife and son went off at a brisk jog.

Then the doctor turned to regard him, still smiling, but with Mary's absence, Lestrade now saw the more numerous . . . and deeper marks of pain around his eyes and graying his hair. "I assure you, the day will grow worse in a few hours. A cup of Mary's tea is just the thing before I head for work."

Veterans were rarely wrong about the weather. Watson's barometer was set in his bones.

Mary Watson had been right about the polish. For a moment, Lestrade thought he'd been trapped in an orangery, or the comfit factory by his childhood home when it was boiling down citrus in clear sugar. Watson sighed in apology and opened the draw in the fireplace slightly. "That should help pull some of the odors out," he hoped. "The polish was a gift from a patient who is mad about patents . . . I confess nothing strips grease off kitchen floors as this particular recipe, but for at least an hour, everything seems to remind one of the tropics."

117

Lestrade chuckled, pulling his gloves into his pocket. "For a moment I thought you were putting an orchard in your practice."

"I shouldn't complain . . . ." Watson looked ashamed of himself. "If it were lavender we were smelling, I daresay it would feel like spring." He moved with his bad leg and arm gone stiff as he poured tea. It was a drastic change from the loose-jointed, cheerful man of yesterday. Still . . . Lestrade couldn't help but notice that with the lowered rate of activity in Holmes's absence – And who could not find their life calmer and quieter? – the doctor moved with less of his old energy. In the past, he recalled Watson had ever been the steadier and quieter of the two, a calming influence who would remind Holmes to pull his thoughts down out of the skies and remember what he was doing . . . .but without Holmes there were no games afoot, and the only midnight chases were from frantic patients.

"No sugar, then?" Watson wondered. "I'm afraid I'm abstaining myself. Too many encounters with diabetic patients of late. Why they call it the rich man's disease, I'm sure I'll never know." A cloud passed over the aging face.

"I agree, the rich can afford themselves what food they need." Lestrade said without apology for his own limited means. "I confess I'm not here on a social call." He swallowed. "Nor am I here for pleasant news."

Watson leaned back in his chair, a very bachelor position. "Naturally I assumed you were swamped with work. When have you not been?" Lestrade grimaced at the aptness of that comment. "No need for regrets there." Lestrade agreed quietly. "What kind of call is it then? Don't tell me you're changing your own physician. Harkess is outstanding."

"No, not at all. There's . . . ." And here Lestrade faltered for the first time since leaving that fog-wrapped street. "There was a murder at the Paddington Station before dawn this morning." He stopped and cleared his throat. "The identification in the man's pockets led the presiding police to believe the man was your friend, Colonel Hayter."

"Hayter?" Watson sat upright, like a crowbar had gone down his back. "Did you see the man? Is it he?"

"No. It is not the Colonel, I verified that with my own eyes, but . . . there's something most strange about this, Doctor. I believe we're going to need you to come to work a bit earlier than we agreed on."

Watson was shocked speechless. He collected himself with an admirable speed. "Lestrade, I'm not a detective."

"Doctor, I need some help in the matter of medicine." Lestrade hesitated until the mouthful of tea cooled on his tongue. "And . . . someone who has had military experience."

Watson's thick eyebrow went up. He was already thinking. "Lestrade, I'm pleased to help however I can, truly, but I am surprised. Your other police surgeon, Pennywraith . . . ."

"Will not be with us much longer," Lestrade blurted. "In fact, if he left today, I feel we'd have a better chance of solving some of our cases."

Watson looked slightly shocked at the blatant criticism, but as usual, let it slide.

"Why did you say you needed someone with military experience?" he asked cautiously.

Lestrade took a deep breath. "Perhaps I should just let you see the body in question. I don't think my attempt at words will do it any sort of justice."

The morgue was not in its best state. Watson actually paused at the step downward into the chill basement, his nostrils flaring. In that light, Lestrade could easily see the veteran of war in the man, and the gleam in his eye suggested no forgiveness for shabbiness. This was a man, the *only* man, Sherlock Holmes trusted as a partner on his dangerous cases.

"Inspector." Gregson was moving away from the cleaner air of the window, touching his hand briefly to his cap. "Dr. Watson, it's good to see you again, no matter what the circumstance."

The hardness in Watson's eyes softened, just a bit. "Good to see you too, Gregson. I'm told there's a case of interest."

"Well, yes, anyone should call it such." Gregson nodded, pulling a slack-featured orderly out of the shadows. "Show Dr. Watson the newcomer, would you, Will?"

The body was resting under a grey-tinged but clean sheet. Lestrade had a feeling Watson noted and disapproved of that too. With a silent flick of his wrist, the man had exposed the corpse on the table.

Things had not improved since Lestrade had last seen it.

Watson did not move. Nearly everyone had taken a step back upon first sight, and the two poor bobbies on the beat had wasted their breakfast in the nearest gutter. But Watson merely stiffened, as if answering the snap of an angry officer, his hand clenched around the handle of his bag.

Long silence in the dim room.

"Bring more light, would you please?" Watson requested with grim politeness. Then he surprised everyone by unbuttoning his coat. Gregson looked bluntly at Lestrade, his breath fogging in the air.

They understood when Watson carefully folded his coat in a wide spot next to the corpse, then placed his precious bag on it. Watson might not openly criticize the way a man held a morgue, but he would not let their foulness contaminate his equipment.

Lestrade passionately, passionately wished Pennywraith was here to see.

"We weren't sure what to make of it, Doctor," Gregson confessed. "The cause of death, or the state of the corpse before death."

"I understand completely," Watson said in his gently. "May I make an examination?"

"We were hoping you'd say that." Lestrade put his hands in his coat pockets, warming them in the coldness. "Gregson, what did Pennywraith say?"

"The usual. Estimated the time of death was sometime before midnight, and called the cause of death as massive trauma." Gregson did not quite keep the sarcasm out of his voice.

Watson's lips set tightly. "No internal examination at all." It sounded like a condemnation. "Gentlemen, this may be unpleasant to your state of mind . . . ." He produced a long white linen smock. "Perhaps you'd prefer to go someplace warmer . . . ."

Outside, Gregson and Lestrade were doing fit to outsmoke their usual ration of cigarettes.

"He's a cool one," Gregson marveled softly. "Always was."

"I imagine he'd have to be, lodging with Sherlock Holmes."

Gregson shook his head sadly. "At least he was makin' some money as Holmes's assistant."

Lestrade sharpened slightly. "What do you mean?"

"Well, I mean the doctor and his wife had to live parts o' their marriage apart for some time, savin' up their money as it were, before he could buy his practice. She was always welcome at her old missus, and he would stay on Baker Street, both saving what they got."

"That's a common tale," Lestrade regretted. "More people I know than not had to do the same thing. If Bradstreet's father-in-law hadn't bequeathed his building . . . ." Lestrade felt his own lips thin, much like Watson had at the sight of the morgue. For all of Watson's talk of publishing, he hadn't mentioned a word about income. *Because he's a gentleman, and his kind do not discuss fees . . . .*

"I wish he was our police surgeon more than part-time," Gregson said with feeling.

"So do I . . . ." Lestrade was still thinking. "What did you mean about 'at least he was making money'?"

Gregson looked embarrassed. "People talk. The Misses Watson isn't well."

"I knew she had poor health in the past . . . She seemed well-enough to me."

120

"Aye, but she *keeps* getting ill. Comes and goes. A month or so she's fine, but then the next, the doctor's using most of what he's earned to her care. London's a bad place to live if your lungs are weak."

Lestrade felt a chill. "You're right about that." They smoked in silence for a few minutes. "Never saw a hint of discontent, though."

"Nah, they're suited for each other, and that's a fact. Misses Watson is just like the Mister. She's always out on charity works, and when he's not workin' you know what he's doin?" Gregson didn't wait for an answer. "He's still going out to the East End, rescuing out what unfortunate collegues of his that fell under the spell."

Lestrade stared at him, his cigarette nearly falling out of his open mouth. "Gregson, that is absurd!" His voice lifted. He lowered it hurriedly. "Mrs. Watson lets him go to those opium dens – I admire that – but the East End?"

"Saw him at The Green Peacock." Gregson took no pleasure in Lestrade's shock. "He's got a friend who keeps windin' up there."

"That's – " Lestrade turned at the click of the door with abject relief. The orderly was standing at the stairwell, nodding at them to step inside.

"I'm afraid the news isn't good." Watson's face was slightly paler than before, and he accepted Gregson's offer from the small flask he carried. Lestrade was satisfied at the smallness of the amount he drank. "The man was alive up throughout most of his ordeal."

Gregson swore, and Lestrade's face went stiff.

"Alive!" Lestrade hissed. "What was the direct leading cause of death?"

"He was tortured." Watson snapped, a bluntness directed at no one. "Flogged, hung by his arms, cut with knives, and finally dispatched with a blow to the head. The throat was cut as an afterthought, I would say, in order to drain what blood was left and minimize the . . . mess of transporting him to the street."

"God almighty." Gregson paused and kicked a rusty nail in the gutter.

"We don't even know who he is." Lestrade rubbed his temples. "The chemical stains on his hands suggest he was a photographer, but he could be a hobbyist just as easily, or even an apprentice learning the trade late in life."

"A likeness at the local chemist' shops would perhaps help," Gregson muttered.

"There's another thing." Watson broke in. They looked at him, dreadfully expectant. "He was in the first stages of influenza."

"How can you tell that?"

"He was running a fever at the time of his death." Watson shrugged.

"How can you tell that?" Gregson repeated.

121

"It's quite simple. I could smell the white blood cells in his mouth."

"Cripes." Gregson stared.

"My thoughts exactly," Lestrade agreed. "I have to say I'm impressed beyond all measure."

"No need." Watson was suddenly awkward. "If you'd had some of *my* instructors, you'd never wonder at some of the bizarre facts I know about the human body . . . At any rate, I'll keep my eye out for anything suspicious at my practice. Whoever did this will be contracting his victim's illness in a matter of days. I, for one, am just recovered." His mouth set under his neatly trimmed mustache. "May I see those papers that led you to think he was Colonel Hayter?"

Gregson could be prescient. He pulled out a flat envelope from inside his heavy coat and handed it over. Watson pulled out a badly torn envelope and peered at the contents. Neat, organized writing shone through the thin paper in the light.

"Rolls from Afghanistan?" Watson was clearly surprised. "Names . . . regiments . . . even ages." His mouth changed direction, a different sort of set. "My card was in – ah, here it is." He pulled it out. "Yes, this is my card, but I gave it to him months ago . . . Why did you think this was Colonel Hayter?"

"Because of this." Gregson had been waiting for the question. He pulled out a tiny japanned box, ornamented with a small yellow *fleur-de-lis*. Lestrade recongized it as a loyalty symbol from the Norman families. It was sturdy, but as expensive as it was understated. A perfect display of wealth and taste. Watson prized the small lid open to find at least a hundred calling-cards.

Watson, a man of words, was rarely speechless. It was almost as good as a theatre to watch him struggle to find an appropriate comment.

"Now why," he asked softly, and cleared his throat, "would this man, whom I don't know at all, be carrying around an entire box of the Colonel's cards?"

"Most people only carry their own cards," Gregson agreed. "Deliveries aren't made unless the cards have received final approval from the purchaser. If you don't know him, then perhaps he stole it from your friend?"

"I wouldn't think this box would be that expensive," Watson said, but doubtfully. "The inside is stained camel-bone and set with low-grade gemstones. The sort's common as sand in the desert."

"In lieu of the circumstances, we sent ahead a wire on Lestrade's recommendation." Gregson puffed his cheap tobacco furiously. "Perhaps he could be persuaded to come to London for a visit?"

"I . . . I suppose so," Watson answered strangely, as if he was struggling to anchor some of his attention back to the Yarders while the larger portion of his brain was busy thinking. "I'll send him a wire myself . . . ."

"Not to worry then." Lestrade sighed. "We'll take this one step at a time."

"We may ask for your help later, but for now, the Yard thanks you." Lestrade gripped his hand. "And of course, compensation for taking you from your work to come in early."

"It was no trouble, Inspector. Do stop by any time. You as well, Gregson."

They watched him go, a veteran from a forgotten war, moving with that war still inside him.

"I," Gregson announced, "have no good feeling of this."

"We've established Dr. Watson is being watched, if not targeted." Lestrade suddenly tossed his tobacco at the remains of a melting snowbank. His breath plumed before his face. "The coincidences are getting a little long in the tooth, Gregson."

"Darts." Gregson said without warning.

"Darts?"

"They're small and sharp and can cause a lot of hurt. They're also hard to see, especially in a crowd. Like stinging bees. How much of our energies are we going to waste on distractions like this?"

It was just as well Lestrade had thrown his cigarette. He might have just swallowed it then. "You call a butchering like that a distraction?" he hissed under his breath.

"I do. Because terrible as it is, our real goal is this case of Hopkins', and we won't be able to give him the help he needs because we're going to be wrapped up in this."

"Let's not discount Watson," Lestrade warned.

"Oh, I'm not. But who, Lestrade, *who else* is not discounting Watson?"

123

Chapter XVI – Eventual Goal

Mary's absence made their new house so chill, even with the fires bright and the coal piled high.

Watson hung his coat up after shaking it out for detritus first. He absently toed a cinder back into the street before shutting the door. Theresa was just emerging, hands inside her apron. The girl spent more time keeping herself clean than actually cleaning . . . .

On the other hand, Watson knew from first-hand experience the level of damage only *one* unhygienic person could wield.

"Good evening, sir. May I bring you a cup of tea?"

"Coffee, if you please, Theresa," Watson said absently. "From the red tin. Will there be supper soon?"

"Yes, sir. The Missus set up a lovely pot of lamb stew before she left, with green curry and pearl onions as you like it. And a dish of lemon rice for the side."

Watson had been putting his hat on the rack. He missed entirely. "*Lamb?*" he repeated. "Where did Mary find lamb? The market's been empty a fortnight!"

"I'm sure I don't know, sir." Theresa shook her head. "She sent me for some winter pippins, and when I came back, she was in the kitchen, dressing it neat as you please."

Watson shook his head, slightly dazed at Mary's unending ability to slip such surprises on him. "She must have wired her friends in Kent . . . they're always coming to London for one excuse or another . . . ."

"Pardon, sir?"

" . . . Nothing, Theresa. Perhaps you could bring some of it up in an hour. I'm finishing up my papers in the study."

"Very good, sir."

Watson spent that hour as promised by sorting papers and filling out invoices (none of which added up to more than the equivalent to an hour's wage). At the end of it, a wild hare sent him on a search through older journals and texts for obscure treatments on influenza.

There must be some sort of pre-existing method . . . Watson grunted slightly as he lifted a surprisingly dense folio of bound books off the highest shelf in his study. *What was that about the Jimsonweed . . . something to do with temporary insanity as a side-effect? That couldn't possibly be sanctioned . . . .*

He grunted to himself and busied himself in the pages – He may as well plumb their depths before the cheap paper fell apart!

Theresa brought in supper. He ate while keeping his mind to the problem. The dead man had been of a poorer class: Holmes's training on reading the callus and skin-tints had been something he could take pride in learning. *Partly because it was physiology, no doubt.* The medical omnivore that was John Watson could memorize and apply *anything* he learned forever, so long as it had something to do with medicine.

Theresa cleared away the dishes. He kept reading. After the clock chimed nine, he glanced at his calendar, decided a later hour would do no harm to the next day's schedule, and pulled out his desk notebook.

A poorer class of man would not always be able to go to the doctor. Financially it was the short route to destitution. Watson disliked the situation and compensated his conscience whenever he could, knowing he had a responsibility to ensure his family's comfort and health too.

The poorer classes had their pride. Pride every bit as stiff and secure and even complacent as anything from the highest echelons. And like any class, they banded together and helped each other.

Rather than go beggar themselves on a consultation they could not afford (and even more for a prescription more expensive than gin, morphine, or an ordinary anodyne powder), they would be reverting to the older methods of treatment. Something that would get this unknown man out of the grips of the influenza . . . .

Watson eschewed faith-healing for the good reason that he saw no overt signs of it on the corpse . . . but also because he had no experience in the field that he could endure. One might as well tell a Middle Age peasant they lived in the middle of a thorny wood titled "Dragon" and expect to have some sort of unemotional response.

Lack of money, a stock in pride and independence, and a large resource would mean some sort of herbal treatment. A folk-remedy that may or may not be useful.

Eupatorium . . . it would have to be one of the Eupatoriums . . . .

An hour after supper he was still researching.

Colonel Hayter put an end to that.

The knock was typical of the old Colonel: Loud, powerful, and shocking – like a nocturnal attack. Watson felt his heart skip two entire beats before it settled. He wiped his brow and went to the front door, knowing very well the identity of the person behind it.

"You're up rather late, sir," he said with that wonderful unconscious irony that was the delight of his friends.

"Late? Are we setting our internal clocks by the *sun*, John?" Hayter paused for a brief clasp upon the shoulder – jarring Watson's teeth – and moved to neatly dispose of his traveling-wear. The old bachelor set his hands on his hips and sniffed expectantly from around his proud waxed mustaches. "Nicely done," he approved. "An orderly layout . . . Is that a shotgun hallway upstairs?"

"Er . . . ." Watson cleared his throat. "I have some stew. Lamb with curry. And lemon rice. Would you like some?"

Several minutes later Hayter was tucking into his meal with enthusiasm, and Watson was politely joining him with seconds. Hayter's gift, a bottle of wine, sat between them.

"Wretched business," the Colonel said around mouthfuls. "One needs to exercise extreme caution. I don't know why I stopped thinking of London as being in enemy territory, but it seems to be a good way to think."

"I always thought of it as living in the middle of a moving cesspool," John answered, slightly dark.

"Just the type of language to persuade a fellow to live here, my lad."

"Well, it is."

"No doubt your opinion is in part due to your family's absence," Hayter said shrewdly.

John poured the wine with a martyred air.

"Not sure about what that man was doing with my cards. I've thought it over and over . . . I'm not even certain I'd know the man if I saw him. Your description is a bit puzzling."

"It's difficult to describe what a person looked like before mutilation," Watson confessed. "Were the cards an order placed?"

"Well, yes. I always keep a standing order at the stationery's . . . McManus and Teasedale. Excellent work, never once lost my accounting." Hayter exhaled. "I suppose I shall have to order another hundred or so . . . there's a large ball coming up, and it's so much easier to give out the cards beforehand . . . The ladies expect it, you know."

Watson momentarily covered his face with his napkin, pretending to wipe his mouth until the smile was back under control. *What an old rascal . . . and what a determined bachelor . . . .*

"I say, do you think Mrs. Forrester would be attending? She lives not so far away."

Perhaps not as determined as I thought . . . Watson's composure teetered over the edge at the abrupt (and disquieting) image of his and Mary's patrons paying court to each other. With heroic effort, he wrenched his mind back upon the proper lines.

"But Colonel, have you had any other problems with McManus and Teasedale?

"Never. All I had to do was select the type of card I wanted, grade of paper, along with the style of type, colour of ink, inscription, what clubs I chose to list – the usual gentlemen's stuff." Hayter looked thoughtful. "I

126

prefer a papyrus or bamboo-fibre weave. It reminds the receiver of my past in the tropics."

"Very astute," Watson admitted.

"One year I had my cards tinted with coffee. It was most attractive, but the popularity was such that I spent twice my normal amount . . . ." Hayter chuckled. "And there was the time I asked for turmeric-grains in the paper. Marvelous job, but the odour remained for some weeks. I gained five unwanted pounds . . . Made me hungry."

Watson wished *just once* Hayter did not exercise that ability to yank the rug from under his feet. It was no wonder Holmes had enjoyed the man's company so much.

"If you are willing, I can take you to the morgue tomorrow morning. Perhaps you could recognize the features of this strange thief."

"I may. He may also be just another pawn on the chess-board." Hayter shrugged. "Where might a man put his kit for the night, John?"

"Oh . . . forgive me. There's the guest bedroom upstairs." John rose and pulled the cord for the maid. "You ought to find it comfortable," he said dryly. "I made it as minimalist as possible."

"Excellent! Is minimalism finally becoming stylish?" Hayter's opinions were obviously hopeful.

"I have no idea, but it is my style," Watson said firmly.

"You should preach that to military families. Especially the wives."

A half-hour later the men were settled into the slow warmth of a low-burning fire. John placed white cedar-cones on top and suffused the air with the sweet smoke. Glasses of cordial rested in their left hands, thin cigars in the opposite.

"Pleasant." Hayter decreed. "Very pleasant. I noticed it is easier for you to look out than for a man on the street to look in."

"I prefer not to repeat my mistakes," Watson said calmly. His eyes were half-closed before the fire, a sleepy look that fooled none of his friends. "London may be my business, but my business is not London's."

"Agreed." Hayter leaned back. "Has there been any word from your publishers?"

Watson was quiet for so long Hayter lifted his eyebrow.

"I would daresay, all is going according to schedule," he said at last, and there was a low, self-satisfied tone to his voice that few people could admit to witnessing. Hayter had, and knew the implications.

"And what would your schedule be, John?"

"Holmes gave permission to write of *A Study in Scarlet* and *The Sign of the Four* while he was alive. Dead, I am now free to demonstrate his methods to the world." Under his dark brown mustache, Watson's lip was frozen in a half-smile. The brown eyes were calm and controlled.

"When you sent that draft of "The Final Problem" . . . Well, I wondered why you were sending it to me. You aren't planning on publishing it just yet?"

Watson shook his head, no. "The atmosphere is not favourable to that story just yet. I sent it to you . . . and to Mrs. Forrester . . . and to Scotland Yard . . . and to a few other . . . ." Here Watson paused, seeking the appropriate word, which was almost unheard of for him. *"interested parties."*

"You sent it without publishing it?" Hayter spoke slowly, feeling his maneuver through unfamiliar territory. "Without a mind to publish it?"

"It will not be ready just yet," Watson answered, soft and satisfied.

"Ready for what?"

"London has managed for years to politely ignore the work of a gentleman who was in a most unusual profession. For the ten years I knew him, he was consulted by royalty as diligently as he was the poor and the rising worker. It is the work of our peers to pretend there is no Sherlock Holmes unless there is need. It was the work of the commoners to adore him. No one else has ever been relied on by so many different folk, for so many different reasons."

Hayter watched, fascinated, as Watson lifted his cigar and inhaled smoke.

"Do you know what kind of letters I saw the most after publishing 'A Scandal in Bohemia'?" he asked. Hayter shook his head no. "The ones that wanted to know grisly details on the late Irene Adler's fate. As far as reaching an audience goes, I am afraid I hit too many sensationalist tastes . . . It was good practice." Watson paused and blew smoke again. "'The Red-Headed League' followed that one, and that was seen as a bit of a more intellectual exercise, but there were some doubts about the humour within . . . Some wondered if it were contrived moments." Watson shrugged as if small minds were not his problem. "I'm certain it caused some disconcerting talk in other circles . . . It did imply that a member of Royal Blood, however diluted, was capable of the unthinkable."

"'A Case of Identity' was similarly received," Hayter pointed out. "I remember the issue a barrister I knew took exception to Holmes's statement that he could not prosecute the scoundrel for taking advantage of his step-daughter."

"But how could justice be met if a scandal resulted?" Watson wanted to know. "The girl would have been harmed and made a laughing-stock, and her mother . . . ." He shook his head. "No. The law is in conflict with society. The lesson had to be shown as it was."

"What is your eventual goal, John?" *There is a pattern here.* Hayter could scent it, like tiger spoor in the mangroves, but he could not . . . yet .

. . see the flash of the tiger's coat. Hayter tapped his cigar-ash into the reservoir, and John found himself caught by the gleam of firelight on the old Colonel's widower-ring.

"My eventual goal?" John echoed. The firelight caught his face, and unlike so many people in Hayter's experience, the effect was far from demonic. Rather, a noble guise like that of a blacksmith from the days when that craft was known for its guile and cleverness and strength and healing. Saintly men, to break the bonds of witchcraft. John Watson.

"My eventual goal is to publish 'The Final Problem'." John answered. "When I am *certain* London is ready to receive it."

And there was a certain set to that chiseled mouth within those bronzed features that discouraged further questions.

Chapter XVII – Answering With A Question

Colonel Hayter was a mixed blessing as far as a guest went. Military to the core, he was down to breakfast two minutes early, washed, shaved, fitted out, and immaculate. Watson knew without having to ask that the man had made his own bed to a camp-cot precision. Theresa's bewildered expression as she emerged to pour the coffee confirmed it.

The doctor hid a smile behind his coffee cup. Theresa no doubt had thought her employer's habits an interesting anomaly. Now there were two men in her knowledge guilty of the same grooming. He wondered if she would survive the sight of Hayter mending his own clothing. Hayter was staunchly and proudly Army, but his family had been the most land-locked of naval officers, and Hayter had grown up with a needle in his sleeve as much as his kerchief.

"The lamb was outstanding last night, John." Hayter tucked into his eggs after burying them in a duff of black pepper. "So. Are we to go to the morgue?"

"If it is agreeable to you," Watson lowered his newspaper (nothing of import, yet again), and picked up his own fork. Theresa hovered, dispensing coffee and fresh butter.

"Best to get the poor devil identified if it's at all possible," Hayter decided. "What do you think?"

"I second that." Watson took up the paprika – Theresa would forever despair of good English cooking at this table – and put it on his bacon.

"Who would be the coppers in charge of this?" The Colonel wondered. "That Lestrade fellow? He's the only one I know."

"Probably," Watson said after a moment's thought. "He's been staying in touch with me of late. If not Lestrade, I would imagine Gregson . . . You would find him an interesting study, Colonel . . . or perhaps Hopkins."

"I hope it is Lestrade. Can't keep up with but so many new acquaintances in the course of a year." Hayter spoke around quick bites that never even wobbled his waxed mustaches. (His valet had sworn the appendages would stop a bullet, if it was mostly spent first.) "I can remember a name like Lestrade. Got too many Gregsons and Hopkins to keep track of as it is."

Watson considered that a reasonable deduction for Hayter was still out of what was considered reasonable for the average man. Then again, there was no point in comparing Hayter with *anyone*. He could all-too easily see the man asking bewildered Inspectors to work with Lestrade just because his name was easy to remember. *Good Lord, that scene would be worth a shilling* . . . .

"I'm sure you'll find Mr. Lestrade easy enough to work with." Watson attempted to exercise tact. He didn't often feel sorry for the little man, but in the burning light of Hayter, they all resembled blackened asteroids. Lestrade was just as kow-towed by Hayter as everyone else. Intimidated in a way he never had been with Sherlock Holmes.

Then again, Holmes had never tried to press a bag of freshly killed squirrels on the Inspector. Hayter had an interesting approach to forging friendships.

On the streets of London, it was difficult to say if Hayter was dressed for business or for war. Immaculate as ever, his breast looked oddly naked when bereft of medals, and his walking stick was a dangerous looking thing that he swung like a metronome down the street. Watson was grateful they found a cab for the largest part of the trip. Hayter was the first to jump out – perhaps "dismount" was a better word – and threw up the fare.

As it would happen, Inspector Lestrade was standing outside the New Scotland Yard building with Gregson and Hopkins. The men were passing a box of the smallest cigarillos Watson had ever seen and giving critical analysis to the leaf.

"Not very strong," was Gregson's unsurprising verdict. "Hallo, Doctor! Is that Colonel Hayter with you?"

Introductions were made all around. Hayter nodded at them all.

"I'm ready to see the poor old remains, sirs," he announced. "If someone would be so kind as to show me where to go? I'm worthless outside of open terrain. Buildings aren't nearly enough like mangrove swamps to suit my compass."

Lestrade never blinked, but his compatriots certainly did. "I'll show you, sir." He politely passed the little box to the newcomers and opened the door one-handed.

"Good man." Hayter swept inside, the folds of his cape swinging after him like the ermine robe of royalty.

Gregson and Hopkins watched them all go inside. Hopkins, not trusting himself to speak at first, concentrated on the geometrics of a perfect smoke ring.

"D'you think," Gregson said at last (and most carefully), "Watson just has an ability to make friends with unusual people, or does he possess a quality that attracts them?"

"I'm certain that *I* don't know, Gregson." Hopkins confessed. "But it seems to suit him."

Gregson grunted.

"Don't know him." Hayter announced in the chilly light of the morgue. "Well, he's a mess, isn't he? But I'm sure I don't know him. Its names I'm not good with. Faces are a different thing."

Lestrade would be glad when the sheet passed over the face again. It didn't seem possible, but the body looked less awful after Watson's methodical examination. It was as if the cool order of the good doctor's work had righted the senselessness of the icy mutilation.

He hoped for some answers, and soon. "Well, Colonel, we'll be pleased to take your word for it." He tucked his hands inside his sleeves in the chill, squaring his shoulders to peer at the ceiling. "Now to find out who he is . . . ."

"What about the cards, sir?" Watson asked.

"Now that," Hayter paused to sniff. "That's a question." He tapped his gloved fingers impatiently. "I had ordered these cards a month ago . . . but they had been misplaced. McManus and Teasedale's policy is to apologize for any wrong-doing, and they felt for their order to be lost in the post was their fault for not sending it by courier."

"Did they normally send it by courier?" Lestrade asked, which echoed Watson's curiosity.

"Well, it seemed to be the grand idea of a new Jack on the trade . . . He was dismissed not long after. Failed to show up for work or something just as fiendish." Hayter lightly tapped his stiff gunmetal grey mustache. "Children these days . . . can't stick to what works . . . ."

Lestrade sighed. "I suppose I'll take his likeness to the stationery's then."

"In case they might recognize him?" Watson blinked. "That is a bit of a long odd, isn't it Inspector?"

"Very long." Lestrade said heavily. "But I might as well confirm or deny the link." Just the thought of being in a shop that reeked of paper, ink, and drafting supplies made his head spin. Martin would be horribly jealous. His brother in law Robert would be insulted not to be asked to tag along.

Watson looked sympathetic to the point of pity. "Well, the Colonel and I were planning on a late supper tonight. Would you care to join us?"

Lestrade weighed the odds of a meal operated by two military bohemians, and his wife's cooking. Just to be polite. "I'm afraid I have a full schedule, Dr. Watson." He smiled wryly. "My evenings of late are spent in a paint-job at the house before the cold weather returns."

"A shame." Watson grimaced. "Well, the offer stands if you find yourself free of time and at odds."

"You'll hear from me regardless, if there's news to report," Lestrade promised. The others nodded politely, but it was clear they thought he was wasting his time and energy.

And they were probably right.

Clea Lestrade looked up from her accounts to see her husband step indoors with an odd expression on his face. She knew that look. Something had given him too much information, and he was trying to sort it all out.

"Had a pleasant day, Inspector?" She rose and finished helping him out of the heavy wool jacket. A tiny flowerpot full of forced saffron crocus were produced from nowhere. He must have shielded them from within from the winds. "Oh, for me? They're lovely." Clea promptly buried her face in the slim petals. Golden threads of pollen dusted her face.

"I had more than this to start out with," he confessed. "But the saddest thing happened while I was going past the Italian district." He loosened his waistcoat to let the warm air in and moved to stand by the fireplace with a sigh. "There was an old woman on the kerb selling sachets." Lestrade shuddered as the heat of the flames began to penetrate his chilled skin. "She wanted to know how I'd managed to come back from Greece with the flowers still fresh." He shook his head. "She's lived in London five years, helping her children and their husbands sell things to keep afloat, and she's not seen a fresh crocus in all that time."

"Poor woman." Clea tip-toed to put a kiss on his cheek. "Other than that, how was your day, Inspector?"

"Interesting," he said finally, after a great deal of silent thought.

"Interesting, but not in a good way, I presume?"

"Well, I don't know," he said honestly. "Where are the boys?"

"They're off with Mrs. Collins, still painting. She wanted some trim-work done by her sills, and I needed the quiet to balance my books."

"Keep it up, both our sons will be waterproofed and permanently blue." Lestrade muttered for a moment. He turned so the fire would throw some heat on his back. "I'll have company tonight," was his final comment. "I suppose I'll keep that samovar of tea on the coals in the study."

"You can also serve them up some sandwiches." Clea said firmly. "I need to use up those walnuts before they turn. But will you be here for supper?"

"Of course."

"So where did you go, dear?"

"Stationery shop. Not completely unpleasant, though. I picked up these," he patted his pockets, frowned, and went to his hanging coat. As

133

Clea watched he rooted in the pockets and pulled out a small, flat box. "Do you think Martin would like these for his birthday?"

"It's paper, isn't it?" Clea chuckled. Ladies did not snicker. She opened the box. A good hundred of paper cards the soft hue of undyed linen looked back at her. "Oh, he ought to love them. I'll wrap them up before he can sniff them out. Geoffrey, these look fine quality . . . How much did they cost?"

"A token two-pence," was his answer. "The customer sent the whole paper back after ordering. Said it was unsuitable. I had to interview the guildsman while he was working, so I suppose it was a profitable day all around." He hesitated and cleared his throat. "They're looking for apprentices."

The fire faltered before the slight chill in the room. "We don't need to send our sons out in the world just yet," Clea said firmly.

"I know that." He spoke as gently as possible. The disagreement had been rising like a Thames-tide, nocturnal and dirty, between them for months. "But Martin wants to learn."

"He's determined to grow up overnight." Clea set her lips.

"He was born old." Geoffrey was not arguing, merely stating what everyone knew. Martin had abilities that resembled adult competence, but he was still young – and sadly, still small.

"You're lucky I got your wire at the station," Gregson said by way of greeting when Lestrade opened the door. He and Hopkins hurried inside with relief, and beelined straight to the fire once their host showed them into the small study that was also a guest bedroom and schoolroom for the children. Hopkins' teeth chattered as he huddled under the mantel.

"We were about to head off to The Elegant Barley," Gregson added and put his hands around the hot metal samovar of tea. "Good God. Where did you find this monster?"

"I didn't. Cheathams never do things in small amounts. This brute is their idea of a *teapot*," Lestrade said wearily. "It's late. Are you up to lime-flower brew?"

"This time of year? Without a doubt. The wife would be making me drink it anyway when I got home." Gregson was still hugging the samovar, making Lestrade wonder if his rival had to worry about nerve damage on top of his cold allergy. "I've said it before, but it bears repeating: Your in-laws are a rather interesting sort."

Lestrade had been faced with the word "interesting" rather much today, and said so.

"Something odd about that wild goose chase at the paper-maker's?" Hopkins' lips unthawed enough to let him speak.

134

"It wasn't a wild goose chase, so to speak, but . . . ." Lestrade made a growling sound. "Gregson, before I forget . . . You really must teach Hopkins that trick with throwing the truncheon. It might save a life someday."

Gregson sniffed. "Why bother? For all we know, the maneuver will be outlawed in a few years. Why contaminate his brains?"

"I'll take full blame," Hopkins assured him.

"On your own head be it."

Lestrade practiced a martyred silence as he poured steaming pale tea. Linden flowers were potent cups. Before long the men were warm inside and out and tucking in to Clea's walnut and lemon-cheese sandwiches.

"What did you find out, then?" Gregson wanted to know.

"You'll see this in my report tomorrow," Lestrade cautioned. "First, the dead man used to work at the stationery shop that the cards came from."

Gregson set his tea down with a heavy sound. Hopkins merely looked astonished.

"They could identify him underneath those wounds?" Gregson wanted to know.

"Dr. Watson, who appears to be as methodical as Moses, drew up a list of characteristics that survived. The colour of the eye. Hair. There was a scar that must have been an excised tattoo on the wrist . . . that sort of thing." Lestrade pulled his cup to the left and went for his tobacco-tin. "I hope you like irony, gentlemen. The man's name was a John K. King, and it was his idea to send the Colonel's cards outside of the usual courier system. As the master guildsman pointed out, he'd been the one to deliver the cards to the post."

"Only they never got to the post, he pocketed them." Hopkins had caught on the same time as Gregson. "He must have known he would lose his position."

"I'm beginning to wonder if coincidence doesn't belong in the bottom of the rock-garden with the other fairies," Gregson grunted. "But this produces more questions than it answers."

"I know. *What was his motive?* What was he going to do with those cards? It's all a mess. Did you know, no one he worked with for his quarter-year employment even knew where he came from?" Lestrade shook his head like it hurt him. "It's like looking in a microscope without being told you're looking in one . . . you can see the smallest detail but it's still gibberish."

"Hayter didn't know him, but it looks like Mr. King knew Hayter."

"Kings are as common as grass-blades in Hyde Park. John Kings are probably half that amount." Hopkins tapped the table. His youthful face was tight and worried. It occurred to Lestrade that, unlike Youghal, Hopkins would not keep his boyish features forever.

"We can go through the records anyway . . . It is a start . . . ." Gregson gnawed on a sandwich. Knowing her male guests would scorn the finer points, Clea had scorned to cut off the bread-crusts. Gregson paused to drink more tea. The lime-flower was pulling a height of colour to his cheeks that was quite out of the ordinary for the man this time of year. "He had to have let something slip to someone. There's no doubt of that. People talk. That's why they have mouths."

"What about the two of you?" Lestrade wondered. "Anything new?"

Hopkins grimaced, mouth full, and quickly swallowed. "I'm waiting to hear back from an inquiry I made on some human remains. It might be nothing . . . got wind of a complaint over some cremated remains. It would seen a few contaigous illnesses render that necessary."

"Yes . . . What are the usual – cholera . . . typhoid . . . diphtheria . . . scarlet fever . . . ." Gregson rolled his shoulders in a shudder. "Once in a while you hear of a pox outbreak. God help us."

"I can understand that, but what was the nature of the complaint?" Lestrade wondered.

"You're Catholic and you wonder what the complaint was?"

Lestrade sighed, bone-weary. "Gregson, we've been over this. Bretons aren't the best Catholics in the world. I don't think any of our saints are even recognized. Besides, I fail to see what the problem is. If the Almighty can assemble rotten meat and powdered bones on Trumpet Sound, how hard can it be to put together a person burnt to ash? That would mean anyone who ever died in a terrible fire was condemned to burn in Hell."

Gregson grinned. "I take it then we needn't offend your sensibilities if we send you word tomorrow?"

"Tomorrow I'll be in the office, catching up with a week of paperwork, possibly interrogating a prisoner or two on that silly fanning case, and if there's time left over, I'll be having a gigantic platter of cucumber smelts with Dr. Watson at The Malmsey Keg." To Hopkins Lestrade explained: "If you ever have smelts with Gregson, be warned. He's got to remove the heads and tails before he bites down. The big sissy."

Gregson sniffed. "Teach Hopkins the truncheon-toss, did you say? Here's a thought . . . Why don't you help? We could use a stationary target to practice on . . . ."

136

Chapter XVIII – Growing Tension

D_{r.} Watson regarded the seasonal special of The Malmsey Keg in a moment of silence. Long used to the Inspector's tastes, the establishment knew what he liked and they liked his presence at the occasional rowdy dinner hour even better.

There were enough cucumber smelts to put two grown men at ease. Lestrade didn't seem aware of the lightly fried delicacies. His hands alternated between playing with his Grozet and his dipping-pot of horseradish. Either attitude was out of the ordinary. With two such behaviors, Watson had the urge to take his temperature.

"Penny for your thoughts?" he offered at last.

Lestrade blinked as if poked sternly in the chest. "Oh." He remembered where he was. "Woolgathering again, Doctor. My apologies."

Watson was tempted to mention that Lestrade's habitual lack of rest was beginning to make him look every bit as unhealthy as he had back in '81. "A man usually thinks for a reason," was his dry response. "And you have the look of a man who is dealing with a thorny problem." *Or four or five of them . . . I believe I've slept more than he has, and I have a newborn . . . .*

"Speaking of thorny, what does one use as a return gift after a bag of squirrels? I was thinking of these hedgehogs that are pestering my father-in-law's country house . . . ."

Watson barely managed not to spew his dark bitter over the table. "I wouldn't know," he said around his napkin. "I wouldn't know, Inspector. Well, they're both considered wild animals, provincial . . . edible plagues upon society . . . ."

Beginning to feel better, Lestrade took up a smelt and dipped it in his horseradish. "As far as my thoughts go . . . there's too much we don't know about that murdered man." Depressed all over again, he slouched. Watson watched the man lean his head into his head as if the weight had suddenly compounded. The mannerism was so unlike him the doctor felt guilty for his fascination. "Hopkins has hit more dead ends than you can imagine."

"That bad, eh?"

"About as bad as betting in a race with a Shoscombe and a King Pyland [1] in it."

Watson made a grimace at the *aptness* of the statement. "What about the wardrobe itself that was used to hide the corpse?"

"Belonged to a very bewildered and dumbstruck man who bought the thing for his wife's anniversary. Now he can't stand to look at it. Can't say's how I blame him. Most people won't have anything to do with an object associated with murder. I think Youghal's going to make an offer, actually." Lestrade shrugged wearily. "He'll get the priest to bless it." He took a desultory drink of his ale. "So, how was your day?"

"Perhaps a bit more productive than yours – or perhaps simply more fortunate," Watson responded cautiously. "I dislike feeling like an invader, but I did feel the urge to enforce some matters at the morgue."

"Thank God," Lestrade said with feeling. "Pennywraith's held that mess for so long. All of the regular Police Surgeons were completely cowed from him."

"That wizened little man?" Watson was incredulous. "What in the world did he possess to let the morgue remain in such a state?"

"Umm." Lestrade swallowed his ale and paused a moment. "He couldn't bear the notion of someone else going, even accidentally, on his authority. That was all well and good when I was a lowly constable on the beat from ten at night till six in the morning – back then he was rather much younger and capable of running the whole show by himself. Man didn't seem to need more than an hour's sleep a night."

"But that was back in . . . Great Jove! Thirty-some years ago?"

"Yes, I'm afraid Time's caught up with him a bit." Lestrade toasted ironically with a smelt. "His need for control has not allowed the delegation of authority. Dr. Roanoke was untouchable. He has a bit of a more prestigious history, with schooling at the Royal College and, if rumour is to be believed, he's saved the lives of enough important people that he's nigh untouchable. So Pennywraith's been simmering in impotent jealousy all this time . . . and no doubt, doing his best to get in the way of Roanoke in ways he couldn't address."

"Sounds as political as a Greek Fraternity," Watson said with feeling. "And you actually *believe* I'm capable of locking horns with this gentleman?"

"Well, I can't think of anyone who ever had any doubt. Pennywraith's an idiot, after all. The man once stitched me up before washing his hands. Why I'm alive wouldn't make sense to an agnostic." He ate a few more of the fish, and paused for a fried masher. "But he has a peculiar allowance for the military. You may be a puzzle to him . . . ." His voice trailed off as he stared past Watson's bad shoulder.

Watson twisted around in his chair. Hopkins had entered and was peering wildly about him. The young man's normally unflappable composure was nothing like his usual mien. Face moist, the Inspector paused to wipe his cheeks from a fresh dew of snow. He must have been snow-blinded. As they watched his eyes gradually pierced the blurry curtain of darkness and he lit up like a Roman Candle, pressing his way across the quiet tavern.

"Hullo, Hopkins. Care for a smelt?" Serious as Hopkins' face was, Lestrade's instincts were to ride that frightened seriousness off the rails. It worked. The standing man blinked and noticeably relaxed.

"Hello, Lestrade. I was hoping to find you here . . . You too, Dr. Watson." Hopkins nodded, just slightly shy as he took up the offer of smelt. Lestrade flipped his fingers in a signal Watson thought was as obscurely intricate as a Freemason's greeting, and a glass of wine appeared by Hopkins' elbow. The younger man promptly seized it up and drained the little bowl. Without a blink, the glass was refreshed.

"A new development, Hopkins?" Lestrade asked hopefully.

"Well . . . perhaps." Hopkins' face crossed as a thought came, and he made a light choking sound. "Perhaps. Are you gentlemen free this evening?"

"I was on the six-to-two shift," Lestrade answered. "I have enough time to give a hand before supper. Dr. Watson might be indisposed with his little righteous warfare with Dr. Pennywraith . . . ."

"Yes. If he doesn't improve his lot, I'll have a bone to pick with him . . . ."

Hopkins moaned softly. "I *wish* you hadn't used that particular word, Doctor."

Watson turned that over in his mind. "Bone?"

Hopkins shuddered. Despite the warmth and the food, he was suddenly pale and chilled looking. "That report I was waiting back on?" Lestrade nodded. "I misunderstood my message. Someone suspected the deceased were being tampered with *before* their cremation . . . ." He abruptly gulped and took another drink. Lestrade wordlessly mixed a glass of watered ale for the man's constitution.

"We followed the intimations in the complaint and found a barrel of human bones in the St. Andrew's churchyard. I know we're speaking of a church that goes back to Queen Elizabeth, but . . . I . . . there's s-something about this that needs a second eye." The Inspector stared in his small glass. "I can too easily see myself at Court, trying to tell them the bones are human, and being told I was not a qualified physician . . . ."

Watson winced with a smile. "Say no more. I am at your disposal."

"*Eat first*." Lestrade said with an unexpected sternness of resolve. "Speaking as an old war-horse, Doctor. It's too easy not to eat after a case like this . . . You need to keep your strength up."

Watson smiled, but it was clear he hated being told what to do. "I can't argue with the rightness of it," he said. "One moment. Hopkins, would you like to help us finish this platter off?"

"Be careful with Hopkins," Lestrade had cautioned under his breath. "He's not going through a smooth patch right now."

Watson had nodded to show his understanding, but the hollow sadness in Hopkins' eyes had somewhat skipped Lestrade's attempt at translation.

He was glad to be back at the morgue, with the barrel of confiscated bones.

And I can't say as how I'd ever planned on owning this sentiment . . . Watson blew out his breath, watching the steam of living warmth hover in the chilled subterranean air. It sank before it settled.

He was alone.

It was strange that he felt so comfortable with that.

I've never been completely alone, he mused. As always, his brain was concentrating on different levels of simultaneous thought while his hands worked. The gloves kept his hands from chilling too soon in the sepulchral rooms.

The bones rattled softly, making a gentle sound at his touch. A barrel full of fragments of human passage.

Does a skeleton miss its lacking portion? There is memory in the stones, the trees, and the blades of grass . . . Does that mean there can be memory within the shaped deposit of calcium and phosphorus?

As a boy, he had smiled at the stories of the old nanny: That the very stones remembered all that had happened. And yet . . . he had wanted to believe those stones could remember the injustices witnessed. He wanted to believe that the stones could remember if nothing else could.

Was a bone so different from a stone?

Holmes would say no. What is limestone but a rock comprised of skeletons of small marine life . . . Chemically, a stone and a bone have much in common once the equation of pressure and time is dismissed . . .

Someone was pushing the door open.

Watson stopped, quite surprised that someone would disturb him in the frigidarium. What met his eyes from the other side of the plank was a tall man, almost skeletal, with hollows upon his sharp cheek-bones and unhealthy tints upon the flesh. His hair was quite dark, but the hair-cream could mimic youth. The eyes were old. Much too old.

The man hesitated, looking from side to side like a trapped animal. Watson nodded slightly to show his awareness of his new visitor.

140

"I was told there was a corpse here . . . found in a wardrobe?" The man stumbled over the last word like a man astonished to find himself in the middle of an avalanche.

Poor devil . . .

Watson straightened, the last of the little bones falling out of his touch. "Permit me to show you," he nodded. "Are you part of the Yard? Forgive me for not knowing everyone."

The man gulped hard. "Yes . . . I am. Inspector Patterson. I've been called out of retirement."

Watson almost stumbled himself. It was a moment his tutors would not have been proud of.

The Patterson that brought down the Moriarty organization from within?

It was hard to believe this walking ghost had sponsored such actions.

"I must warn you," Watson spoke as gently as possible, sensing dangerous waters beneath, "the deceased is not in good condition."

"I know." Patterson nodded. A fine dew of sweat shone on his temples. He nodded again, too quickly for the doctor's liking. "I am prepared, Dr . . . ?"

"Very well." Watson again felt that whicker of warning in the back of his mind – a soft voice that had sounded well in battle and in the times just before Holmes had advised him, *Bring your revolver.*

"Please, follow me."

NOTE

1. The two stables mentioned in "Silver Blaze" and "Shoscombe Old Place".

Chapter XIX – Personal Feelings

"And there it was, bold as you please." Hopkins had (finally) come to the end of his story. Lestrade and Gregson had perhaps plied too much tobacco on him, but it was a safer addiction than the drink. *Something* wanted to steady the man's nerves.

Gregson was privately concerned. Hopkins was a worrier, though careful and methodical. That his emotions had risen up suggested a few unpleasant possibilities. It just wasn't like the man to be this way. Steady and reliable since his first days in the constabulary, making Chief Constable sooner than men twice his years but managing to avoid any resentments in the tight-knit crèche. His rank to Sergeant had been slower, but it had given him a few more years' needed experience on the street.

Lestrade said it first: "Hopkins, have you been letting this case get to you . . . just a bit?" The older man managed not to make it like an accusation. Hopkins' glare was reassuring. "I'm not attacking you, Inspector. You didn't make rank from nothing. But there's always the case that strikes a bit close to home . . . ."

"Or you get a case that's so dashed knotty that you can't stop thinking about it. That's when your sleep suffers," Gregson grunted. "There's no shame in asking for help. We couldn't get anything done without it." Unspoken was the common knowledge: Men who could solve problems by themselves rose faster in rank, took promotions and rewards.

Could afford to marry.

"It's a shame most of our informers can't allow themselves to be as clean as Mr. Holmes," Lestrade muttered, obviously reliving an unpalatable memory. "Let's see . . . informers who were fawning and eager to please and unwashed . . . and then Mr. Holmes, who was certainly well-groomed but less-than-amicable."

Hopkins had gone from red-faced to slowly smiling. "I suppose I've been thinking about it too much," he confessed softly. His eyes slipped downward frequently, still clearly uncomfortable with the advice of his older peers. "But it does strike close. I admit it. These funeral homes . . . What if we can prove they've been padding their purses with poor, dead veterans?"

"I know. It'll be a snorter at best, and at worst . . . the scandal will be strong enough to blast the Serpentine to a dead crater." Gregson perked up. "Ah, Watson must have found something. He's coming at us at a good two horsepower."

Gregson instantly wished he could take back the light remark. The doctor's face was severe in the gaslight.

"Would someone kindly tell me why is it Inspector Patterson retired and then came back to Scotland Yard?" he demanded. For some reason, he was looking at Lestrade. Mr. Holmes used to do that . . . just before he either attacked his intelligence or sent him off on some sort of godforsaken pursuit in places that made the Great Grimpen Mire look like a Morris Dance at Glastonbury.

Lestrade slowly lowered his pipe. "He retired because of the strain of the Moriarty case, as I understood it," he answered carefully. The truth and nothing but the truth, but possibly not the whole truth?) "He felt ready to return a week ago . . . ."

"Well I'm not certain he's in fit shape to return." Watson scowled. He folded his arms over his chest. Muscles over the former rugby player's bones bunched under the fabric. "He wanted to see that corpse found in the wardrobe, so I obliged . . . The man fainted dead away."

There was a greatly lengthened minute.

Watson grew impatient over the round-eyed silence. "I'm telling you, gentlemen, he was cold as an oyster. Now I have him in that little broom closet the Yard calls a makeshift infirmary . . . It has a draught, by the way . . . and he's propped up under something that resembles a horse blanket with a cup from Gregson's teapot."

Lestrade grimaced.

"I think it is a horse blanket, Dr. Watson," Hopkins ventured bravely as those flashing brown eyes settled on him. "None of us really want to get messy on a good blanket."

"Ay, we might have to take it home and the wife wouldn't want to wash it," Gregson supplied.

Watson's eyes dilated for a moment, but he was a good man for his composure, and only a single quirk of lip under the mustache betrayed his opinion. "Most practical of you," he said at last. "But I can't say I've ever seen such extravagant colours on a horse blanket before . . . not outside a carnivale."

"Rumour has it, we got it at auction to save a few pence . . . but I really think we have it so's we have fair chance of bleeding on something that's already red." Lestrade puffed on his pipe. "Fainted, eh?" He shook his head sadly. "I suppose I'll have to have a talk with him. He was determined to return to work after that mess in Exeter . . . ."

"You call an accidental food poisoning on top of a deliberate drugging by a corrupt Inspector a 'mess'?" Gregson wanted to know. "Lestrade, *you* are a mess."

"Now, Gregson, you'll embarrass us both." Lestrade smirked at him and slipped inside. Watson followed, his limp heavy on the polished floor.

Lestrade's CID credentials had been hard-earned. It was a part of the parcel. Still, gazing upon Patterson, who was shaking inside the horrid rough-wool blanket for the cot and latched around the tea-cup in a sweat.

There were many things I did not see, and I was glad of it.

"Will you be all right, Inspector?"

Patterson rallied with a will. He took a large, indecorous swallow of tea and set it down. Lestrade wordlessly put a dash of his hip-flask in it. "I . . . I believe I know that man," he said slowly. "He was one of my informers within the Professor's gang."

No wonder he's shook up. "The report can wait a bit," Lestrade said as gently as he could. Whatever strength the man had drawn on before all this, Lestrade hoped he would find it again, and soon. "I'm sorry to hear that, though."

Patterson shook his head sharply. His neck-joint popped. "I'll get started on that report." With a last swallow he rose and let the blanket fall off his shoulders. Still grey as homemade soap, the man strode out of the small room, an astonished Watson staring after him.

"Good Lord," Lestrade muttered. He closed his eyes for a moment, suddenly overwhelmed with fatigue. The camp-cot became a settee in short order. He sank down, elbows on his knees as he stared at the out-of-true floorboards. "I belong in Bedlam. I didn't try to convince him to stay out of this . . . ."

Watson breathed out, a low sound in the air. "I confess that's the first time I recall putting eyes to him and knowing it truly was Patterson." He rolled his bad shoulder slowly. Helping Patterson to the room had done little for his old injuries.

Lestrade let that soak in, but could see no overt anger aimed at the absent Inspector. Watson showed nothing more than a steady hardness in his dark eyes that suggested a battle somewhere. "Dr. Watson, will you have a problem working with him? It's understandable if you say yes . . . ."

Watson's eyes snapped. "I am a professional, Mr. Lestrade. My standards are not affected by personal feelings. However," he added cautiously, "I must state that I am concerned at the depth of his motives."

"His motives?" Lestrade echoed. "I'm sorry, I don't follow you."

"The man isn't well. You can see it as well as I. If he was compelled strongly enough to return to duty, he may not be paying attention to his own health. That can lead to an infirmary within the Yard itself." Watson suddenly looked down at his nails, and scowled. "It should be handled judiciously," he said at last. "No man likes to be recognized as the weak link in the chain."

The silence grew between them, thick with the unspoken.

"That's true enough," Lestrade heard himself agreeing.

Watson had said his piece. He was now vaguely embarrassed. "Is there anything we can do to stop this draught?"

Lestrade laughed without a sound. "As I recall, we all voted to keep the draught a few years ago . . . It keeps us from worrying about coal-gas poisoning from the other side of the wall."

"Gentlemen, behold our dilemma."

Watson approached the barrel with a thoughtful face, absorbed the sight in silence, and without a word, reached into his pocket and pulled out a pair of thin-kidskin gloves. He pulled out a double handful of brittle objects, turned, and gently poured them out on the table. He repeated this procedure three more times, each pile of bones at a different quarter of the examination table.

Lestrade swallowed without a scrap of moisture in his mouth. He could tell Gregson was being struck by the same unpleasant empathy. Hopkins had been perfectly within his lights to react so poorly. These were sad, pathetic remnants of remnants. Only in a few cases were they clean and pale. Most were wrapped in a terrible, thin gossamer shroud of their own tissues.

Gregson was staring at a fingernail that had dislodged and was lying by itself on the table. He sealed his mouth shut, hard, against his gorge.

"*These are all fingerbones,*" Watson announced. "*All adults.* There are no children present that I can find so far. Most of the relics appear to be from the left hand. A fraction are from the right hand . . . ." He frowned softly, deep in thought. "The implications in that are quite disturbing."

Gregson did not want to be the one to say it – Hell, he didn't want to be the one to think it. Hopkins gulped over and over in the small room. Morton was slowly draining colour, beginning at his temples, and Lestrade, sitting in front of the other Inspectors, had the show of a man who was facing a long-buried nightmare.

Long-buried . . . that's a terrible play on words and I didn't mean it . . . I don't want to say this . . . Gregson gnawed at his morals, and opened his mouth just as Watson was beginning to do it. "Doctor," he rasped, "are you suggesting these finger bones are . . . ring-fingers?"

Watson's lip thinned. "It is a certainty. The greatest damage is on the proximal phalange – that is the first joint on the hand itself, which is where the ring rests. Most of them would be on from the wedding ring, or the widow-widower ring corresponding on the right hand." He held out his own left hand, where his wedding ring gleamed, and pressed his right index finger against the joint as if it were the blade of a knife. "A single, quick stroke of the knife through the joint would have been quick. It wouldn't even have to be a very sharp knife."

"Lord above," Morton said under his breath. "It's been decades since we last dealt with organized grave-robbers." The man sunk into himself, huddling within his wool jacket. Normally calm and businesslike eyes were dilated and bleak. "What was it . . . those ghouls at the wreck of the *Princess Alice*?"

"The *Princess Alice*," Lestrade agreed softly. "More than six-hundred-fifty men, women and children drowned." He'd been on duty during the collision. He hadn't slept for days after. His first encounter with Sherlock Holmes . . . The tired man winced away the memories.

"There would have to be a place where the bodies were robbed to begin with." Hopkins was gnawing on a cold supper of sausage roll. "The question is why would they be stored in that little keg like that? Why keep it all in one place where it could be discovered?"

"No one looks for remains among human remains," Watson pointed out. "It took a complaint to get the Yard's attention . . . Finger-bones scattered about would have even more chances of discovery. I agree it is inefficient to our perspective. There *had* to have been some reason."

"It wasn't a good reason," Morton said under his breath.

Watson sighed. "Agreed." The strain was tinting his temples and cheek-bones, causing a severe gleam on his skin. "It was no doubt a foul reason." His head lifted slightly to peer down his nose at someone who had just entered the room. Dark eyes went black and his shoulders went straight and solid, the same moment his spine re-locked itself into a position as tight as a telescope's.

There was no doubt that Dr. Pennywraith had just entered the conference room.

Chapter XX – Intelligence of Women

The Lancashire Rose Cooking School:

"**M**arianne, take a look at these ledgers." Mrs. Lestrade spoke firmly as she tapped two different sheets of columns. The girl was young, earnest, and slightly near-sighted. She peered uncertainly at the paper before her.

About the two, the steady rise and fall of conversation in the small kitchen continued as usual. (The headmistress, as she was called, liked to get the girls used to their arithmetic among the cooking environs they would be expected to work in). Mrs. Lestrade was a small woman but had a presence about her to be obeyed.

Marianne licked her lips and stilled the motion as unladylike. "The one on the left, Mum, it's much neater an' cleaner."

"Yes . . . Anything else?"

Marianne hesitated so long Clea shifted her weight within her shoes.

"It . . . looks like the sloppy one is the right one where the numbers come together . . . ."

"Very good." Mrs. Lestrade pulled a small pencil out from behind her ear and tapped the blunt end on the paper in question. "These ledgers are for what purpose, Marianne?"

"The week's food, Mum," Marianne answered promptly. "And the coal or the gas accounts. How much it costs for the staff and messengers."

"Now, imagine you are the lady of the household. It's been a very long, tiring week. The social season is about to open up. You very much want to be a part of all the balls, the music, taking your daughters and nieces out to meet the fine young gentlemen . . . ." Long experience had taught Clea Lestrade that an ignorance of her students' interest in 'fine young gentlemen' would not help things. Marianne's lips went up in a quick smile, perhaps dwelling on a hopeful memory. There. She had the girl's attention now! "You're going to need to budget out your accounts *very carefully*. Those dresses aren't cheap, nor are the flowers, calling-cards, comfits and season tickets. You *can't* make an error or that will set you back as long as an entire month. Looking at these papers, Marianne, which ledger would you choose if you were tired and thinking of other things?"

"The wrong one, Mum. Because it *looked* like it was right." Marianne nearly melted with relief now that she understood what this lesson was about. "The messy books might be right, but who's to tell at a quick look?"

"There you are." Mrs. Lestrade smiled her approval. "You have a duty to the lady of the house in tracking your work. She won't always have time to manage her accounts and if you are in a position of trust, you shan't have to ruin it with a careless error. Keep to your own end. I know it seems like it can take a long time to put down everything neatly and cleanly, but it takes much longer to re-do everything!"

"I understand, Mum. Thank you."

Clea Lestrade carried her teacup to the small office-nook just off the kitchen and set to her own paperwork with a will. The older students were to the point they could run the business by themselves. She liked giving them that responsibility. A cook does more than prepare the food. She holds the house together.

Yet I could be taking my own advice, she thought ruefully. Her own ledgers were clear but nothing near her usual meticulous graphing. Abbreviations, which she tried to avoid, were sprinkled throughout the pages. She sighed at what was before her . . . and she sighed at herself.

If only there was some way to alleviate Geoffrey's growing anxiety. She knew the basic methods of slipping extra nutrition into cooking, but she did not know how to improve a medicinal quality. Books were terribly scanty on the subject. In the meantime, he was working himself to exhaustion. When he was home he was still working. The walls were all painted. The creaking board in the stair replaced. Geoffrey had gone as far as to re-treat the ironwork facing Paddington Street and tighten the stone walkways. For all his efforts, his sleep was still light and easily disturbed, full moon or no full moon. The nightmares were continuing. Clea had never comprehended the term "hag-ridden" until now.

He eats as well as I give him, so there's no improvement in that area . . . There must be something I can do.

Clea gnawed the tip of her pencil without knowing it. This was something even Hazel Bradstreet couldn't answer. Hers was a boisterous gang of boys and Amazons, but no matter how much trouble they got themselves into, or how hard matters were . . . they never skimped on sleep. Clea had sent a letter asking her for advice. Hazel had not known of anything outside of the usual cup of cham or skullcap. So many people would just offer a bit of opium to their drink, but Geoffrey's bad history of the drug ruled that out.

The problem was, Clea could only ask for Hazel's assistance up to a certain point. If it looked like Geoffrey was failing his duties, and Roger knew his wife was consulting Geoffrey's on sleep aids or anxiety disorders, he might be obligated to report the matter. Clea bitterly regretted sending Hazel that letter in the first place, for the accidental burden she placed on all of them. It was foolish. She should have –

She looked up at the tap of knuckles on the door-frame. One of the older girls was peeping in.

"I beg your pardon, ma'am." Janet said softly, "but there's a lady to see you."

"A lady to see me?" Clea repeated dumbly. "Did she give her name, Janet?"

"No, ma'am." Janet blushed. "I asked, an' she said that you knew her."

Clea's mind gently rolled that stone over. Not giving one's name was unfathomable in London. There were too many reasons why a person should announce themselves.

Why would they not? "Janet, would you describe her, please?"

"Yes, ma'am. She's a little taller than you, older by much with dark grey hair and verra dark brown eyes. Almost no eyebrows. Couldn't help but notice that. Way of talkin' is a little funny, I can't figure out where she came from. Wears respectable enough clothes, ma'am. She's a lady."

Clea pulled in her upper lip and held it as she reached up to the tiny watch pinned to her blouse. She snapped the casing off to peer at the numbers. Time enough before they prepared for the evening lessons. "Janet, show her to the back garden. Have a pot of litchee brought out for us, and try to see that we're not disturbed. Irene will be teaching the younger girls how to set up the soufflés."

Janet nodded and left to her duties. Clea stood. Her hands were shaking.

Before her marriage and right after the marriage bans were posted, Clea met a little woman who looked so much like Geoffrey there was no point in either woman pretending they didn't know each other. Aware of Geoffrey's disownment, Clea had said nothing, served the tea the woman purchased, and watched her go in silence.

There was no telling when Jeanne Lestrade would show up at the cooking school. Months could go by. Once she visited twice within two months but it was a unique event. In 1885, she had only shown herself once. It must have been a bad year for slipping away from the rest of the family.

She ordered the same cup of black litchee tea every time, and Clea would pretend not to watch as she sat and slowly sipped the rose-scented cup until it was empty. Sometimes a younger man would accompany her.

Jeanne Lestrade never asked about her son, never inquired about her grandsons, but she must have known about them. The silence was final. Geoffrey listened carefully to the description of the young man and decided it was his nephew, Marcus.

149

It was a terrible matter, and Geoffrey never knew if he would accidentally discover his mother on the street or not. He had to have drawn anguish from knowing his own mother would see his wife but not her own son.

But she sounds alone this time . . . and she's never announced herself. Clea stepped into the little garden-plot with her shawl about her shoulders. In the sudden calm between the storms, it was as mild as day as the season could give. She was worried at this sudden change in her life.

The little woman stepped out with her hands tucked into her sleeves. By now Clea knew what to look for in Breton styles. The dress was black, but instead of the bright floral embroideries that told of her birth-place, she wore a more sober English abstract. Her hat was English. Beneath the collar of her coat her blouse was blue, not frilled white lace.

Those lovely dark eyes fastened on her, so dark it was difficult to fathom her true thoughts – one had to look elsewhere, for facial traces and posture. The worn mouth softened in a light smile.

Hang this shyness. Clea hadn't reaffirmed her reputation for boldness in months. She reached forward and took the frail hands within her own.

Scotland Yard:

Pennywraith was not a handsome man, nor had he ever been. A cool, methodical gaze swept over the room, slow and deliberate as fungal growth. Watson's first note was the man had been in that subterranean morgue for far too many years. His pallor was unappealing. In offensive contrast, his clothing was so clean and crisply starched it was a marvel the man could even move in them.

Watson could not miss the fact that Inspector Bradstreet was carefully schooling his face to impassive lines behind his mustache. It was a common reaction, he realized. Some of the Yarders were carefully looking elsewhere. Lestrade pulled out his watch and pretended to study the numbers. He scowled and went through a production of cleaning the lid with a tiny handkerchief.

Watson had faced a great deal worse than a senior official in a questionable sense of power.

The old man met his gaze from the other side of the table and nodded his head in an arthritic show of professional respect. For the thinnest moment, something flashed under his filmy eyes and Watson was glad he was not about to pledge friendship with him.

"I fear I was delayed by my practice," the senior police surgeon said. It was neither an apology nor an excuse. "I came to see the new discovery."

"How do you do?"

"How . . . do you do." Mrs. Lestrade said to Mrs. Lestrade. Her accent was halting, rusty in spots from lack of practice. "I came to see how you were. If you were well."

Such a contrast from her father-in-law. Potier was an old rascal, but vibrant and alive and brimming with energy. His daughter Jeanne only had ghosts of that spirit within her. Yet they were there . . . Clea took hope from that.

"Shall we have some tea?" Clea asked softly.

They settled their winter-weight skirts at the plank table kept out for sorting the vegetables from the plots. At this point there was little more than kale, which broke apart into tiny pieces when one harvested it frozen, but it was still fresh. Leeks and onions would be set before long. Clea looked forward to it.

Jeanne Lestrade took her tea with no more than a drop of honey, and held the cup within her hands, letting it draw warmth before she drank. Clea almost smiled to see that similarity with her husband.

"Your grandsons are strong," Clea decided to lead. "Martin favours you and it's true. Nicholas is a strapping one, and seems to have his father's love of fixing things."

Jeanne Lestrade smiled at that. "Geoffrey was always careful when he took things apart to see how they worked. I don't think anyone noticed what he was doing until after it happened . . . ." She looked down. "His father is unwell."

Clea took a drink. "I am sorry."

"I thought you should know."

Clea felt a tiny prickle, like too-stiff lace, at the nape of her neck. "Is he so poorly then?"

"There is no knowing yet."

Here it was. Clea held her breath. "Is there anything we can do?"

"*Nann.*" It was said in a whisper, with those gorgeous dark eyes looking at nothing in particular. "*Nann.*"

The Malmsey Keg:

"Lestrade, for someone who got a large portion of unpleasantness passed on to the more qualified . . . you aren't looking too happy."

Lestrade stirred slightly, a barely visible movement in the dark of the old Tudor-style tavern, and finally picked up the heavy pint off Bradstreet's hands. Just in time. A bar-maid stumbled into the space his arm had just occupied.

"Hoy, miss!" Bradstreet snapped. "There's more than one way to abuse the drink!" The Runner huckled his shoulders over his own choice protectively. "Blamed if I pay for a drink the establishment spills," he said under his breath.

Lestrade felt a low chuckle coming on. "Well, thanks for the comedy, Roger. You're about what the doctor would order."

"I'll settle for being an approximation." Bradstreet settled in stages into his wooden chair and took a prodigious swallow. "Ah," he sighed. "When was the last time we had a drink together?"

"Too long." Lestrade said with finality. "You got caught up in those outhouse murders, and I've been wrapped up in . . . well . . . I don't know whatnot since last spring." He scowled at a water-drop on the table and thumbed it aside. "We could at least take the wives out on a Sunday."

"Aye, they couldn't get into too much of a fashing with us to stand guard." Bradstreet tried to be optimistic.

"Let's see . . . Hazel's two-shot peashooter and intimidating presence – I'd sooner face Queen Elizabeth on the battlefield – and Clea, small, under-estimated and armed to the teeth." Lestrade shuddered. "She's started carrying *two* knives since that horror with Constantly Mad Jackson."

Bradstreet's eyebrows popped skyward, like a hot-air balloon. "They ought to behave a bit around the children." He slapped the smaller – much smaller – man in the shoulder blades. Ale sloshed. "Well, except for Hazel. She's back to her old broody instincts again. Makes her tetchy on occasion."

Lestrade grunted. Hazel was well above the usual height for a woman, to the point that she wore low-soled shoes to keep from causing too much consternation in society. Why she even bothered was a mystery. Even without the height, she was a bit of a Boudicca with flaming red hair, snapping eyes, and an occasional foray into the rougher dialect of her childhood.

Lestrade disputed the notion that Hazel Bradstreet looked for a quarrel. He always suspected she simply operated under the assumption that some sort of fool would try to disrupt her day in some way . . . so she remained eternally prepared for the moment when trouble came.

Bradstreet lifted his head and said something in a quick banter to someone against the wall, laughing once at his response. He looked considerably younger than his companion, but that appeared to be a family trait from what Lestrade understood. His age rested in his eyes, with the deep-set wrinkles of laughter and sorrow.

"What did you say, Roger?"

152

"I said," Bradstreet was patient, "How often does Clea work at her cooking school now? Is it still most the week?"

"Yes, but usually not a full day. She's trying to teach the older girls management skills . . . though she's gotten herself into a real pickle with that Owens girl. I think she doses herself with opium before she heads to work."

"Remind me to be careful what I ask for in her hearing," Bradstreet said thoughtfully. "Well, let us make it so, Geoff. Sunday with the family. Almanac says the weather's mild enough for travel." He gave a crooked smile and slapped Lestrade again. "Come on, Geoffrey. We shouldn't be afeard of the intelligence of women."

"I'm not afraid of their intelligence, Roger," Lestrade protested. "Unlike the two of us, they appear to be able to get out of the messes they get themselves into."

"So very true. It's a shame we can't have women on the Metro. Can you think of what they could accomplish?"

"After what happened today?" Lestrade demanded with a bit more volume than intended. "Roger Bradstreet. The way that old grasshopper tried to attack Watson's training was enough to make me arrest myself for assault."

"I noticed when I had to slam you back down in the bench," Bradstreet said dryly. "Not that I didn't feel sympathy, but thoughts of what Hazel would say to me if I came home late because I was posting my own release would not go over well. She's planning to have the vicar over for supper tonight."

"Well, it wasn't Hazel in my head. It was Clea. One of these days she will follow through with her threat and toss me into a wall with one of her father's wrestling moves." He took a deep breath. "I still feel cheated. Here I was preparing to defend Dr. Watson, and he takes care of the situation rather well."

"Yes . . . I think Pennywraith was expecting anything but to be ignored." Bradstreet snickered. "Shall we adopt that policy for our very own?"

"Let's wait and see what Gregson's memo tomorrow says . . . ."

The Lancashire Rose:

Clea Lestrade felt alone at the plank. Beside her rested the upside-down teacup her mother-in-law had left in her passing.

I haven't felt like crying in such a long time . . . I'd almost forgotten . . . .

153

She sniffed loudly, and blew her nose. There was no chance of going inside with the girls to see her like this.

Feeling powerless always does this to me . . . I'm a mess when it comes to things out of my control . . . She sniffed again.

Janet emerged from the back-door, and Clea quickly lowered her head, pretending great interest in pouring out a cup of tea she did not need. "Mrs. Lestrade? Message for you."

"Bring it here, thank you." Clea said firmly.

Janet pressed the paper down by the tray and stepped gratefully inside the kitchen where the stoves kept all red-hot.

Clea blinked her eyes free. She studied the little paper without truly seeing it, and then slowly opened the flap. Hazel Bradstreet's neat, beautiful script flowed across the stationery:

Talk to Mrs. Watson.

HRB

Chapter XXI – Puzzles

"*F*ascinating. *Where did you learn these methods?*"

In the corner of my eye, Lestrade was ready to stand. A quick temper darkened his face. Just as quickly, Bradstreet pushed him back down in his chair. Pennywraith's eyes glittered at me, an unblinking serpent waiting to strike . . .

. . . John grimaced as the cab slowed even further. At this rate, he would have his own memoirs written, re-read, proofed, and ready for his publisher by the time he reached his home!

He set his pencil within the crook of the little book and blew on his fingers a moment, collecting warmth inside his palms. The cab-ride smoothed out. He resumed writing down his impressions of that less than warm meeting with a man who intended to catalogue him under 'rival' . . .

. . . I confess, I was not completely unprepared for the man's enmity, but I had also trusted to wait for my own judgment. When faced with his antagonism, my first reaction was astonishment. In the silent expressions of the Yard, I read a forlorn hope that Pennywraith would at last be taken in hand.

Only a few months ago John Watson would have attacked any man for questioning his reputation and his teachers – even if the fight would be lopsided.

Months have a way of being as entrenched as the centuries.

"As you can see – " I turned his back to the grasshopper man, and faced the chalk-board. " – the bones are all adults. Comparison of the size is the least effort in this identification. Other traits, such as wear on the bone, smoothing of the joints . . . and of course, the partial dissolution of age which makes the bone look spongelike . . . all these factors besides the size separate the bones from that of children or physically mature individuals." So saying, I sketched quick lines of comparison on the slate.

Pennywraith was left standing, his own audience of one . . . .

The mildness of daylight suddenly vanished like it never existed. John peered hopelessly at the paper, and finally closed it up and secreted his journal into his pockets. With the growing dark came what his grandmother would have called the "*sna*" season. London was acting as though it had been given the wrong month. February was far enough away to be a myth.

Soft winter illumination had melted coldly into the dark *that* quickly. The snowfall was resuming. Watson couldn't recall in his memory such an erratic winter. Or perhaps he had simply ignored it? With a wife and newborn child to think of, thousands of obstacles to their safety and happiness materialized in his mind –

The cab jolted, nearly sending him flying. The doctor caught himself in time by flinging his good arm up. The driver from above swore like a highwayman and just as quickly apologized.

"Sorry, Doctor. Bit of a spill up ahead."

"It's all right, Parkinsson." Watson paused to open the door a crack and peer out. About twelve ells ahead he could see the disaster of an upturned chestnut-cart. As a man who had a secret weakness for the roasted wares, Watson had to wince at the loss. The vendor looked barely old enough to shave. While he more than matched Parkinsson's skill with language, he was also making use of his time with cleaning up the remains steaming in the road.

Remains.

Watson tried to fix himself a pipe during the wait, but his hands were cold and the renewed jostling of the cab helped not a whit. He gave up and thrust them back into his gloves, feeling the familiar tremble in his spirit spread outward to his muscles.

The finger-bones haunted him. Finger-bones. Small, delicate relics of what had been an assembly of parts that created that strange total known as a human. Mortal clothing for the immortal soul. Watson had been drawn to the wonders of the human creature, but it had been Holmes with his brilliant, logically faceted mind that had drawn out the particulars of his thoughts. For a man that professed to place little interest in large fields of learning, his friend's maieutic [1] tricks had shown Watson they were both philosophers. Holmes had merely been more aware of his self-questioning.

There were few people who could be defined by their intangible traits. Such language was usually reserved for the pious or spiritual. The holy men of India had affected the young soldier with their calm dignity, just as the desert dervish struck him with the raw power behind their eyes. They were not defined by their physical presence so much as the presence behind their bodies – the way a man notices the lit lamp first and not the unlit one closer by. Holmes had carried that quality – all the more remarkable because it was not a trait nurtured among Englishmen. It was something that was such a part of his being that it could not be ignored, or submerged, repressed . . . discounted.

Holmes had felt his true legacy had been in the mark he left behind. To that end, he had pressed his methods upon the few he felt were capable of continuing. Still. There was the matter of his mortal passing, and that should have been addressed in a decent manner. Holmes had not said specifically what his desires were, and Mycroft had not been helpful the one time he asked for information.

I fear my brother never spoke of his wishes to me . . .

Battered within and without, he'd accepted the even voice of the large man and left with a final apology.

Do not mourn him, Doctor. My brother was not a sentimental man, and he would not have wished that of you.

Perhaps, sir. Perhaps . . . but I am a sentimental man, and he would have told you there was no logic in changing a man's nature.

Something flickered in those sharp grey eyes – so much a Holmes. Those eyes had nearly broken him then and there. Giving his last regrets, he left quickly before he could embarrass them both.

So tired . . . tired beyond reason, and his control had fractured. So many things he'd wanted to say to Mycroft. So much he'd tried to do.

He'd tried so hard to find the remains.

Remains . . . He'd argue with me even now. He would tell me his true remains are the methods he left behind. Methods I can publish now that his conditions are met.

Holmes had been adamant that anyone could learn his ways . . . but he was still in possession of his own vanity – and justified it was. His work was his primary livelihood and his disdain of those who would ape him without truly understanding . . . Well, it was the same as finding one's neighbor had polluted the well. *Publish after I am gone*, he had said. *Let them know me in the wake of my life.*

Very well. Watson could keep his word.

He'd kept far worse commandments.

The cab lurched. He gnashed his teeth as his bad leg hit the door.

This case was pulling more out of him than he'd dreamed possible. It hurt deep as Shakespeare's well, and there was nothing to end it.

Lestrade turned the key in the lock, shoulders slumping as he made his way in. Now that he was home, gravity couldn't be put off any longer. One of the women in the building had been cooking something with orange peel. It placed warmth in the atmosphere he needed.

Someone in the other floors – children – were thumping about in a game. Probably the new neighbors. Nicholas was doubtless with them. He'd fallen in love with the oldest son's wood-carving set.

He hung his coat and hat up and finished his trod upstairs. Clea was just opening the door as he cleared the landing of the first storey.

"There you are, Inspector." In her house-slippers she was even tinier. "I've just set down the dishes. I hope you've an appetite."

"No fear there." He paused on his way to the wash-room to tap her nose with his cleanest finger-tip. "Smells like beef and barley, but not quite."

"Right you are. I had to use up some pork roast, so that went in instead of beef, which I would have had to buy." Clea produced a hand-towel just as he was turning, wet-handed, to the cabinet. "You look ready for a meal. There won't be any soot falling off your collar and into the plates, will there?" He produced his collar for her inspection. "Nice to see that new coat is doing the job."

"Have the nippers et?"

"Since they were good enough to finish painting Mrs. Collins' rooms, she was good enough to stuff them with cabbage rolls. They're both asleep, but they did their lessons first."

He flexed his dried hands, wincing at how the cold seemed to chap them even within their lined gloves. *Gregson must be in agony*, was his thought. "I'm more than ready for supper, *ma-mel*."

"Sweet words will get you nowhere with me." Clea chuckled. As *mel* was the word for honey, it was not a bad play with words. Clea seemed to be developing a skill in those lines.

Inside their rooms the fire had settled to lava-like coals. Lestrade had been in the act of loosening his tie when something grey and fur-covered caught his eye by the grate. "What in God's name is that?"

"It's some sort of cat," Clea answered. "Mrs. Collins rescued it from some beggars this morning.

"*That's a cat?* It's got to be a stone-and-a-half! Why would it need rescuing? It's big as a French beagle!"

The cat in question paused while licking a massive paw. *It looked at him.*

"It's sensitive to paint. I told Mrs. Collins we could keep it here a few hours."

"Well, perhaps it can take care of those Thames-rats that took up housing in the basement." Lestrade decided he could move on with his life. He resolutely ignored the new tenant. The cat returned the courtesy. And he *would* introduce that monster of a feline to the latest unwanted, unpaying lodgers.

"Doctor Watson! You'll catch your death!"

For once – and only once – Watson permitted Theresa her fretting. "Thank you, Theresa. I trust your father will be picking you up soon?"

Theresa patiently pulled his coat off and hung it in the warmest nook of the foyer. "He'll be ending his shift in a few, sir, but let me take care of this first. I took the liberty of setting some tea out in the sitting room. I put your mail on the tray . . . ." She stopped at the state of his gloves and wordlessly placed them on drying-hooks. "The stew Mrs. Watson set out to simmer in her absence is well tender by now. Shall I make you a bowl?"

"Please do," Watson sighed. "I'll be downstairs in time to give you your wages for the week. We'll need you back on full time when Mrs. Watson returns."

"Thank you, sir." Theresa parted with his gloves. John went to his bedroom for a much-needed change of stockings and house-slippers.

Geoffrey was grateful for the sudden quiet settling upon the building with the late hour. Soft snow burst against the windows, and once in a while the snatch of holiday bells rang down the street.

"I've always enjoyed listening to that sound," Clea smiled. In concession to the chill, they were wrapped under a quilt. "When I was a tot, the farmers would deck out the brightest brass bells on their sleighs as they took their families to church."

"And here in muddy old England, we just have the thrifty cab driver who wants to make a few extra fares by the young, romantic crowds leaving the theatres right now." Geoffrey chuckled lightly as he measured his watch-time with that of the mantel clock. "Well, I hope they get it. By tomorrow it will either be a sheet of ice or a curtain of rain."

"I suppose that's the lot of life." She was pleasant enough, but her usual mood was slightly off. Geoffrey knew his wife and knew when she was self-censoring. That meant something was upsetting her.

And it was hard to say what. Clea had been determined to forge her life with his from the beginning, but there was a great difference between her family (*comfortable, deeply respected, close-knit if overbearing*) with his (*disowned, family fortune lost* decades *ago, family not all that honest or respectable to begin with*).

Past experience said it had something to do with her family. Spending occasional week-ends with her loving folks meant someone, most likely a sister-in-law or her brother Andrew, had been noting again how Clea's husband could be doing better. The Cheatham households held enough wealth that husbands and wives could afford separate bedrooms. No one had to budget their meals. Sewing was a matter of skill and pride, not necessity. Clea had often sworn it meant nothing to her, but the fact remained that his income was a bone of contention with her pettier kinfolk, and some had a cruel streak to their teasing.

The Cheathams had stopped trying to cause trouble (and thankfully, no more fights), but they rarely came to visit. She visited them. By degrees things seemed to get better . . . .

159

Lestrade still found it strange that the men had been the first to accept him after nearly killing him in a bar and Clea's wrestler-brother breaking not a few of his bones before the engagement. Once they understood that he cared about their sister as much as they did, the resistance had dropped. (He still had no idea what would have happened had they decided his affections were false. Best not to dwell on that).

Best not to dwell on too much of anything right now. He was tired enough to try sleep a bit earlier than normal, but he was loathe to let go of the peace and quiet.

"Clea, you appear to be a bit on loose ends."

She leaned her head back against his shoulder. "I suppose I am. The day started out so pleasant and mild."

"Nothing like that now." He paused to yawn behind the back of his head. "We've got some time to ourselves before bed-time. Anything about your day you wish to speak about?"

"No more than you do, I suppose." She rested her head against his chest and they both fell silent, listening to the fire close by, while the bells continued down the street.

Mycroft Holmes?
John turned the paper over in his hands. The name remained the same.
Mycroft Holmes . . . and I was just thinking of him.
But why?
Shaking his head and suddenly wide awake, the doctor split the seal and opened the folded-over notepaper.

Dr. Watson,

Your presence requested. Diogenes Club at your convenience.

MH

Of course the man would be too lazy to write a proper missive! John blinked in wonder. What was this? When they'd parted ways all had seemed . . . well, not joyous of course, but neither had it intimated there was something amiss between them.

Presence requested. Mycroft was as steady and unsurprising as a neap tide. If he didn't have something to do, he wouldn't expend the energy to ask for him.

I should go then, tomorrow . . . and see what he wants. He was suddenly quite sick of puzzles. In a flash of insight, John understood why his old friend solved puzzles and then moved on to the next one *post haste.*

160

There were days when these things were thick as weeds – and just as hard to eradicate.

NOTE

1.   A Socratic method by which a person draws another's latent thoughts into actual consciousness.

Chapter XXII – Do I Know You?

Mycroft Holmes: The antithesis of his younger brother, as if Sherlock had been made up of the bits and pieces left over or unwanted traits, like the need for some sort of physical activity.

He was standing by the window, one foot drawn up against the thick wainscot as he peered down to the streets below. John could see the glitter of his heavy watch as it swung on its chain off his vest. There was no other ornamentation on the man. Another contrast. His brother had worn jewelry given him by royalty, used their mementos such as ornate snuff-boxes, and then just as carelessly forgot about the nobility's largess for months at a time.

Watching people. The brothers had shared that love.

Standing in the doorway, John felt a pang of something deep. Mycroft would watch the world alone now.

"Ah, Doctor," Mycroft said without moving. "The weather must be working against the wishes of the meteorologists. Your limp has not improved."

"I doubt it will for a few days," John agreed as he moved in. Across the room the pale winter light glinted off the gilt-work of hundreds of leather-bound books. He'd once dreamed of a room such as this for himself. A room to conduct his work at the end of the day within arms'-reach of useful references or quotations. "I trust you've had a peaceful season?"

"Peaceful enough to be sure." Mycroft grunted and chose his usual leather-backed chair. "I felt it might be an appropriate time to discuss some business with you concerning my late brother."

For one awful moment, John thought it was a criticism of his writings. "Business?" He repeated as his heart slammed against his clavicle.

"Yes." Mycroft took a pinch of snuff. "Sherlock had his loyalties to you of course, Doctor. He even chose to set some portion of his earnings aside on your behalf. And now that the legal courts have finished their say in these matters – "

John found himself sitting down without the memory of doing so. "What do you mean?" he asked sharply. "I fail to understand this talk of earnings. There was never a mention of anything like this . . . ."

Mycroft only shrugged. "Sherlock was never voluble in matters he deemed personal."

So true. John's mouth drew into a tightly sewn line beneath his mustache. "Please explain." His tone of voice was not encouraging.

Mycroft paused slightly before resuming. "Sherlock left a sum of money to you. A comfortable sum. It should be enough to alleviate any concerns you may have for your finances for a year or two."

John felt his face grow cool as it paled. "And why would he do such a thing?" A stranger's voice was coming out of his mouth.

Mycroft may have held his brother's remote view to emotions, but this was outside even his ability to anticipate. He straightened his square shoulders and leaned forward slightly in his chair.

"Doctor . . . why would he not?"

Before his eyes the doctor rose to his feet. His cheeks had paled to a dull transparency against his too-bright eyes. Mycroft recognized the signs of shock, but his intellect could not comprehend the origins.

"Mr. Holmes," Watson's voice shook with barely constrained emotions, "my thanks you for your kind offer, but I am afraid I must refuse."

"Refuse?" Without knowing it, Mycroft had risen to his feet. It was a mistake he usually avoided. He knew he was intimidatingm but Watson was immune to such ordinary impressions. "Doctor, I assure you, this was what my brother desired."

"He should have given it to the Irregulars!" Watson's teeth set together so sharply it must have hurt his jaw. He swallowed hard.

"Thank you," the smaller man said at last. He was still not fully under control. "But I must . . . respectfully . . . refuse."

And before Mycroft's swift mind could calculate *this* possibility . . . he found himself alone.

"Hoy!" Lestrade gave up. He let his arm drop, the note and coin still in his hand as the messenger vanished down the street. It would be another fifteen minutes before he came back.

More of the same luck for the day . . . the small man trudged back inside the front doors, and returned to his office. Today it was just safer to be there.

His shift – his day-had not gone well. Somehow – and he wasn't sure how it even started – Clea had firmly announced that Martin was not going to take any sort of apprenticeship at any stationery's shop or anything approaching one. Taken aback by what had resembled a frontal attack, he'd held his tongue in silence while Martin stared unhappily into his oatmeal. Nicholas, God bless him, had only looked puzzled at all the fuss. How to even explain? Martin had been close to his mother for years, and now that he was stretching his wings she didn't seem to be ready for it.

No one in her family started work so early, she pointed out several times.

No one in her family needed *to work early*, he thought without saying. Reminding her of their less-than-ideal finances would have been a low and unworthy response. Keep silent, he'd told himself.

The Yard had been no refuge from conflict. Lestrade had caught a note from Hopkins practically begging for his company at the wharf . . . but the note had reached him too late. What human bones and stolen bodies had to do with the waterfront he didn't want to know anyway, but the disappointment soured his mood.

The next few hours were no better. Patterson had left a message claiming to be hunting the dead man's relatives . . . but there were rumours that he was actually in a seedy bar drinking himself into a stupor. Lestrade had gone digging in the records for several suspects in a recent string of robberies in the Paddington Station . . . and found two of the five men had identical features to the much darker business of burying lonely widows soon after marriage. With ash in his mouth, Lestrade informed the records department that a discrepancy had been discovered. If anything, the backlash to that was the lowest portion of the day yet. The cataloguer responsible had been appointed his role as a last-minute attempt to make him useful in "the family trade".

"So the Yard's now the family trade?" Lestrade wondered glumly as he found a weak cigarette in the bottom of his little case. With compelling reasons, he'd chosen to spend the rest of his shift in the office with the door shut. Gregson had found him with his head in his hands and surrounded by sheets of foolscap.

Gregson only shrugged at that. "I suppose it is if your last name is Miller."

"Just bloody-all marvelous. He hates me enough as it is without adding grounds for dismissal to his useless third-cousin's nephew or whoever that little blabber [1] is."

Gregson gave him a mighty slap on the back – his usual form of sadistic affection for a fellow Yarder. After years of being just his rival, Lestrade found his promotion in Gregson's eyes no easier to endure.

"He doesn't hate you personally, Ratty." Gregson's idea of comfort was equally unnerving. "He just hates everything you stand for. Being a Frog-eater and all that, living on good English soil like the thief you are, taking honest jobs away from people who were here first. No, it's not personal."

Lestrade's hands twitched. "Your idea of counsel is so uninspiring I should tip you off to the salt-box, [2] Euclid. Just *think* of all the already-condemned men who'd find reason to confess to *just a few more murders* under your form of good cheer."

"It wouldn't be much of a challenge this time of year," Gregson pointed out. "Even Two-axe Anderson is getting mopey. He asked me if he could have his date of execution sped up a bit. All the carolers on the streets are starting to get to him."

Lestrade made a sound suspiciously close to "*Agh!*" and struck his last match. "Frog-eater," he said under his breath. "You'll never see *me* pay for frogs in a restaurant. I'll just have the wife dip a chicken in swamp-water and serve it up with dill."

Gregson was proud of himself for not guffawing, even though the effort made his nose sting.

" . . . sooner eat another baked toad than chew up a scrawny little frog-leg and risk death by bones in the stomach . . . ." Lestrade decided he needed a stronger form of tobacco, and fished in his drawers as he muttered.

Gregson shuddered. "'Another baked toad'?" he repeated. "Dare I deduce from the statement that you were deemed a sickly asthmatic in your halcyon youth?"

"Halcyon youth?" Lestrade glared. "Where do you find the time to enrich your education, Gregson?" He lit a grotesque-looking cigarillo off the first smoke. "There's nothing halcyon about youth." He puffed ferociously. "So how do you know about those horrible folk-cures?"

"You think parents won't try everything else first before they spend money on a crow?" Gregson chuckled. "I had a cousin they did everything to. Even made him swallow a ball of spiderwebs."

"I do hope they blew the dust off the webs first." Lestrade snorted. "The toad was the worst of it for me. I told my parents I'd run away into the Haunted Forest and live with my cough in a hollow tree rather than do that again."

"But it must've worked . . . you're not the least bit asthmatic."

"I never was to begin with!" Lestrade complained. "I had the draftiest room in the house to sleep in! Once they moved me to the inglenook [3] I was fine!"

Gregson finally laughed. His reserves were not indefinite. "It's not like you to let Miller get under your skin."

"It's just this whole day . . . What did you call it – *darts*? I've been getting a bellyful, and it's distracting me from the real work." He held up the pages of reports and dropped it. "Speaking of distractions, what are you doing here?"

"I've been demoted to distraction?" Gregson sniffed. "I like that. 'Scotland Yard's best' now an ordinary distraction."

"If there was anything ordinary about you, Gregson, your parents would have locked it in the attic with the other horrors." Lestrade could be

165

scathing when the occasion demanded. "Unless you've come to gloat because you got your lead on the parade-toolers – " [4]

"Nothing so simple, Ratty." Gregson looked serious for the first time. It was almost a relief. "After you missed that note from Hopkins, we got word not ten minutes after . . . there's something going at the St. Andrew's all right . . . but . . . ." The big man actually squirmed. "Hang it!" he blurted. "I don't know anything about you Catholics!"

Lestrade stared, utterly nonplussed. "I didn't know you *had* to, Gregson."

Gregson was so agitated he started pacing. "It's a matter of making one's career, you fool! What if the Yard does something . . . steps over the line somewhere? The Home Office doesn't want any sort of scandal from us."

Lestrade sighed and looked at his hands. "I don't know about any of that," he said at last. His voice sounded like a poorly cast bell: Dull and flat. "If you want to avoid scandal, then you find the sexton or vicar or whoever it is and ask them to come along."

"We're going to need you tomorrow just in case." Gregson said stoutly. "You're the only Catholic on this case."

"Yes. And such a perfect example I do make . . . ." Lestrade said sourly. "What exactly is happening tomorrow?"

"We're going to check out the graveyard. Lord knows I don't want to think of what we could find. There are enough horrors on a good day."

Lestrade rubbed at his temples. Why did he feel as though he'd not slept a wink? "Well, what else?" He asked. "What needs to be done?"

Gregson gnawed on the end of a stick of dried meat pulled out of his pocket. The waxed paper crackled in the small room. "See if you can get Dr. Watson on this," he said at last. "It's short notice and we can't keep asking that of him. It's too unprofessional. But of all the things not to trust Pennywraith with . . . ."

"Cozen him, eh?" Lestrade leaned back. "I suppose I could." He chewed on his bottom lip. "I don't like using him, Gregson."

"You name me one – *just one* – man within our reach who approaches his level of expertise." Gregson said, not completely without feeling. "You've heard the other physicians and doctors and even the corner chemists talk just as much as I have. Watson's an entire encyclopaedia all to himself. If there's something out of the ordinary, he'll notice it. He might not recognize it, but he'll see it and point it out all the same."

Blast it.

Lestrade took Gregson's advice with a block of salt (he was still officially in charge of this case) and clocked out exactly one minute after his shift was over.

166

Instead of heading straight to Watson's practice, he detoured to Bow Street. Bradstreet was sharpening a small army of pencils and lining them up in precise fashion on his desk while the messengers piled a staggering amount of foolscap into the little box he reserved for ingoing problems.

"It's not as bad as it looks," Bradstreet grinned sheepishly. "I take it you got my message?"

"No, not at all. What message was that?"

Bradstreet cleared his throat. "I . . . don't think I'll be able to do this Sunday outing, Geoffrey. A few things came up that I need to take care of . . . that's all."

Roger had always been a terrible liar. Lestrade thought about asking him why he didn't just come out with it instead of avoiding the issue, but the weight of the entire awful day pulled at him with cold, soggy fingers. He sighed.

"Perhaps next time," he said softly. "Good thing I hadn't spoken to Clea yet."

"Aye." Bradstreet swallowed. "Perhaps we can do this later. I'll . . . I'll see you soon."

He didn't remember if he said goodbye to his best friend or not. His head was starting to feel too full. A fairy tale from a man who had served with him on the force for almost half their life-spans . . .

People lied to him all the time. He hadn't thought Roger would be one of them.

This day is still getting worse . . . I know when to read the signs! The detective kicked something wet and soft into the gutter. Rain was starting to fall. It might be melting the snow, but it was as cold as snow could get. Slow dank fog began to rise off the streets. Stop by Watson's on the way back home . . . that's all you have to do. You can stay out long enough to do that.

He was more than glad to see the familiar door. Office hours had passed, but the doctor tried to be available outside of them. Lestrade shivered inside the growing chill of his wet clothes and rapped on the brass-plate.

No answer at first. Lestrade could hear movement upstairs in the dull thud. A troop of children ran by. Two of them shoeless, the third wore pampooties [5] against the weather. He absently barked at them to find a drop door-way for the night and jumped at the squeak of wood and metal.

"Just a moment," Watson's voice was muffled through the thick door. "Key's . . . a bit dodgy I'm afraid . . . ."

He sounds queer, Lestrade thought. A moment later while the metal clicked: *Oh, stop it, Geoffrey B. Lestrade. You're letting this day taint everything else . . .*

167

The door scraped open. Watson swore softly as the bottom part caught on the scraping-mat beneath. "That girl doesn't believe in more than half-a-job," the detective caught him saying.

"There." Watson leaned on the door-frame, and blinked down at Lestrade. Despite the thankless weather, he was in nothing more than his shirt-sleeves and a wool waistcoat. "Hullo, Lestrade. Care to come in? I'm waiting for the water to brew hot enough for a pot of tea."

Dear Lord Above. Lestrade stared, too astonished to react. For the first time in his life, he was witnessing John H. Watson in his cups.

NOTES

1. Fool
2. Condemned cell
3. In older rural homes, the fireplace was a gigantic affair with room to place benches or sleeping-crannies on either side.
4. Toolers: Pickpockets
5. Scottish version of moccasin.

Chapter XXIII – Needed Distractions

"Geoffrey!" Clea forgot their usual banter at the doorway. One look at her husband and she quite forgot. "You're as wet as a ship's cat! Inside with you! I'll have some red tea!"

"I'll be fine," he started to say, but suddenly had the sense to give up. "I'm going to change into something dry," he amended.

" . . . you still look awful." Clea decided when he returned. Without waiting for his response, she pressed a warm cup in his hands. "Drink that and rest yourself."

"Where are . . . ?"

"The childer are about to go to bed."

"I'll see to them." He stood to drain the cup dry and started down the hallway without putting it back on the tray. She intercepted him at the doorway and set the cup down with a sigh of exasperation mixed with genuine worry.

He returned a few minutes later and showed no interest in eating. As she ladled the soup into bowls and floated the toast on top, he watched her with a dull politeness that said he was not attending.

Clea's past silence about her visitor at the 'Rose had created its own particular guilt that only worsened her attitude over Martin's desire to work that morning. Seeing him like this did little for her fast-melting peace of mind and she knew that was a very bad thing. Wives weren't supposed to admit to having bad days. It placed extra burdens on the rest of the family.

"Geoffrey, are you needing something stronger?"

His wife's soft voice sank inside his ears. "No," he murmured. "No, certainly not, but thank you." A shudder moved his shoulders and he sat up. "A bad time to drink anything stronger than water-cider right now . . . ."

"Was your day truly that terrible?"

"It . . . wasn't a very good day, Clea. There's a chance the weather had part of the blame, but . . . I think I ran out of the month's bad luck all at once."

"Just before the holiday, isn't that a good thing?" Clea tried to be supportive, but she didn't have enough of her usual wit to carry it the way she intended. With a sympathetic look, she slid the bowl forward and dropped a single sprig of parsley over the dark broth. Clea's little touches

169

at the table. She could stop them no more than she could stop breathing. It made him soften inside, for it was her own way of demonstrating her feelings. "You're home now, Love. That's all that matters. Eat, get yourself the rest you need, and tomorrow will be another day."

"I certainly hope so," he whispered. "And I hope tomorrow will be nothing like today."

"At least it won't be as cold."

"Oh?"

"Mrs. Gregson stopped by to drop off her part of the quilting-blocks for the stitching tree. She let me know in no uncertain terms it would be a day for waterproofing!"

"I wish I'd been there to see that for myself." Geoffrey picked up his spoon and dunked the toast under a few times. "How she could marry a man with such an imperfect sense of humour, I'll never know."

"I think it has to do with her sense of the absurd. And I argue with you that your comrade has a fine sense of humour . . . so long as you're not smaller than he is and can keep up with his strange observations."

"I'm glad you said that before I started eating," he confessed. "When I recover, I'll tell you all about the conversation we had about baked toads."

"Asthma and folk-remedies?" Clea wondered. "You know it does work. When I was in boarding school, this doctor decided to analyse the chemicals in the skin of – "

"I believe you," he said quickly.

Clea smiled, relieved that some of his natural personality was re-surfacing. "If you need to talk, dear, I'm just across the table."

"And thank you for that, Miss Cheatham . . . ."

What am I supposed to say? That I saw Dr. Watson drunk? His wife is your friend, and you have so few of them in London. Hazel was your first, but I don't know what's happening with Roger. What is going on with Roger? He's never hid his eyes from me like that before, never openly lied . . . .

Lestrade closed his eyes for a moment, listening to the snap of the coal as a flame caught on a flaw in the mineral. Clea had found the water-cider and was pouring out a glass for each. He heard the ring of liquid inside the tin cups.

He wasn't even all that drunk . . . It was just the grief. My God, the grief in his eyes I've never seen such a thing in that man. Couldn't have been more than one glass of wine out of that bottle by his desk. Couldn't have. *Didn't smell drunk, didn't slur his voice . . . just . . . the way he acted like he was half out of his mind . . .*

170

A thought happened just then, causing his eyes to flip back open. Clea was just reaching out with the cup. He thanked her and took it.

It was like assembling a puzzle in the dark. You had to know you were close to solving it by means other than your eyes.

As long as Watson had someone to look after, he was perfectly fine. Stolid underneath his surface flaws (such as his inability to make small change or his impulse to help first and think later), but he depended on being depended on. Sherlock Holmes had been quite enough to keep an army busy, more so an army man.

Asking if he'd be free tomorrow was enough to break a heart. He was so damned glad of knowing he could be of use somewhere . . . *like the Yard was a distraction he needed . . . .*

A sound ruffled in the hallway. Nicholas sneaking out again. He watched as Clea cheerfully went to the doorway and sent their youngest son marching back.

. . . Watson's family needs to come back to him. And soon.

Chapter XXIV – Worsening

The clock chimed the early hour. Watson stared at the numbers in distaste and snapped the lid shut with a sharp set of his mouth. Rain patted the door-step and windows while the night's snow melted, casting an eerie fog to rise up from the streets.

It looks like wraiths rising out of the earth, he thought. A melancholic observation, but the way the plumes slowly twisted and spiraled as they reached for the higher aether was compelling and unsettling.

You have death on the mind, John Watson.

Memories of last night – Mycroft's inadvert re-opening of old wounds – still scraped raw and hot behind his eyes. He went to the kitchen and poured himself another small cup of coffee. Three cups a day now. He was growing dependant on the brew to keep going.

Alone, the doctor moved to the warmth of the fireplace and settled his back against the old stones. It felt good, but every nerve jangled and he knew he could not stand being in the house alone for much longer.

It was wet. It was chill. It reminded him of Switzerland. But there were people out there.

Millions of people.

He would not be alone this time.

John looked at his hands as he sipped his tea, and at last the compulsion he had fought all last night . . . won. He lifted one hand, then the other, turning them over to peer at every line and mark.

The abrasions had faded at last. The stains of moss and lichen were still in his mind. Deep scores against the flesh that scabbed over into thin shrouds and finally . . . finally sloughed away.

In the heat of summer he had not looked at his hands. The Pleistocene waterfall had branded him. The marks were memories of the hours below the falls where the sun could not sink. The roar inside his bones as he searched for something of Sherlock Holmes . . . something to have survived.

The marks were the memory of the alpenstock splintering inside his grip as he prized a boulder for the glint of metal.

His desperate reaching for the metal, thinking it was a length of watch-chain, a fob . . . something of Holmes's to track the rest of him.

When you were a boy, you found a drowned woman in the kex. You pulled her to the high bank against the rise of the flood. You pulled her out of the mill-pool and ran for help. You succeeded as a boy . . . but you couldn't find your own friend when you were grown.

The metal glint had been a buckle, blotched with rust and age.

He waded into the swirling white pools and plunged his hands up to the limit, still searching.

He'd offered a reward for the body – for both bodies, thinking that if one would be found the other could not be far. Holmes's writing had left no doubt in his mind that the two, so matched in their opposition, would remain clutched in death. Holmes had sworn he would face his own death as worthwhile if he finished Moriarty as well.

John could not argue. He had known the Professor's brother in Afghanistan. He'd experienced for himself the venom inherent in that family.

When his hands were too raw and swollen to move, he staggered back up to the village and paid out of his pockets for the search party to continue.

In the end, all they'd found was a shoe.

Not Holmes's but a fine gentleman's all the same. Holding the sodden shape as it soaked into his bandages, he felt the slow horror as it pulled the bile up his throat until he had to fight to keep it down. He knew then, that Sherlock Holmes's oft-repeated statements had come to pass: That his methods would be his last mark upon the world. There would be no grave, no marker of stone with some comforting or philosophic phrase. No quotation taken from *The Book of Life*. No thing at all.

But he had tried his best.

It had cost him more money than he had owned, but he had tried.

He swallowed hard, wondering if his composure would splinter like his alpenstock.

It's always worse on days like this. It brings back the cold and the wet . . . when the storms rage it echoes the Falls . . . When I smell the melt-water and the ice in the air . . .

. . . It was easier in the summer. It was endurable . . .

He would go out today. He would work. They needed the money. Mary had offered to sell one of her pearls. John had refused so stridently he knew it hurt her feelings. In the end, he had managed to soften his reaction by pointing out their child deserved a legacy. The pearls should be kept for him or her.

"For him, you mean of course," she had responded. *Just that quickly, he knew he was forgiven.*

It was the second time he'd ever hurt her. He'd vowed there would never be a third time.

A familiar-looking cab pulled up as he keyed open his door.

Theresa hopped out, dark eyes even darker in the awful morning light. "Doctor, I'm so sorry I'm late!"

173

"Had t'go around, Dr. Watson!" Savoy Nash touched the brim of his hat in respect against the elements and his daughter's respectable employer. Falling rain created a dim halo of light around the pipe he furiously puffed. In concession to the weather, he wore a black slouch hat, a sort of umbrella against the drench of his smoke. "High Street's been clotted up with water. One of't' pipes t'the T'ames wuz a-clogged!"

Watson was getting better at verbal deciphering. "Thank you, Mr. Nash!" He called up. "I trust your business will not suffer in this weather!"

"P'r-haps na! Who wants t'walk in such a curtain? Now if th'roads'd behave umselves . . . ."

Watson shut the door and ensconced himself inside the cab with deep relief. Just the quick dash had splotched his shoulders and left the first of the mud on his trouser-cuffs. It would be a wretched day for the laundress!

Lestrade and Bradstreet met him outside the Yard. While they were hardly any drier, the shared warmth of their bodies was welcome. Steam hovered inside the glass, forcing Bradstreet to grumble under his mustaches and wipe frequently with the raveled end of his thick muffler.

"Give it a rest, Bradstreet," Lestrade finally said after they crossed two more streets. "We'll get out when it's time to see something and you're just getting that dirty."

"I hate waiting," Bradstreet answered with more temper than Watson was used to seeing from the man.

The detectives were sitting in the same bench opposite from Watson, but it did not seem to be from their usual bond of friendship. Three more streets down the Thames and Watson decided that he did not want to know what sort of trouble was fermenting between the two. Normally they were friends, but when there is a fissure between friends . . . .

"Does Hopkins have any more details?" he asked without much hope. Lestrade and Bradstreet had abruptly plunged into an angry sort of truce. Perhaps restarting conversation would cause trouble.

"Just information about the churchyard itself." Lestrade sighed. "Are you familiar with the St. Andrew Saltorel?"

"A bit. It's really just the usual St. Andrew. Saltorel means '*narrow saltire*', and a saltire is the emblem of St. Andrew." Watson told him. "The church itself was destroyed during one of the bouts at the Reformation."

"It was burned to the ground." Lestrade nodded. "There were some horrible jokes that the blaze warmed the Protestants for a week. Many of the valuables like the gold cup and a washing-bowl given by the Archbishop of Canterbury vanished in the fuss . . . Rumour said 'twas tossed down a well with the other treasures, but it's just as likely someone melted the whole bit down and re-cast it into coins or something else."

Bradstreet snorted under his breath. "Easy enough to dig out a well."

174

"It is if you know where to look. This is one of the older parts of the town, Bradstreet. Once every while the engineers run into a Roman villa or something even older. There were twelve wells dug out in the records, and they're all rather buried in the mess by now." Lestrade huddled inside his clothes, speaking mechanically without much in the way of feeling. He looked smaller and strangely frail in that moment. Watson hoped it was just the light, but his premonitions were rarely comforting.

He'd felt something similar not so long ago . . . escorting poor Henry Baskerville to his ancestral home. Something about the earth itself had stirred up a sad strangeness inside his breast-bone, and he didn't know what to do about it.

Holmes would have called him needlessly romantic. Coloring events past recognition. Try as he might, Watson could not bury his upbringing like so much rubbish. The bottom truth was . . . something was wrong.

"What a mess!"

Bradstreet's sharper eyes and insistence on wiping the glass bore fruit. They jumped to look out the rubbed circle to a small army of miserable-looking constables, digging implements on the standby against the remains of what had once been a small church. It was now nothing more than a three-sided box, and one side slanted in a worrisome way. The graveyard was little over an acre. A soupy brown morass.

"Poor devils," Lestrade said with feeling. "Those awful shoes just don't keep the weather out." Watson thought at first he was talking about the sorry state of the graves, which looked every bit as bad as the hosting church.

"Why wasn't the church ever restored?" Watson wondered.

Lestrade grimaced. "You might as well ask the same question to all the hundreds of little churches razed. But if you want to know the honest truth, there were rumours the fire was started from within."

"I don't understand," Bradstreet scowled.

"Old superstition." Watson suddenly shuddered. "A house destroyed by fire will be destroyed by fire again. I'd almost forgotten that old chestnut."

Hopkins was running forward, nipping around the stones like a rugger. He braked himself and flung open the door before Bradstreet.

"We found something in the old out-building." He puffed great clouds of steam as he spoke. His face was fever-bright with excitement as water ran down his cheeks. "They were going to restore the graveyard . . . built up this little structure on the other side of the wall. Come and take a look for yourselves."

It took some time to walk to the place in question without sinking into the loosening soil. Hopkins hopped nimbly from firm spot to firm spot.

Again, Watson thought uncomfortably of the past. Stapleton's way of running across the soft mire with his butterfly net.

The out-building was dank but dry . . . on the ceiling and two of the walls. Elsewhere it seeped in the wet from outside. As simply as that, the pale sunlight vanished in the gloom over their heads. They could hear the faint roar of the rainfall as it increased.

"This looks like some sort of . . . ." Watson dropped his voice. "It reminds me of an archaeological dig I once saw. The weather was poor enough that they were forced to put a building over the site."

"Stranger things have happened," Lestrade muttered. "I'd rather see a building for the living."

Bradstreet grunted and caught himself in agreement. He looked away.

"Gentlemen," Hopkins tucked his hands under his arms and faced off, smiling broadly. "What funeral home would you think would be interested in the charitable act of restoring a lonely forgotten graveyard for the sake of the poor? And what bank would be persuaded to partially fund this endeavor?"

It took a moment – Gregson felt as though his brain had slowed in the cold – but the numbers tumbled into place. "Your man George Blake?" he demanded harshly. "The one who has that brother at the Bank of Thames?"

"One and same." Hopkins was very proud of himself. "For a while I couldn't understand how a lowly teller could have influence on one of the investors, but it would seem investors have their secrets to keep too . . . and tellers are excellent in tracking accounts."

"Time to switch banks," Lestrade said under his breath. Next to him, Watson was stiffening up.

"The bodies are being moved quickly," Hopkins continued, oblivious to Watson's frozen expression. "The crews have been pulling the coffins – if there even are any – out of the ground and putting them in the storage area to protect them before they're moved to the their new plots. But when certain workers are present . . . ." The young man's face stopped being so cheerful. "They don't have the time to risk getting caught by stripping jewelry off the bodies, so . . . ." He knelt a moment and held up a tiny knife. It was just about the size of the small apron-knife Lestrade's wife kept close to her.

"Oh, my Lord – they've been cutting the dead?" Bradstreet demanded harshly. "Hopkins, that's bad enough, but why are you needing me in on this? Grave-robbing has nothing to do with me."

"I'm afraid it does when there's extraditing required," Hopkins said softly. He cleared his throat. "Several of the major parties are out of country."

"How far out of the country?" Watson spoke at last, with a voice like sand. "Is this involving other countries?"

"Not directly and of course not with government approval. But there's a faint trail from here all the way to Kandahar."

"This is too much." Bradstreet held his head as if it hurt him.

Lestrade looked away, ashamed of what he could see in Watson's face. It was sheer bad luck he was seeing it. No one else had the doctor at that angle. They were all looking at Bradstreet as he ranted. A gust of wind in the hollow mausoleum went through his coat and down his neck. He shuddered and stuffed his hands in his pockets, stepped backwards away from the focus of attention.

"Lestrade, look out!"

It was already too late. Even as something caused Watson to turn his way and call a warning, he felt the weight of his good foot sink downward. His twisted foot lacked the sudden strength required to balance and a second later there was no point in trying.

Lestrade had no control over himself. His mouth opened in a startled cry as the ground crumbled underneath, pitching him backwards into a wet black pit. A sharp, stabbing pain struck like a thunderbolt between his shoulder-blades, and tumbling dirt filled his eyes and mouth. The stench of the grave filled his world. He choked, more frantic than any drowning man to be smothered in death itself, but his gasps for air only opened the way for more of the grave. Around him the walls were giving way, filthy dirt filled his eyes and then the wall by his left had burst open. A skeleton half-clad in graveclothes and flesh rolled on top of him, its bony arms folding over his neck in a gruesome embrace.

Chapter XXV – Vinegar For
Four Thieves

Lestrade was never so glad to see Gregson's pasty face as when he was in the bottom of a grave, trying to blink mud out of his eyes from around the grip of a skeleton. He clawed past a rotting shroud. Gregson's large cold hand wrapped around his wrist and yanked him like a carrot out of the ground. Bones rattled down in his wake.

"*Inspector?*"

"*Inspector . . . .*"

"*Back off, man! Give him some air!*"

"*What air there is in this godforsaken place . . . .*"

"*Would you just hand me the water, please – *"

The detective's mind and body abruptly came to an agreement. He came back to reality in spasms, trying to breathe, spew, and gag all at the same time.

"Steady now, Inspector." That familiar voice was the owner of the strong hands that held him up. "Steady . . . your system has had a terrible shock. Give yourself some time to come to yourself." He turned his head and bellowed: "Bradstreet! Where the devil is that bottle?" (*mumbling sounds*) "Then give him what he wants, for the love of God!"

Watson . . . .

A final bout of retching struck. Watson nary blinked, but sponged the charnel filth off his face and neck before holding up a scrounged cup of water. Lestrade filled his mouth and spat it out before he thought about what could be in the church's well-water. He tried to throw up again.

"Don't worry, its clean water." Watson read his expression. He lifted the side of his mouth ruefully. "I recognize the look on your face, Inspector. Many a man in the field has worried about plain water when the enemy was firing corpses into all the known wells."

Lestrade braved a drink and began to feel better, but like putting his hand on a wire with an electric charge, the memory of the corpse falling over him kept happening over and over. *OhGodthesmell* . . . Watson leaned him back against a sepulchral pillar holding some kind of sculptured flowers. The rest of the men were hovering at a respectful – and awed – distance. Lestrade had a terrible suspicion of the kinds of rumors that would fuel the Yard for the next month.

"Well," Lestrade croaked. "Has anything else been found of interest?"

PC Harris stepped up, awkward with discomfort. "Sir. Inspector, sir. It's hard to tell, but it looks like a few of these graves have been robbed."

Watson sighed through his nose. "There's unmistakable signs." His face cleared as he noted something behind Lestrade. "Good man! Good! Bring it here!"

"Dr. Watson, are you sure about this?" Constable Peterson looked uneasy in the extreme as he passed a dark brown glass bottle into the doctor's hands.

"As sure as anything. After what your Inspector went through in the line of duty . . . ." He unscrewed the cap and sniffed the contents, jerking his head back quickly. "Perfect. Inspector, as a physician, I am ordering you to drink at least half of this bottle down before we allow you back on your feet."

Lestrade's shaking hand closed over the glass, and then the odor hit him. "Watson, have you lost your mind?" He demanded. "Are you trying to get me thrown behind bars?"

Watson glowered at him. "Gentlemen, did anyone here hear me ask Peterson to bring back a bottle of *poteen* from O'Flagherty's?" There was a universal flutter of *No's*. "I distinctly said a bottle of the finest." Watson passed Lestrade a droll look. "We could have given you vodka, but it tends to give Englishmen severe headache the next day." He tapped the bottle. "Three good swallows, Lestrade. I guarantee there won't be a germ alive in your body after the third."

Adding to the latest of humiliations, Gregson helped him to his feet. Now they were both filthy.

"Your wife is going to murther you," Stress combined with alcohol sent Lestrade's speech down an earlier path.

"Watson, not that I'm completely grateful that Lestrade proved beyond a doubt this bone-yard is dangerously unstable, but we need to get him home."

Watson looked dubious. "We should do it now, but I'm aware there are reports to write about this . . . ."

"By God, I can do it." Gregson responded with an honesty that frankly surprised Lestrade.

"He's been exposed to dangerous elements." Watson pointed out in a grim tone. "I'm afraid that requires a quarantine."

"You leave that to me." Gregson sounded really rather grim. "If they can't give him time off to recover, I'll know the reason why."

Lestrade closed his eyes. The whisky was not helping his head . . . His emptied stomach had not taken the foul concoction very well . . . not at all.

179

"Inspector," Watson was saying, *"I don't think I have to list the reasons why someone needs to keep a close eye on him right now."*

"Right you are at that," Gregson grunted. He actually sounded worried. *"Will he be all right, Doctor?"*

"If we are all vigilant, and keep a close eye on him. He's hardier than most."

"But the way that . . . thing . . . fell on him . . . ."

"It wasn't his fault. We have to get him home and check him for scratches, cuts, scrapes – any sign of broken skin. I can do that simply enough, but he's going to need some permitted time off . . . .

Silence. The rocking of the cab and the sounds lulled at Lestrade's consciousness.

"Truly, Doctor, will he be all right?"

Watson chuckled very softly. *"He's got enough poteen in his blood to kill a wharf rat. I doubt he'll thank me for the precaution tomorrow."*

Lestrade kept his eyes closed. He was afraid grave-earth would fall off his lashes and into his lids. There was a rustle of cloth.

"I need to get a message to my wife. She'll be coming in on the 4:15 and I shouldn't go home tonight. Not in her condition."

"I can send a message simple enough. My wife can see if she needs any help."

"Not if it will indispose your own wife." Watson protested.

Gregson laughed out loud. *"You don't know Mrs. Gregson! If I didn't tell her there was something she could've done and she didn't . . . Well, I might as well camp out at Lestrade's with you, Doctor . . . ."* A sound of cloth and leather. Gregson was peering upright. *"What in God's name . . . Who the bloody devil is that madman?"*

Lestrade heard Watson lean forward. *"I was about to say it was George Bernard Shaw,"* the doctor confessed, *"but I don't think he dresses in pea-jackets . . . ."* There was a pause. *"You know, dressed like that, he – "*

"Holy God, I think that's . . . It's the Seagull!" Gregson gasped.

Lestrade's eyes shot open with a mixture of gladness and unease – the usual reaction to his grandfather. Naturally, dirt fell into his eyes.

"Here in London! Are we at war with France again?"

"I've never seen him in the flesh." Watson was clearly shocked. "You know, he looks just – "

"We don't have anything in common." Lestrade rasped. He struggled to sit up as they started. "He made some sort of vague threat about coming to visit a while back . . . I suppose the seas were clear enough."

"If he calls that clear seas, it's no wonder they call him the seagull. He *can* fly," Gregson snorted.

"Witticisms don't become you." Lestrade coughed so hard he choked. The cab was trying to find a place to stop where they could dismount to the kerb.

"*Salud!*" The little man was scampering forward. In his sea-gear, he looked like the only natural element in dripping London. "*Jafrez!*" Heedless of his grandson's condition, or perhaps because, he nipped straight to him and helped him down, rattling in his native tongue: *("What are you doing with these big English clowns?")*

"*Saozneg, Tad-kohz . . . .*" Lestrade gasped. "*Saozneg.*" (*"English, Grandfather, English."*)

Potier switched to English. "I'm very sorry forgive my manners it was a shock to see him like this you didn't look this bad back in April."

"We need to take him inside," Watson broke in. "A quarantine, sir. He fell in an open grave."

"An open *occupied* grave." Lestrade said wearily.

Potier's eyes expanded to their natural limits. "I'll send the small ones out. Will they go their Cheatham grandfather?"

"Clea too." Lestrade knew it was a mad thing to be standing out and talking fine details while an icy rain poured on them, but he wasn't about to go inside and infect the house while they were in it. "She can't risk getting sick again. Send them out that old side-door by the snicket. I'll go in the same way. That should keep the neighbors and Mrs. Collins from dealing with this."

"Ya, give me moment . . . ."

Lestrade would have preferred not to remember what followed. His family evacuated with gratifying speed, but the farewell looks they passed were awful. Watson paid the driver extra to take an early day and wash down the inside of his cab . . . the barest mention of the Ministry of Health was an effective persuasion. After that, Potier paid a disgraceful amount of money for a boy to bring back a horrendous concoction that smelled like Saffron Hill upwind of the vinegar factory.

Together Potier and Dr. Watson searched his skin for abrasions and perforations while Gregson got the hot water going, and some chaos erupted as Watson discovered a tear in his skin behind the left shoulder blade. What happened next was a blur of a severe scrub-down, stinging salves, and more salves. Finally, another dose of that rubbing alcohol Watson insisted was perfectly respectable Irish contraband.

"You've got to use this," Potier didn't exactly snap, but he was firm about the vinegary-garlic-rue-concoction in his hands.

"What is it, Mr. Potier?" Watson wasn't going to let anyone's grandfather medicate him to his detriment.

"What do you think, you nouch? It's the Vinegar of Four Thieves. If it can stop the Bubonic Plague, it won't be impressed at a dead man's germs."

"I'll take some of that." Gregson lifted his hand. "For all we know, that grave was dug back during the last plague!"

"Someday I'm going to have someone analyse that brew," Watson grumbled, but did as he was told. "I loathe a mystery."

"Don't worry, I'm used to it," Lestrade mumbled wearily. "I'm also used to this Vinegar. The family puts faith in it."

"I didn't live this long by living on luck," Potier returned. "Where can I get a glass?"

Gregson left like a relieved bandit, but not before Potier could fob off some of the foul concoction. Lestrade didn't envy him – he knew what the stuff was and the man was about to have a hard time of it. Mrs. Gregson had the nose of a perfume-mixer, and wouldn't take to garlic-drenched vinegary husband happily.

Twenty-four Hours Later:

"I'm afraid your comrade's condition is worsening, but at least it does not appear to be from the direct effects of the grave itself." Watson decided a delay of the news would do no one at the Yard any favours. Bradstreet, Gregson, and Hopkins looked a bit like children about to be scolded for something.

"He was *bound* to come down with something! A *mucking grave* collapsed under his feet, man! *He fell in!*"

"No, Gregson, I mean . . . ." the doctor sighed. "It appears to be influenza. In which case, he would have *already* begun to contract it before he even set out. The shock of the graveyard in turn shocked his immune system. At this point he's in strict need of rest."

"Then what?" Bradstreet rubbed at the back of his neck. "Lestrade hardly ever gets sick. Not after the fogs of the seventies."

"Has he been under an unusual amount of strain lately?" Watson asked point-blank. He was surprised and unsettled to see the number of glances that failed to meet his own.

Well. Spilt milk. Watson let the moment pass. Self-recriminations were harder than hearing someone say it. He glanced at his watch to allow them a moment to prepare their thoughts. "Considering the experience he had . . . it would be a good idea to ensure he was quarantined a fortnight."

"I can see the sense in that, now," Bradstreet said carefully. "But there's different levels of quarantine."

182

"His grandfather is more than willing to be the go-between, and I don't think we could stop him." Potier had in truth practically dared the Yard to try to keep him behind bars when his grandson needed him. There was probably a lockpick or three under that thick grey beard. "Let him do so then. It will be hard enough on the family as is."

A fortnight. Lestrade would miss out on all of Christmas, from beginning to Belsnickle's. That was assuming he'd even be aware of it. The guilt in the room grew. "We'll do as you say, Doctor." Gregson said. "And we'll see to him. Now you need to go home to your family. No sense in the Missus Watson chewing me down for forgetting this is your first holiday with Little Arthur."

Watson spluttered, but trying not to laugh made it worse. "I don't think I've forgotten for a minute!" He shook his head, the tired lines smoothing as he smiled. "I think the entire street mobs me on congratulations and good advice." He was still smiling as he bade his farewells.

Alone, the silence of the three Yarders grew thick.

Hopkins spoke first. "I didn't know he was that poorly."

"He's been pushing himself since spring." Gregson grumbled. "Holmes's dying had a lot to do with it." He fixed another cheap cigarette and defiantly lit it. "No use bein' angry at a dead man, but Lestrade is as angry as they get."

"I'm angry as well," Bradstreet protested. "It isn't right for a civilian to take our risks. He's dead all right, and we're *still* paying the price for an amateur's bravery."

"We'll be paying for it a good sight longer," Hopkins said soberly. "Mr. Holmes was right by his own lights, and I don't think he could have moved out of true to himself . . . but we're going to be taking the blame for this for a long time."

"Oh, Hell." Gregson shook out his match furiously. The vapour wafted before him like steam off a locomotive. It matched his red face. "What's one more punch for the Crown?" He asked rhetorically. "We're used to it. Someone's always blaming us for something. Corruption, laziness, bribery . . . illiteracy, nosiness, going beyond our station . . . ." The bitterness was worsened by his flat acceptance of the truth. "Bradstreet, please tell me your extradition duties will not extend to Khandahar."

"Certainly not. Not without approval from the highest-ups." Bradstreet was shocked. "I have better odds of getting approval of going through the Blake's ancestral home off the coast of Ireland."

"Well, I know you'll do what you can." Gregson hesitated. He clapped Hopkins on the back as he left, but blocked Bradstreet from following.

The office door shut for a moment. "Lestrade's on a narrow path right now," he said in a low voice.

Bradstreet turned dark. "I'm aware of that."

"I'm saying it for the record. He wasn't with us but for part of the raid that took Moriarty's gang down. There's a lot he didn't see,

and there's a lot we didn't see of him. But you're the one we trusted to go get him when he sent his coded message out. You're his best friend."

Gregson's face hardened at the blocky Bow Street Runner. "And if there's *anything* going on with you that might interfere with your duty, Roger Bradstreet . . . I'm sure I don't want to know about it."

Bradstreet paled but said nothing.

The story continues in:
The End of All Things

MX Publishing

MX Publishing is the world's largest specialist Sherlock Holmes publisher, with over six-hundred titles and over two-hundred authors creating the latest in Sherlock Holmes fiction and non-fiction

The catalogue includes several award winning books, and over four-hundred-and-fifty have been converted into audio.

MX Publishing also has one of the largest communities of Holmes fans on Facebook, with regular contributions from dozens of authors.

www.mxpublishing.com

@mxpublishing on Facebook, Twitter, and Instagram